One Please
By Mia Coffin

Copyright © 2012 by Maile Bartholomew

All rights reserved. Without limiting the rights under copyright reserved above, no part of this publication may be reproduced, stored in or introduced into a retrieval system, or transmitted, in any form, or by any means (electronic, mechanical, photocopying, recording, or otherwise) without the prior written permission of both the copyright owner and the above publisher of this book. This is a work of fiction. Names, characters, places, and incidents are either the product of the author's imagination or are used fictitiously.

We must let go of the life we have planned, so as to accept the one that is waiting for us.

Joseph Campbell

for my ohana

Contents

Choco & Scar   1
Indonesia

Promises   68
Tanzania

Crazy   130
Lebanon

Call Me Ishmael   198
New Zealand

Choco & Scar
Indonesia

Sumatra

Chapter One

Most girls my age are married or about to get married. They have Z gallerie furniture, Ralph Lauren bath towels, send Christmas Cards and have wine parties. I'm not like most girls my age, or any girl really. I spend my money on plane tickets to travel the world instead of all that American dream lifestyle stuff. All six of my sisters have the husbands, treadmills, Saturday soccer meets and maxed out credit cards. I don't. They all think that I will snap out of it, settle down, find a man on match.com and start having babies. Unlikely. I'm not gay (my mom lets me know it's OK if I am, every year) I just haven't met the right guy to buy designer towels with yet.

Traveling, exploring, learning and experiencing other cultures is my life. It's not really the life I chose. It chose me. People tell me I'm brave to travel alone to 'all these crazy places.' I think my sisters are brave to raise children and be married to the same man year after year. It doesn't take much bravery to buy an airline ticket and escape from ordinary life for a few months.

Today I have four hundred dollars in my checking account. I work as a waitress. I live in an illegal garage in back of my parents' house. I have no fairy godmother or a trust fund to rely on. I *do* believe that when a guy takes me out, G.D.P. (girls don't pay). I drive a crappy 1992 Ford Ranger and wear hand-me-down clothes. I'm the fifth daughter of nine kids. My parents finally got their boy only eleven months after I was born, actually they got two. My twin brothers (dubbed the golden boys) were a huge relief to my parents and grandparents who feared my mother could only produce girl children.

As a fifth daughter I felt like a disappointment growing up. My parents certainly never said that. They loved me equally along with my eight siblings. However, I felt a bit ignored, lost in the crowd, overshadowed by my four older sisters who were all over-achievers. They excelled in sports and academics, were funny and naturally beautiful. Everything came easy to them. I couldn't compete with them for positive attention—so I sought negative—and I got it. I was the bad one, always getting in trouble and acting out. I hungered for my parents' approval, love, attention, acknowledgment. I wanted them to be proud of me. But I couldn't do anything that my sisters hadn't done a million times better.

When I was fifteen—still in high school—as part of a ROP program, I took a job as a hostess in a seafood restaurant and by the time I was seventeen, I had saved four thousand dollars. It was Christmas, I had enough credits to graduate early my senior year from all my ROP classes. I had no clue what I was going to do, but I hated high school and I knew I wanted to do something different from my friends. I was idly turning the pages of my favorite magazine—National Geographic—when I saw an ad that said "Speak French like a Native. At the illustrious Sorbonne." My heart leapt! I instantly saw myself on a bike, with a beret on my head, a baguette under my arm and the Eiffel tower in my sights.

Paris! I was moving to Paris! I had the money, I had a passport, I could do it. My dad always says it's easier to ask forgiveness than permission. So, Monday morning I met with my high school counselor, requested my diploma and announced I would not be coming back—ever. He discouraged me, but admitted I *did* have enough credits to graduate. Enough said, pal, I was outta there. Next stop, Laguna Travel. I bought a ticket to Paris and left three days later. The only person I confided in was my sister Rose who was supposed to tell my parents the next day. I didn't want to worry my mom and dad, but I didn't want them to stop me either.

I had never been alone in my life. I never had my own room. I never even had my own bed. I shared a bed with a sister for as long as I can remember. Paris was a rebirth for me, an escape from who I was in small town California. When I signed up for classes at the Sorbonne, my student living arrangements were taken care of. I lived in a dorm for two hundred dollars a month and took a French class every day on the Boulevard Raspail. I ate at student cafeterias around the city for six francs a meal. I was seventeen, so I got into all the museums for free. I went to my French class every morning from eight till ten then the day was mine. I went to the Louvre, Muse D'Orsay, Muse de Cluny. I hung out at flea markets. I found myself making friends from all over the world—Denmark, Bangladesh, Pakistan, China, Turkey and Nigeria. I thought I was so cool sipping espresso at a café, reading Hemingway in French. I mastered the metro and took in every square inch of that city and, still, I missed my family.

On my first day in Paris, my mother reached me—in tears. She just wanted to make sure I was safe and happy. She forgave me for the pain I caused when I left so abruptly and we talked regularly during my six months in Paris. When the course ended and my money was spent, it was time to go home. I had changed. A lot. I was no longer the spoiled, rebellious girl who had run away. I had learned to live on my own and, what's more, I had learned to appreciate my family. The perspective that I had gained by going away was invaluable.

But I had also tasted freedom. I had had the chance to grow up independently of my siblings. I was a different person. No way would I ever again be content to go back and live a regular life. I had always been interested in other cultures and dreamed of one day traveling, but now I had connections. I had been invited to visit my fellow students who lived in Bangladesh, Turkey and Denmark. I realized that I *could* travel. There was no excuse not to. I wanted to see the world. I wanted to experience other places and now, with Paris under my belt, I knew I could do it. But first, I had to go home.

Home it was. But only for eight months. Enough time to save money for my next bite of the world—a round-the-world-ticket. I visited four of my fellow students from Paris. On a stopover between Bangkok and New Delhi I stayed with my Bengali friend. Imtiaz proudly showed me Dhaka, his humble hometown. We babbled in French and ate curry served on a banana leaf. This was the beginning of a year-long journey that took me to fourteen countries. Starting in South East Asia, I went through India, Europe, North Africa and finally back to the States. Even then, my wanderlust was not satisfied. For me, returning home is what I do between traveling the world.

But my life is complex. Traveling is my passion, yes, but I also wanted a college education. It was waitressing that enabled me to make those first trips and paid my tuition for college. It's a job that sustains me today. I'm grateful for what it has given me. Waitressing is no dream job, it's not who I am, it's what I do so I can travel.

Over fifty countries later (my sisters say that stop-overs don't count so that takes it down to forty-eight) I've also earned my BA in anthropology—and managed to stay single! And after 'running away' to Paris that time, it turns out my family is my life. When I'm gone I desperately miss my six sisters, two brothers, parents (who are still married) and twenty-eight nieces and nephews. I get sad sometimes when I'm traveling alone for months on end. During down time while I'm gone I begin to question my choices. I am my hardest critic. I doubt myself, but never more than when I am hounded by questioners who ask me, when are you going to settle down? What is your future? How can you live without health insurance…or a television? I don't know. I just know this is my life and I love it. I thought my wanderlust would wear off. But inevitably an intriguing prospect comes along—a study abroad program, a job offer or just a new place I haven't been that looks fantastic in a National Geographic.

National Geographic became the one constant in my life. I never allowed my subscription to lapse. Tonight, after a grueling waitress shift with fifteen percent tippers all evening, I was anxious to come home and crack open my new issue. An article about China's mighty fleet detailed the sophisticated trading networks with local societies that existed a century before Columbus was even born. Beautiful glossy pictures stared up at me depicting Sumatra where much of the trading took place in a port city called Sabang. Chinese ships would harbor there for weeks, trading with the locals and resting in paradise before moving onward to India and Africa. These mysterious pictures and fantastic stories captured me.

I read all night. I learned that Sabang harbor is on the island of Weh, the western most tip of Indonesia off the coast of Sumatra. Strategically placed in the straits of Malacca, its maritime history is incredible. Hoping I wouldn't find information on a civil war, recent kidnapping, or hatred for my country, I spent the following morning on the Internet searching for traveler's tales, blogs and advice on traveling to Sumatra. It all checked out, budget travelers go there, it's safe, it's cheap, it's beautiful and yes, of course they hate America and have demonstrations where masked men burn effigies of our president. But I would simply avoid large groups of angry boys. I was going to Sumatra!

I'd been to Indonesia before, but only to the more touristy islands of Java, Bali and Lombok. Sumatra was something different, the Africa of South East Asia, the unexplored, wild, rugged, exotic spice island. Of course, I had no money saved, but, Sumatra called me and I intended to answer.

Chapter Two

I'm not motivated by money. I'd rather sit on a beach and read a book than be bothered to work. But when I have a goal I am on fire! My goal was to earn enough money for a plane ticket and spending money for three months in Sumatra. It was summer in Laguna Beach, and I was lucky to have a job at the most expensive restaurant in town and live with my parents to save on rent. Besides picking up as many shifts as possible at the restaurant, I had four garage sales, baby-sat for my sisters and sold all my Turkish kilims on Craigslist. Any free time I had during those 'working months' I was on the Internet forums, chatting to backpackers, or in the library researching everything Sumatra.

If I could be a contestant on Jeopardy and have categories like, Sumatran History, Famous Anthropologists, Parisian Street Food, Pagan gods of Mesopotamia, The complete works of Thomas L. Friedman, Bantu Dialects, Napa Valley Wine Varietals, Word Origins, and Birds of California, I could quit working completely and live off my winnings. Unfortunately Alex Trebek didn't contact me, so I spent the next few months slowly saving and met my goal of $3,000 by Halloween.

It takes me about ten days to pull the trigger on buying an airline ticket. I sit at my computer and compare discount travel companies until I have memorized flight times, city codes, every possible discount, and flight connection. I save about three hundred bucks by stopping over in one or two places instead of flying non-stop. Knowing how much three hundred US dollars is worth in developing countries, I convince myself, when in the comfort of my parents home, that I can handle the extra two stops. In fact, somehow I fool myself into the fantasy of how exciting a few layovers will be. Inevitably, when sitting at some airport after a twelve-hour flight with another fifteen hours of travel ahead of me, I go to the nearest restroom, search my tired eyes in the mirror and right there make an oath to myself that never again will I save a few hundred bucks for this hideous discomfort. And, yes, staring at myself in a bathroom mirror at Hong Kong's airport, I said exactly the same thing to myself.

After a fifteen-hour flight from LA to Seoul, a six-hour layover, a five-hour flight to Hong Kong with a quick two hours between connections and a six-hour hop, I arrived in the lovely equatorial city of Jakarta, Indonesia.

I had landed at Jakarta's Soekarno-Hatta International airport before. It was just as I remembered, an open air baggage claim, taxi drivers with official tourist guide cards speaking perfect English, each one convincing you that he is the most experienced guide in the universe. Vans park curbside, stuffed with passengers waiting to take you into the city. These vans, the locals call 'bemos' are actually efficient transportation. You just stand on the side of any road in Indonesia, flap your hand in a downward motion and they usually stop for you. If it looks full, opting for the next bemo is not a choice, so be ready to squat between the seats with a basket of chickens or perhaps become an instant foster parent with a child or two on your lap.

However efficient bemos are, at this point I need a taxi. I introduce myself to a couple waiting at the end of the taxi queue. They are Swiss, Nick and Elana, just arriving from Bangkok—a pang of jealousy rips through me that this adorable couple have been traveling for five hours compared to my thirty-four. I offer to share a taxi into the city with them, assuming they are headed to Jalan Jaksa. Every city has a budget tourist area, and in Jakarta, Jalan Jaksa is it. They agree to have me ride along and contribute to the one hundred seventy thousand rupiah fare the forty-five minute ride costs. This amount is clearly documented in the bible, AKA; Lonely Planet guide book, that all backpackers rely on for accurate prices, accommodation, transportation, maps, sightseeing, history and of course the quick reference guide to the local language with important phrases like, What kind of meat am I eating? Or, how far to the summit, because I don't think I'm going to make it?

An old silver Mercedes pulls up and behind the wheel emerges a tiny man immaculately dressed in a button-down shirt and pressed trousers, ready for his next prospect. The Swiss couple begin to load their backpacks into the open trunk. I wait at the curb to establish a price before relinquishing my backpack. "How much to Jalan Jaksa? I ask. The driver takes out a paper and pen from his shirt pocket and writes 220,000. I smile, and think, let the bargaining begin. I take his pen and write 150,000 and say, "good price for you". He acknowledges my offer with mock anger and quickly retorts, "OK, special night price for you" and writes 200,000. The Swiss couple are watching me from the back seat of the Mercedes. The driver hands me the paper knowing that there will be one or two more attempts before a deal is struck. I write 160,000 and add, "last price." He does not make eye contact with me but goes for my backpack sitting on the curb beside me and says, "Ok, one hundred seventy thousand, good price for you, we go. I allow this tiny man to heft my backpack into the trunk while I get into the front seat and slam the rusted door closed.

"Did you come to a good price?" Nick laughs from the back seat.

"Yeah, we'll each pay sixty thousand."

Nick adds, "It is so cheap to begin with, why spend the energy to make it lower?"

I'm too tired to explain that bargaining is a system that is respected and expected. I pride myself in the nuances in the art of bargaining. The driver is a good bargainer and a hard worker and after all that haggling, to pay him ten thousand more is not expected but appreciated. I look at his Taxi driving permit displayed on the dashboard and read his name, Mohamed Halim. He eases himself into the driver's seat covered in a lining of wooden balls that looks like a torture device made to refresh memories of terrorists at Guantanamo, but Mohamed rolls his back into the wooden balls and cringes with apparent delight. "Help blood circulate" he smiles at me with four front teeth. I love Indonesia—it's so far from Orange County California in so many delightful ways.

While I am instantly asleep riding shotgun, Elana and Nick are wide eyed, anxiously watching Mohamed negotiate the largest city in the world. Most business in Jakarta is conducted in the evening, after the oppressive heat has diminished. Sharing the road with our Taxi are bemos, tuk tuks, horse drawn carts, thousands of people buying and selling goods from makeshift shops along the road, or actually *in* the road. We arrive at the famous Jalan Jaksa in tact and happily pay Mohamed the agreed upon price of 170,000 rupiah plus an extra 10,000, which elicits another toothless smile of thanks. Mohamed deposits all three backpacks onto the curb and speeds away, into the humid night.

Nick and Elana see the neon sign of their hotel just three buildings down the road and begin walking, then look back at me and ask if I have booked a hotel. "Oh, yes," I reply, "nice to meet you, have a good sleep."

"OK, bye-bye." Probably glad to be rid of the bargaining American.

I didn't book a hotel, but I didn't want the Swiss couple to worry, or invite me with them to their hotel that I definitely couldn't afford. Jalan Jaksa is a short, four hundred meter road, packed with over forty hotels, or losmens. So, to go door to door in search of a place to stay is easy.

Bagus Losmen was the first place I came upon, it was almost eleven at night, but the family was still up, five members all on a mat on the floor, watching TV, two little girls were playing with another baby boy about eight months old, while three cats groomed themselves on nearby chairs. The woman got up and said, "Hello?'

"Do you have a single room for just one please?"

"Sorry, no room tonight, but my brother have room next door."

After thirty eight hours of travel, I think, fine, I'll sleep with your brother if that's what it takes, but my expression gives me away, and the woman laughs and adds, "He have other losmen."

"Oh, yeah, OK, I'll try his hotel, where is it?" I ask, starting for the street. The woman yelled something to her oldest daughter and the girl responded and quickly took my hand and started to guide me down the dark street.

"What your name?" the girl asked.

"Mia, and what is your name?"

"My name Anna, you come from Holland or Australia?"

"I come from USA."

Anna, quickly responded, "Mister Bush no good."

Wow, an eight-year-old Indonesian girl knows her politics. We arrive at Wisma Losmen just in time to save me from defending the Bush administration to Anna and hopefully leave her with the idea that all people from USA are not horrible. Anna walks ahead of me into the front room where a family that looks exactly like hers, including an eight month old baby boy, three cats and a blaring TV, sit on a mat. Anna announces me, "She from USA, she no have husband." Not sure how Anna determined that information, but she is correct, I am an unmarried American even though I do wear a ring on my left hand while traveling. Anna runs over to her cousins and immediately they start laughing and playing.

"Welcome, we have a room for you tonight, but tomorrow we are fully booked." Anna's uncle is soft spoken with kind eyes.

"No problem, I just need a place for tonight. I come long way today."

"You need fill out register, and I need passport." He hands me three pages to fill out, and I deflate, tears are actually brimming. He sees my reaction to the lengthy registration and quickly adds, "Come, join my family, please sit, and drink tea." Anna's aunt smiles at me and hands me a glass cup of warm, sweet amber tea. I crumple onto the mat, lean my back up against the wall and use my backpack as a table to begin the registration process for my one night here at Wisma Losmen.

Country of origin? Flight number? Sightseeing planned? Contacts in Indonesia? Visa number? Number in party? Family name? Mothers maiden name? *Really*? Is the Wisma Losmen doing genealogical research? But in true postcolonial tradition, paper work is king. I completed the essay fully so it may be safely filed away into the bureaucratic archives. Another register is pulled out and I must sign and date this as well. I scan the previous names, passport numbers and countries then notice the name before mine, Dirk Diggler, Australia. Funny.

"You pay now." Anna's uncle is kind but firm. I'm sure it is not easy managing a hotel on one of the busiest roads in Jakarta. Jalan Jaksa boasts 60,000 foreign tourists a year averaging only two nights stays at a time. That's some serious laundry to do.

"Berapa?" I ask

"Oh, you speak Indonesian?" Anna's uncle beams.

"Not so much, but I want to learn." I can hear the children laughing and mocking me, "Berapa, berapa, ha ha!"

"Sixty thousand rupiah for one night, you get discount if you stay three night."

I pay the man and remember him telling me that it is booked past tonight, so the discount couldn't apply, but stop myself, and smile.

"Room satu," then he holds up one finger, "tiga" he holds up three fingers, "lima" and holds up five with a huge smile.

"Terima kasih. Room one, three, five?"

"Yes." he hands me a set of keys and wishes me Slamat tidur, as he walks back to join his family.

Room 135 is a windowless cement block with one single bed against each wall, a small table between them with a thermos of hot tea, two small glasses and a plastic ashtray. I flip on the ceiling fan, put my backpack down on one bed and sit on the other. The mattress is covered with a clean, white flat sheet folded under each corner. I am tempted to look under the sheet at the condition of the mattress but don't. Why torture myself with visions of what lies beneath? I inspect the bathroom with low expectations and hope I don't see any cockroaches. I know they're there—I just don't want to see them. There is a moldy smell, like nothing ever quite dries in this box. I flip on the bathroom light and am pleasantly surprised. It is a gleaming blue tiled room with a drain in the middle of the floor. A squat toilet is situated on a platform. A tall skinny tub-like bath is filled to the brim with water. A small bucket with a handle sits on the ledge of the tub. This is called a mandi, both noun and verb. You pour buckets of water over your head for a shower, or in the toilet to flush it. What a great invention.

I find my most prized possessions –my sarongs – folded neatly in my backpack. I use my sarongs for everything. They can be used as a towel, a skirt, a blanket, a pillow, a scarf, or a bed cover for a questionable mattresses– the possibilities are endless. Really, they are just a meter of thin, cotton material, but they are lifesavers on the road. I undress and go into the bathroom for a mandi. I dip the bucket into the water and pour it over my head, washing the long flights off my tired body. I wrap a sarong around myself, make sure the door is locked, flip the light off and lie down on my back. I watch the fan swirl, hear its rhythm, shuh ruh ruh shuh ruh ruh shuh ruh ruh.

Chapter Three

Ahhhlllahhaooooohhakkbahh! I would be the worst Muslim on the planet—there is no way I would get up out of bed to go pray at 4:57 a.m. I roll over on my side and fall back to sleep. Not until 10:38 do my eyes open again, my stomach is growling and the heat punches through the concrete walls. I squat on the toilet until my thighs start to shake, then douse myself under another mandi. Despite the stifling heat, Indonesia is still the largest Muslim nation on earth and conservative, consequently I wear long pants and a long sleeved T-shirt. No skimpy clothes for me, my blonde hair and blue eyes are target enough—I discourage attention when I can. I retreat from box number 135, happy to have slept and washed, but looking forward to getting out of Jakarta and onto my real destination, Sumatra. I have been guilty of choosing my destinations by how their names slip off the tongue – Zanzibar, Timbuktu, Istanbul, Zambuanga. And Sumatra was one of those names that conjured up images of tigers, maidens and headhunters. Did I mention I romanticize places?

I took a Renaissance art class in junior college. Four months later, I went to Florence where I cried my eyes out standing in front of Bernini's Ecstasy of St.Theresa. I ran around that city like a crack addict, searching for the pieces I had studied. I stood in front of Bertoli's gold doors, drinking in the battle scenes. I hiked up Brunelleschi's dome, and saw myself in Botticelli's Birth of Venus. Ever since, my Italian orgasm, I research my destinations like a scholar before I go, so when I'm standing in front of a crusader castle, a crumbling ruin, or temple, I appreciate what it is, who built it and for what purpose. And so, for the last four months while researching Sumatra, I had developed my must-see list and was anxious to get out of Jakarta and begin to check it off.

"Helllooooo?," I called at the front desk, but no one was around except two sleeping cats, so I set my key on the counter and walked across the street to the Memories Café where the Karoke is in full swing.

"Take me to the magic of the moment on a glory night, where the children of tomorrow dream away in the wind of change!" You gotta love the drunk, old, white, expats belting the Scorpions at eleven in the morning over a whiskey and a bottle of Bintang. Usually they have a beautiful, young (I mean young) Indonesian girl sitting by their side. I must leave this city today.

A stunning young woman approaches me and asks, how many?

"One, please," I respond with a hint of disdain, like do you see anyone else behind me pal? Take it easy, Mia, your just hungry and sweaty and need to find a way out of this city. The Indonesian super model hands me a menu and gives me a glamour shot smile.

"Terima kasih," I say, surrendering any ill will to her. I order nasi goring—a fried rice dish and a mixed fruit smoothie. There are two very important phrases I pride myself knowing in about every language known to man. One is 'It's too expensive' this term is exclusively saved for my shopping extravaganzas. It's an icebreaker and a bit of comedic relief before the commencement of the very long and arduous bargaining process. The other phrase is 'no meat please'. So, I try that, "Tidak daging" and of course, the supermodel waitress responds in perfect English, "Oh, are you a vegetarian?"

"Yeah, if the cook could make sure there's no meat or fish in the rice I would appreciate it." Way to use your Indonesian, Mia.

I take my map of Indonesia out of my handbag and spread it on the table. The letters spread evenly over the island located to the west of Java. S U M A T R A. I have planned this trip for months, I have studied anthropological journals, National Geographic articles, histories on Marco Polo's visit in 1292, the spice trade, Dutch colonialism, and rounded off my research with the depressing data on the critically endangered rainforest housing dwindling numbers of elephant, tiger, bear, rhino and orangutan populations. Add the strategic location and a few natural resources, namely gold and oil—and presto, War! Still, this place held a romantic illusion for me that would remain unquenched until I saw and felt and tasted it for myself.

    Everything from travel stories to girlfriends are swapped on Jalan Jaksa. Catering to backpackers, this short street holds everything we need to satisfy our desires. In my case, it was a way out. I left the Memories Café and walked next door to an Internet café, in compliance to my mothers contact treaty. Signed after a misunderstanding in India, the treaty states that I contact her within 48 hours of arrival in a new place, then make regular contact with her every ten days. If twenty days elapses with no word from me, my mom has my permission to worry. Pre-Internet world, I would fax letters to her work line, hoping her boss didn't intercept my strange messages, *Safe and sound in Angola, please don't worry, Ebola is miles away!* My parents have accepted my macabre sense of humor but I adhere to the contact treaty for their sanity.

    I hit a travel agent/book exchange next, with a faded copy of a Dean Koonz paperback in the window and flight specials written on a board outside – 'Bangkok, Manila, K.L, Bali, Bus and Ferry tickets available, trade books, new and used.' The air conditioning felt delicious and a man smoking a sweet clove cigarette said, "Welcome, what you need?"

    "I need to go to Sumatra," I answered. And an hour later I walked out with an airline ticket to Medan, a Wilbur Smith novel and a wicked cold from the freezing temperature of Batavia Travel Tours and bookseller. Only bummer was my flight didn't take off until nine the next morning, which meant a whole day and night in Jakarta… splendid.

During my hour in the igloo office I was faced with several travel choices. It came down to taking a three-hour minibus ride from Jakarta to the port city of Merak, then a three-hour ferry across the Sunda Straits to Bakauheni, Sumatra. From there it was a 1,600 kilometers to Medan, a trip that would take about two weeks. Or a free lift to the airport and an hour and forty-four minutes on Garuda Air. I knew I would fulfill my adventure quota without putting myself through the horror of being stuffed in a bemo, with the worst drivers in the world chain-smoking clove cigarettes, while the lethal roads paved across active volcanoes and dense rainforests threatened to kill us. Oh no, not I.

So, off to find another hotel and catch up on a few national treasures. My sights were set high. First I would visit the National Museum. It houses the largest and rarest collection of Oriental ceramics outside China. Then I'd visit the Immanuel church built by the Dutch in 1834, followed by a tour of the puppet museum with its priceless collection of puppets from around the world. Next, I'd round my day off with a ride up to the top of the 137 meter high MONAS monument and gaze down at the entire city below. In fact, I found another hotel, decided to take a nap before my lengthy excursion, and woke up much later to my alarm. It was six the next morning. I'm just in time to catch my shuttle to the airport. All that potential sightseeing exhausted me.

If I had a dollar for every hour I waited at airports I'd be rich. I have my ritual–find an empty gate area, set up a bed of sarongs, snacks, ipod, novel and guidebook and settle in. Once, I fell asleep in the Nairobi airport and missed my flight to London, so I set my alarm now. But today would be a different story. I entered my waiting area and noticed a salon advertising a one-hour massage. A massage parlor in the airport, I love Indonesia.

An hour and a half later I emerged, loose as a goose, smelling like eucalyptus and jasmine flowers. And, with a new contact—which is the best while traveling alone. The massage girl, Sarah, gave me her parent's name and address in Blangkejeren, Sumatra, which I was going right through on my way to Sabang. I always take people up on invitations, always. In western countries it's considered a polite offer that will likely never be accepted. However, South East Asia is a different story. Two years ago I showed up, hungry, tired and alone with some random contact in Lombok, and left as an adoptive daughter three months later. These people clearly carry the hospitality gene.

  I boarded the plane feeling clean and refreshed and excited to finally be off on my adventure to Sumatra. My father taught me to ask for what you want, the worst thing that could happen is they say no, so half way through the flight I asked the stewardess if I could see the cockpit. She asked me to follow her which I did—to the front of the plane. She knocked before opening the door, and a cloud of cigarette smoke billowed out the door.

  "Welcome, please sit, my friend," one of the two pilots said to me, like it was normal procedure to have a passenger come visit the pilots in the cockpit during the flight. I sat on a jump seat behind the two pilots and all I could see was blue sky through the front windscreen. "Where you come from?" said the short guy on the right.

  "I come from USA," I replied. The other pilot began to cough and laugh at the same time saying, "George Bush no good."

  "Yes, I know." I rolled my eyes and smiled back at him.

  "You smoke?" asked Shorty, offering me a cigarette.

  "No, terima kasih."

  "Oh, you speak Indonesian!"

We continued with a bit of small talk about what I do for work and where I live, when I saw the rainforest appear and the clouds begin to clear. "Wow, it's beautiful," I yelled over the noise. They both laughed and lit up their eighth cigarette in forty minutes. I watched the pilot to my left flip several switches and respond to a radio transmission that I could not hear.

"Yes, tower Garuda niner zero zero, requesting landing." We were losing altitude and I thought it was time for me to return to my seat. "Well, thank you for allowing me to sit with you" I said standing to leave. They both looked back and Shorty said, "No, you stay for landing, put seat belt on." I was kinda freaked out, but sat back down and figured out the seat belt comes over your head and buckles between your legs. This time both pilots were switching levers, pressing buttons and I could feel in my stomach the plane was landing soon, but all I saw from the window was the tops of trees below us. Where the hell is the airport, I thought. We were totally surrounded by trees, I couldn't see a city anywhere.

"How much longer until we land?" I asked, my eyes must have looked frightened. Shorty looked at me and laughed, "Don't be scared, I land plane with eyes close!" He shut his eyes and mocked driving with his hands stretched out. Then opened his eyes and continued, "we are like bus drivers, we go to Medan and back to Jakarta four times today!"

The other pilot lit up a cigarette and spoke again into his mouthpiece, "Copy that tower, landing number six, Garuda niner zero zero." Still wondering if we were going to land in the rainforest, a clearing appeared, then a road, an airport, and civilization. The pilots never extinguished their cigarettes even through their perfect landing. The other passengers deboarded past the door to the cockpit and down the stairs. I thanked my pilot friends again for allowing me to watch the landing up close (with my heart in my mouth). Shorty asked if I wanted to go back to Jakarta with them. I declined but said I'd be back in a few months. I ran back to my seat to collect my backpack—and walked down the stairs onto the runway.

The equator runs directly through Sumatra, and I'm telling you it's very warm— incredibly hot, in fact. But here I was, finally, on the island of Sumatra. Sixth largest island on the planet, where tigers, elephants, rhinos and orangutans co-exist. Where the Kantoli kingdom thrived in 489, where Chinese ships docked in 1017, and Marco Polo stood in 1292. Well, maybe he wasn't at the Medan airport, but here I was, on the Island of Gold. Finally. I watched the stewardess escort my fellow passengers into the small airport terminal. I followed behind dripping with sweat. I had no checked luggage, just my backpack, so I by-passed the carousel where passengers waited for their bags and went straight to the arrivals hall. Not exactly a hall, just a small room with high-speed fans mixing up warm air.

Excited family members waited outside the arrivals area for their relatives coming from Jakarta. No one was waiting for me. I saw them searching for their loved ones, and their disappointment when they saw it was only this foreigner coming from the baggage claim. I felt like telling them, your family is right behind me. I've never been picked up at the arrivals hall.

I found my way out past the waiting taxis. Bemos aren't allowed curbside at the Medan airport, you have to walk a street over to find those dependable minivans. "Medan city?" I asked a bemo driver. He sucked his teeth and pointed to another van a few feet away. "Medan city?" I questioned the next driver. He sucked his teeth, took a long drag on a cigarette and lifted his eyebrows clearly meaning that, yes, this was the vehicle to take me into Medan city. I sat in the back row and waited for the bus to fill.

High noon in downtown Medan, Sumatra– time to make a plan. The bemo dropped me at the Padang Bulah Bus Terminal, but before I make any decisions I have to sit, evaluate my situation and decide what to do. This routine keeps me from making hasty choices that I will later regret. One of my crucial rules is: never arrive in a new place late at night without a pre-booked hotel. I landed in Cairo at midnight once, and got screwed out of a hundred bucks for the crappiest hotel on earth. It took two more late night arrival horror shows, one in New Delhi and one in Frankfurt, to convince me that I should never land in a new place a minute later than six. It's vital to check out a new spot while it's still light out—to case the joint. And, room rates aren't jacked up beyond belief.

I knew before I landed that I didn't want to spend the night in another big, dirty city. My plan was to go to a small village called Brastagi, only seventy kilometers outside of Medan. I wanted to begin my introduction to Sumatra in Brastagi which boasts a higher elevation, and means an escape from the oppressive heat. Another rule, which again was learned the hard way, is to limit daily travel to four hours. Notice I don't refer in miles or kilometers but in hours, because until you have traveled the roads in India, Africa or Guatemala you couldn't know that a mere seventy-kilometer journey could take twenty hours! Good times.

Hopefully *this* seventy kilometers would take the normal one hour. With that thought in mind, I happily boarded a bus to Bastagi and chose a window seat. In no time at all, the beauty of Sumatra was gliding by me. Rubber tree plantations by the miles, little kids playing on the side of road, water buffalo swatting flies with their tails in the rice fields, old men squatting on their haunches waiting for the next call to prayer. I was filled with excitement and nostalgia. This life of travel is not glamorous or easy. I sit on busses not knowing where I'll stay that night. I complain constantly about schlepping my backpack around in 100 degree heat. I get lonely. I get bored. But the rewards far outweigh the misery and occasional disappointments. For me traveling offers up mystical contrasts filled with surprises (not always good ones). My wanderlust drives me to endure the obvious nightmares that can define a trip. Even then, I pinch myself to realize my amazing luck. During my trips I may be exhausted, my sunburn might hurt, I may smell foul—but, all those discomforts can be restored, healed, or washed away. I'm living the life I want. I felt happy sitting on that old bus, looking out the window at sights I'd imagined—but now were real, dazzling my eyes. I wish I could express it like a poet, but I'll simply describe my feelings as contentedness.

Chapter Four

The scenery went from miles of rubber tree plantations to a deep valley surrounded by hundreds of volcanoes. We were higher now, the air, clear and crisp and I see the blue sky for the first time in days. In Jakarta and Medan the air was smoggy, as if a distant forest fire was burning. That haze has been replaced by a vivid blue sky, fluffy white clouds caressing the cones of green volcanoes. After an hour and a half, I stepped off the bus in the cool hilltop village of Brastagi. What a welcome change from Medan and Jakarta this little paradise was. I checked the map in my guidebook and found where I was standing near the city center, I walked up a main road past an outdoor market until I arrived at the losmen I had already chosen from the book. The Karo House Losmen did not look too inviting, the windows were broken and a family of chickens nested in the front room. Sometimes the guest houses recommended in guide books get so much business they can't keep up, looks like another one fell prey to guide book syndrome. I continued up the road looking for another losmen. And there it was--the Karo House Two, which was perfect.

At the check-in desk, a young woman greeted me—and, as usual, I was immediately asked why I was alone. Indonesians would never travel alone! I filled out all the registers and informational forms, wondering if some government employee was accumulating all this visitor intelligence to promote tourism or if millions of pages of travelers' information was gathering dust in a government office in Jakarta. Didn't matter, I was happy to have a bed, a cup of jasmine tea and a mandi all for eight bucks a night.

Four days later I was still holed up in the gorgeous little mountain get away of the Karo House Two. I spent my days wandering through the market, tasting fruit straight out of Dr. Suess's imagination– white jello flesh with tiny pink seeds covered in a spiky red peel, papaya five times larger than I had ever seen, mangos so sweet I thought they were injected with sugar. Monsanto, however, has yet to trademark this fruit, so it was all organic, delicious and affordable.

And the hiking! Every day I found a new trail that wandered through the dramatic volcanic landscape. I got lost in dense bamboo forests clinging to the slopes of Mt. Sibayak. I never summited the 7000 foot volcano but I checked out a hot spring, waterfall, a traditional Adat house and took in breathtaking views of fluorescent green rice paddies on the valley floor terraced all the way up the pitch of the steep mountain.

All the backpackers I had met during my stay in Brastagi told me that Lake Toba was a must-see. So when I climbed into a bemo and headed out on the thirty-minute drive south I was armed with a list of places to stay, to eat, hikes to go on and museums to explore.

You first see the lake from spectacular vantage points as you drive down the mountain road. The water looks like someone poured blue paint in it—the minerals give it an amazingly brilliant aqua color. Surrounded by a pine forest, I had been transported to Austria. Complete with the Tudor style cabins, I heard the Von Trapp children singing in the distant hills. With his missing front teeth and huge home-rolled cigarette between his lips, my bemo driver brought me back to reality. "Toba" he bellowed between puffs. I got out and went looking for a guesthouse that was recommended to me by a German guy I met in Brastangi.

The largest volcanic explosion on the planet formed Lake Toba. I spent hours reading about the super volcano in the museum—this volcano had been big—like Texas big. A ferry takes people to the small island in the middle of the lake, formed by a resurgent caldera. The Toba eruption generated 2800 times more pyroclastic material than the eruption of Mt. St. Helens. Whatever exploding geological monster it was a million years ago, now it's a serene place of beauty. However, I was not alone. Millions of tourists have despoiled its purity. The tranquility that should be there is lost. Prices are sky high, oblivious litterers leave their boxed lunches and trash on the hiking trails. Lake Toba must once have been a peaceful place, but, for me, two days of picking up trash and paying triple for my guesthouse was enough! I was filled with rage. It was such a shame to see what careless people will do. I turned my back on this desecration of nature and began my trip to Bukit Lawang.

Even though I had only been away from home a week I started missing my family. I wanted to hug my mom, eat a Chicago style pizza, watch a movie and have a conversation without having to think of the words in a foreign language. The grass is always greener for me. Toba had depressed me—my expectations were thwarted because of a poorly run national reserve. I hoped the Orangutan sanctuary, my next stop, would be better managed and not upset me even further. How pathetic that this pristine land was being decimated faster than any other in the world. I would have to visit a sanctuary in order to see the once abundant species that thrived here. In truth, the once prolific American Bison withered to humiliating numbers in my own country, barely survived the same plight. I was homesick, disappointed with Toba and depressed with the world, I needed my mom.

I found an Internet café and e-mailed her. I didn't express my disappointment with Toba, I didn't want her to be worried or upset. I wrote that I was safe and having a good time, that I missed her and I was already looking forward to seeing her in January, getting a pizza delivered and watching a movie with her and dad at home. I closed with a P.S.—When you pick me up from the airport will you come into the arrivals hall, not just curbside, like usual? She must think I'm nuts, but I kind of am.

My bemo left at just after one p.m. to Bukit Lawang. Me and an Australian guy called Tim shared the dreaded backseat—Indonesians hate the back. True to form, the minibus was packed with twelve adults six kids and several baskets of live chickens. I made Tim laugh with some bad-luck travel stories and he shared his Marie biscuits with me as the hours went by. The easy four-hour ride evolved into a moving torture show. We were crushed into that bemo, sucking up second hand smoke, breathing in the smell of vomit and chicken shit for hours. My friendship with Tim was cemented like fraternity brothers through hell week. If he hadn't been with me, I wouldn't have any one on this Earth to corroborate my insanity.

We rolled into Bukit Lawang eleven hours later, at midnight—yes, both travel rules broken—exhausted and smelly. Tim and I shared a room at the Garden of Eden Guesthouse right along the banks of the Bohorok river. Each bed had its own mosquito net draped over clean white sheets. A quick mandi, a clean sarong and T-shirt and I was in bed, glad to be out of Toba, over that hideous bemo ride and lying in a fresh bed listening to the river flow by.

Tim and I had breakfast at the Garden of Eden restaurant early the next morning. I inhaled a banana pancake dripping with lemon and sugar, and sipped a very strong cup of locally grown coffee. Tim was headed home after spending two months surfing on Pulau Nias, an island just off the coast of Sumatra. I told him I was headed up to Pulau Weh and he tried to change my mind by convincing me that Nias was heaps closer. But I was on a mission, to see the famous Sabang harbor where Chinese sailors harbored in 1017. Tim rolled his eyes at me and said, "No worries mate, go do what you have to do. I get it girl, but enough about the old Chinese sailors already!" I guess I had mentioned the National Geographic article a few times on the endless bemo ride. He talked nonstop about a killer left off the reef and how stoked he was on the rad swell. *Surfers*. Tim and I didn't have too much in common but since both of us were on tight budgets, sharing a room worked out perfectly.

We hung out together for three days, me talking about the culture and history of Sumatra, Tim asking me about awesome surf spots in Hawaii and California. We rented tire tubes and floated down the river that bisects the city. We visited the Orangutan sanctuary. It was run by a Swedish couple. I was relieved to find that this place of rehabilitation had found the right caretakers. And the baby orangutans were adorable as they clung to their mothers, swinging from tree to tree. Tim and I went for a dozen hikes into the rainforest. At night we ate big plates of fried noodles, drank a lot of beer and exchanged travel stories at the restaurant as we watched the river glide by. He was a perfectly tanned surfer boy with gleaming white teeth, a set of abs you could bounce a quarter off and a delightful singsongy accent. Why, you ask, didn't anything but sleep go down in our lovely little Garden of Eden hut? I'm a romantic, and hooking up with travelers just isn't my deal. Not to say I haven't had some love on the road, I just know myself and hurt will ultimately follow.

After four days we parted. Tim took a bemo to Medan where he flew back to Brisbane, while I headed west, getting closer to Pulau Weh, my final destination. Of course Pulau Weh was about 500 kilometers west and according to my bemo tripometer that's like hundreds of hours in hell. That's what travel is about—rough situations that are miserable at the time but that later—sometimes, a lot later—make fantastic and hilarious stories. I read in a travel blog before I left that said, "Whatever can go wrong, will go wrong in Sumatra." I understand that I am not on a pleasure cruise and I need to keep my expectations low and my patience high. With this in mind I found a bemo going west and chose a town that was only a four-hour ride. Again.

Bemos are not express vehicles, these minivans don't budge until they are chock full, and I mean full. They stop when passengers want off, and pick up other customers on the roadside, even when you think there's no room, another commuter is admitted. I usually sit in the back seat near a window so I can see out and breathe a bit of air even though it's mixed with the endless thick cigarette smoke. In this case, I found my usual spot and got comfy for the journey. I was headed to Kutacane, a town half way to Blangkejeren, where I had my one and only contact.

Sarah, the massage girl at the Jakarta airport had given me the name of her parents and promised to tell them I was coming. Periodically, in my travels contacts have not come through—once I ended up sleeping in my car at a rest stop just inside the Pennsylvania border because my only contact to whom I called for directions informed me that it wasn't *convenient* for me to sleep on her couch. That sucked. But in this case it wasn't actually the people who had offered, it was their daughter so my expectations were low, if Sarah's parents were busy or unavailable, I could easily find a cheap guesthouse.

Willie Nelson's, On the Road Again was playing over and over in my head as my little bemo pushed westward through the highlands of Northern Sumatra. Beautiful scenery, more volcanoes, rice paddies, boys playing soccer, goats, chickens and mangy dogs running across the road. The sky was filled with dark rain clouds, then moments of dazzling sun. I didn't drink water because I didn't want to have to pee. I just enjoyed the ride until the first flat tire.

Everyone out, then decision time, do I wait for a spare, or flag down the next bemo? The driver stopped a guy on a moped and sped off. I waited, along with my fellow passengers on the side on the road for about an hour until the driver returned on the back of another moped with a new tire strapped to his head, not a brand new tire, but new enough. There is an expression in Indonesia, 'Jam Karet' it means rubber time—translation, if it doesn't happen today, could happen tomorrow and if not then, sometime soon. It's always said with a smile and a shrug of the shoulders and seems to be an acceptable answer for most questions in Indonesia. Tire changed, passengers file back in and we're On the Road Again.

Another full day spent in a smoke-filled bemo. It's eight o'clock at night when the driver wakes me up, "Kutacane!" Of course, since I am in the back of this crowded vehicle, everyone has to disembark to allow me to get out. I create an impromptu pit stop. The driver takes my 10,000 Rupiah, about a dollar fifty, jumps on the roof to untie my backpack from the luggage rack and hefts it down to me. Everyone loads back in. I smile and wave to the group I've just spent the last eight hours with, they all smile back and wave back as they continue westward. We only went four hours over the predicted time, I feel giddy!

Blangkejeren is another (estimated) eight-hour drive the next day. I am dreading it! For now though, I'm tired, hungry and need a mandi. I find Wisma Gunung, just steps away from where the bemo dropped me and it seemed as good as any place at this point. The check-in procedure commences. I fill out the usual forms, give the guy at the desk my passport to make a photocopy and am given a key to my cell. Not the most inviting of places I've stayed—one barred window opened to the main road, a toilet that I had to take a picture of to show my sisters because it was *so* bad, the mandi basin was filled with wiggling mosquito larvae that I pretended not to see as I lifted the first bucket of water over my head. The walls had little peepholes that someone had stuffed toilet paper into. I returned to reception and asked the guy, "Makan?" Indonesian has no tenses so I guess it means eat, ate, and food—but he got my meaning and pointed out the door to a street cart. Awesome… street food in the middle of nowhere Sumatra. I made my best small talk to the man cooking some meat on the cart. "As Salaam Alaikum."
"Wa Alaikum As Salaam" he responded with a smile.
"Nasi goring, sayur saja." I doubted I was going to get vegetable fried rice without meat, but it was worth a try.

"Saya tidak punya." No have. All right, smile Mia, and take what he's cooking. Pretty sure I ate dog that night, washed it down with a warm Coke, thanked the man for the stomach ache and went to bed. No fan, no mosquito net, cars whizzing by the open window, and horny men probably watching me through the peepholes. At 4:57 a.m. I discovered that the loudspeaker to announce holy Friday morning prayer was actually wired on to the bars of my bedroom window. My body jolted out of bed not knowing where I was or what was happening—it took me a second for it to register, then I just had to laugh or else I'd die crying. No need for wake-up alarms in Kutacane. At least I would get on the first bemo that morning!

More driving, more cigarette smoke, more questioning why I didn't fly to Banda Aceh and skip this bemo hell? I know—I talk about life being the journey, not the destination…horseshit! Distances were deceiving on that map—a map that had been so romantic to me only days before with its letters S U M A T R A spread across the long skinny island. I had referenced that lying-piece-of-crap map so many times along my journey, now I only wanted to shred the exotic paper and throw it out of my moving bemo.

Next stop, Blangkejeren—my only contact and another eight hours closer to my final goal of Pulau Weh. Starving and tired I watched in horror as my driver holds a cigarette in one hand, laughs with the three guys sharing his bench seat, all the while taking hairpin turns at high speeds. Maybe I should switch up my priorities, I thought, and instead of complaining about being famished, be glad I was alive to experience hunger.

At one point the road was gone, completely gone under a mountain of dirt and rocks from a landslide. A makeshift bridge of two logs was placed over the twenty-foot mound in the middle of the road, the little van screamed in first gear up and over and on we went. Several areas of the drive, the pavement had fallen down one side of a cliff and the road suddenly became one lane, where the driver would play chicken with whatever vehicle was coming the other way, mostly with huge logging trucks going 100 mph piled high with freshly-cut ancient trees from the annihilated rainforest. Still the little minivan would putter up and up the mountain road, and then speed down and down until I was conscious of my jaw locked so tightly my head burned with a migraine.

The bemo stopped for an hour break at a roadside restaurant and fruit market. I took advantage of getting out of the van and making a break for it. There were several giant tour buses parked nearby so I approached a driver and asked, "Blangkejeren?" Not only was he headed that way but he spoke a little English. I returned to my bemo driver and paid him the full amount to Blangkejeren, grabbed my backpack and thanked him for the last three hours. He looked a little confused, but I smiled, thanked him again, wished him a safe journey, "Senang Perjalanan, terama kasi." I wanted to thank him for facilitating the re-examination of my entire life thus far but was unsure how to convey that in Indonesian. I knew one thing though, I was finished riding in bemos. Forever!

The humongous bus seemed safer than the bemo only because I could not see as well through the front window. At two o'clock I made it to Blangkejeren exhausted and frazzled but alive. I did have the address—Jalan Besar 143—of Sarah's parents, but I thought it would be better if I got a hotel for the night. Perhaps they weren't really ready for a houseguest even though I intended to bring a gift. I found a little losmen and bargained for a room for one night. Searching my purse as the paperwork ensued I realized that I didn't have my passport. I must have put it in a different spot this morning when I was awoken by the morning prayers, I fooled myself. I *never* put my passport in a different spot—it's always in the front cover of my little plastic address book. My heart started pounding. My passport was gone.

Chapter Five

Well, not exactly gone since I was pretty sure I knew exactly where it was. Left in the copy machine at the Wisma Gunung last night. Meeting time.

I have been calling meetings with myself throughout my travels. Instead of going into panic mode with news of a certain magnitude, I quietly excuse myself from the situation, find a place to sit, have a drink of water (oftentimes beer) and think through all my options before crying, screaming, or throwing myself off a cliff. OK. I'm not getting on a bemo for eight hours to retrieve my passport. I am not going to go anywhere without my passport. I am not going to start weeping and throw my body in front of a bus. I am going to walk to Sarah's parents' home, explain my situation and ask for help. Meeting adjourned.

I walked along Jalan Besar until I found number 143. A modern, cement house with a screen door. "Helllooo?" I called. An angelic little girl about five appeared, then cocked her head upwards staring at me through the screen. "Hello?" I asked. "How are you? Apa Kabar?"

"Hello missus, give me candy." She demanded with a smile revealing rotten front teeth. Clearly someone had obliged her command. Then Sarah came to the door behind the little girl. "Sarah?" I asked, surprised she was home from Java.

"I am the younger sister of Sarah, my name is Ratu, this is my daughter Princess. Please come in, Sarah telephoned and told us you were coming." Ratu swung open the door, I slipped off my flip-flops and joined the girls inside.

I dropped my backpack in a corner and sat on a comfortable couch. Ratu went into the kitchen and returned with a bowl of freshly cut watermelon and a neon pink drink for me. I thanked her and she sat down while Princess played with a Little Mermaid doll on the polished concrete floor. "I cannot believe how much you and Sarah look alike, you could be twins!"

"Yes, we fooled our teachers in school many times."

"You speak English perfectly."

"Thank you, I think my English is not good, I completed a language course at the American school in Medan last year but I have no one to practice with."

"What are you doing in Sumatra?" Ratu asked me. I went into why I travel, that I finished my University course in Anthropology and love to learn about different cultures. I told her I was headed to Pulau Weh and Sabang harbor. I asked Ratu what she would do with her degree, and about Princess.

"I won a scholarship for a computer-engineering course at the University. I travel to Medan each week then return home to be with Princess on the week ends."

"You go to Medan every week? Please tell me you don't travel in bemos!" I begged. Ratu laughed, "No, I take the express bus, it's not so long." Note to self... take express bus. We sat comfortably for an hour talking about our families, she told me that she and Princess's father were planning on getting married when she finished University. He worked on a ship that is usually harbored in Jakarta so they only see each other once a month, sometimes once in two months.

I always bring a little photo album when I travel, photos are a great cultural bond especially when a common language doesn't exist. Ratu flipped through the shots of tow-headed babies, laughing sisters, my favorite beach, kids blowing out birthday candles, mom and dad smiling in front of the house, more babies. "Your sisters look very much like you."

"Yes, we also fooled teachers, and boyfriends too!" I detailed my passport situation and Ratu called the Wisma Gunung to make sure it was there. It was, and they told her they would put it in the mail that afternoon headed to 143 Jalan Besar. I felt relieved and a little annoyed at myself. I consider myself an expert traveler and that was a very amateur mistake.

Ratu, Princess and I walked to the open-air market to buy fresh vegetables for dinner. Ratu told me my passport would probably arrive tomorrow or Sunday, so I could spend the weekend with a real Indonesian family to get experience for my University work. She explained that her mom would be home around eight, but her father came home too late from his job to eat with the family. I thanked her for her kind offer and looked forward to being part of a family for a couple days.

Ratu's mother arrived home later that night. She worked weekends doing accounting for a school, then watched Princess through the week when Ratu went to University. She did not speak any English except for hello, so we exchanged smiles and used Ratu as an interpreter for small talk around the dinner table. She asked about Sarah, and I told her how talented her daughter was at massage. I helped wash the dishes, watched an Indonesian soap opera with the girls then went to sleep in an upstairs bedroom under the safety of a mosquito net. I was happy to be with this loving family and looking forward to reuniting with my passport tomorrow.

When I woke up the next morning, I heard Ratu talking to her mom and dad. Princess was watching TV. It felt like I was home. I walked down stairs and was introduced to Ratu's father. He spoke no English, so again, smiles and nods all around. Ratu announced that since they had a special guest we would go to the lake for the day.

We all piled in the family car and drove about an hour through the mountains to a lakeside resort. Small campsites equipped with a picnic table and a fire pit (to burn your plastic bottles) surrounded the lake. Local fishermen set up kiosks where you could buy their fresh catch of the day. They also offered a cooking and delivery service. We chose the fresh Tilapia and an hour later the angler/chef showed up at our campsite with eight barbecued fish (heads, tails and scales still on) accompanied with five individual banana-leaf pouches filled with white rice.

I tried to pay, but Ratu's father was offended. I was the entertainment that afternoon as they all laughed at the American girl trying to dissect and eat her fish with no utensils. Just hands. It was gross, but I ate every morsel, like a good guest should. We threw our banana-leaf plates and fish bones into the lake as the clean-up ritual.

After lunch, father napped under the pretense of reading a newspaper. Ratu and her mom chatted on a blanket near the water while Princess and I went for an adventure in the forest. We discovered, the lakeside resort included a small zoo. There were two sad elephants chained to a concrete cylinder and jailed by a polluted moat. Cages of Gibbons and monkeys squealing for release and Sun Bears pacing in their feces littered pens. All the animals looked like they had gone insane years ago in their confined enclosures. Princess wanted to go see the panther, but I couldn't stomach anymore of that neglected menagerie. I pretended to be a horse, let out my best neigh and ran back to the lake. Princess followed me giggling with delight.

When we returned to the house, Ratu checked the mail for my passport. It hadn't arrived. "It will be here tomorrow," she assured me.

"Tomorrow's Sunday, do they deliver mail on Sunday?" I asked hopefully.

"Don't worry Mia, it will come tomorrow and you can be in Ache on Monday. My father said he would drive you to the bus station early Monday morning on his way to work." I felt relieved. I appreciated this family but I was uneasy about my passport. A passport is worth money on the black market, and I began to worry. I took a cold mandi and retired upstairs to read in bed while the family watched TV downstairs. My dreams were filled with those poor elephants.

Sunday morning I joined Ratu downstairs and asked if there was a restaurant where I could treat the family to breakfast. She laughed at me and told me that was an American tradition—she saw it on TV. She was right, I hadn't seen an IHOP for a while. Fried noodles with shrimp cakes again. I didn't want to dwell on the missing passport, but I couldn't help it. I asked Ratu what time the mail was usually delivered. "The post usually comes at two o'clock, so we have to wait, but it will be here today Mia, don't worry!"

Ratu was taking the night bus to Medan so she spent the day saying goodbye to Princess and getting her things together. I took a walk around the town, but there was nothing to see or do. It was desolate and small. There certainly weren't any tourist shops, Internet cafes, or anywhere else for me to go. Locals nearly fell off their mopeds staring at me. I was glad to be leaving the next morning. I returned to the house, went up stairs, read my book and waited for the mailman.

The mailman never came. Ratu insisted that post *was* delivered on Sunday—but sometimes if there's not enough mail, they wait until the next day. Another case of Jam Karet, rubber time. Just then I had a waitressing fantasy about telling a customer when they demanded why their food was taking so long, sorry pal, rubber time!

We all gathered downstairs for dinner and a prayer for Ratu's safe journey. I gave her my address in California and told her she was always welcome to visit. I was genuinely sad to see her go, she was my sole interpreter, I felt abandoned and frustrated with my predicament. But she reassured me that my passport would be there tomorrow and not to worry. Father drove her to the bus station, I played a video game with Princess until bedtime.

At five the next morning I heard Ratu's father leave for work. I made my way down stairs to said hello to Ratu's mother. Nods and smiles. I was already longing to have a real conversation with someone, anyone. Princess was watching cartoons. I sat at the dining table and ate the noodles and shrimp cake mother had made for me. I was miserable. I didn't want to impose on this woman in her own home. I smiled up at her, "Terima Kasi." She said something back. I went out on the front porch and read my book. It was about Magellan's circumnavigation and it was good, but my passport crowded out the words.

If it doesn't come today, should I get on a bemo and go back to Kutacane? I should have gone back on Friday, but I thought it would be here, and if I go now and miss it then I won't know. Stop it Mia! It will come today—you can have a going away dinner tonight and be on a bus in the morning. I was confident that I would leave tomorrow. I couldn't stay another day here. It started to rain. I went back inside the house, and back upstairs to my little mattress and book. Magellan had just arrived at Mactan island. I heard a knock on my bedroom door, "Hello?" Ratu's mom asked in a quiet voice. I jumped up and she and another lady stood at the entrance to my room. "My fren Anisa give good massage, she teach Sarah, she do for you now."

That's how my next five days went. After my noodle breakfast and shrimp cake, Anisa would come to the house around noon, she would slather me down with sweet smelling oil and massage me for an hour. Mama would heat pots of water on the stove so I could have a hot mandi after my massage. Princess and I would play video games and Barbies while Mama prepared dinner, did the washing, cleaned the house and mended clothes. I was anxious every day until the post arrived with no passport. I couldn't communicate with anyone, so I waited and got massaged, and read, and babysat. I almost stopped caring when Ratu showed up on Friday afternoon from Medan.

"Mia! What are you still doing here?" It was so good to hear English and see Ratu. "Where is my mom?" Princess ran to her mom while I explained, "I let your mom go to work early, I told her I'm fine watching Princess until you got here." Ratu hugged her daughter while listening to me. "This is crazy Mia, let's go down to the post office and talk to them." We walked the five blocks to the Post office. Ratu spoke to a lady behind the counter for a few minutes, I recognized 'America, Kutacane, passport'. Ratu turned and asked me what other form of picture identification I had with me. I dug into my purse and brought out my California drivers license, my Costco card and my expired student ID. The post lady scrutinized the photo on my license then looked up and scanned my face to compare the likeness. Perhaps I was an imposter. She walked in the back and returned with an envelope sent from Wisma Gunung. It had arrived last Sunday. I tore it open and there it was! My passport! My beautiful passport! I gazed at the gold eagle emblazoned on the blue cover—his left talon gripping the thirteen arrows and his right, an olive branch, his promise of peace.

Immediately I thought of my dad and his clichés: Take time to smell the roses. Things you think are the worst often turn out to be gifts. For the past week, my passport was sitting five blocks away safe and sound while I was desperate to leave. I felt like I was imposing, I was uncomfortable and feeling sorry for myself and would have left if I could have. But look what happened! What a gift it was! I got to spend time with mama and Princess and get massaged by Anisa every day. What I thought was one of the worst things to happen, turned out to be the opposite, just like my dad predicted.

"There must be a restaurant that we could go to Ratu?" I asked, knowing it was truly my last night with them. Princess, Mama, Ratu and I walked to the nearest street food cart that evening. It was raining, so some local boys hoisted blue tarps up and over the plastic tables and chairs. A man ladled out his delicious noodle soup in bowls then added pieces of fried chicken and white rice for each of us. We drank Sprite's and shared a delicious, spicy dinner under the tarps together. I was happy that night. Rain drizzled down through the tarps onto the tables, the townspeople stared at me while mama was beaming with pride that she had a westerner friend to show off. I paid the six dollars for our dinner and piggybacked Princess back to the house. We waited for lulls in the rain under awnings, and then raced out to the next dry spot until we made it home.

Father gave me a ride to the bus station early the next morning. I got off the moped, then with my inadequate Indonesian, I tried to convey how deeply thankful I was to him and his gorgeous family. More smiles and nods, but he understood. I made sure to send them a care package when I got home. I sent Princess a set of Barbies and a dress up Little Mermaid outfit. I didn't send candy, for the sake of Ratu's future dental bills.

Chapter Six

With my passport safely stowed, I watched out the window as the bus chugged over the steep mountains. The mist held on tight to the peaks while the sun warmed the slopes of tea plantations. Lush, verdant tea plants were rooted deeply in the red soil. Women picked the fragrant leafs and dropped them into baskets strapped to their chests. Several workers had babies tucked into sarongs across their backs. I was on my way west again. I felt content. I was not in a hurry. My stay with Sarah's family helped me put time into perspective. Eckhart Tolle rang in my ears, live in the moment. I felt lucky to be sitting on a bus in the middle of Sumatra with Willy Nelson singing in my head. Girls my age back home were trying on designer jeans, going nowhere on treadmills, worrying about how their Coach purse would look with their Jimmy Choo shoes. Thank goodness, all I had to worry about was my bus hurtling off a cliff with me in it.

Three hours later I arrived in the picturesque mountain village of Takengon. I found a guesthouse on the banks of Lake Tawar. The air was cooler than anywhere else I'd been during my month in Indonesia. I actually took a hot shower, found a sweatshirt at the bottom of my backpack and strapped on my running shoes. Coffee plantations thrived on the steep hills off the lake. I packed a day bag with a bottle of water, my new book and a sarong and set out on a mountain road. I followed it for a few miles and to my delight, discovered a tiny store perched on a rise overlooking the crater lake. There was an Italian espresso machine that looked like it had been there since the 20's. A withered old Chinese man with no teeth welcomed me in. For two hours I sat on a plastic chair sipping strong coffee reading a Michener novel, which I had swapped for my Magellan book at the guesthouse. I was in heaven. I felt alive. Magellan didn't fare so well—but I had. The temperature dropped with the night. I walked back down the hill to my little room and slipped under my wool blanket, fully dressed. I fell into a deep, dreamless sleep.

The last leg of my western migration to Banda Aceh beckoned but I stayed put. For four months I had been anxious to get to Sabang harbor but that morning I felt I could wait. I couldn't get out of my warm bed. I listened to the loons on the lake, to mopeds whizzing by, to schoolchildren laughing. It wasn't in me to get onto another bus, not right then. I lounged until hunger finally triumphed. It was cold—like seeing your breath inside, kind of cold. OK, maybe not that cold. But I kept my sweatshirt and shoes on, wrapped a sarong over my head and hit the mean streets of Takengon in search of food.

My day was spent wandering around the hillsides. There were no other westerners there, no Internet café's, no English speakers. Just lots of stares and smiling faces from the locals. No grocery stores either, so I found a local Chinese market that smelled like dried fish, bought three large Bintang beers, a bag of Doritos and some pistachios, found a grassy spot on the bank of the lake, laid my sarong down and perched up against a tree to waste my afternoon.

I put the beer bottles into the cold water of the lake, sat under my tree and read. After an hour the beer was ice cold, I had my picnic of chips and beer and watched some women doing laundry on the rocks. Naked children played near their mothers, jumping off the rocks into the icy water. The mist hid the sun all day. I was drunk. I made my way to my bed and slept, alone. That day, I wished I had someone to share my lovely afternoon with. It was magical.

I woke up to the sound of a plane around six the next morning. It gave me an idea. Screw driving to Banda Aceh, I would fly! I grabbed my Indonesian dictionary and made my way to reception. The woman who helped me check in was there, writing in a logbook. "Selamat pagi," I smiled as I wished her a good morning.

"Selamat pagi."

I looked up airplane in my dictionary, "Pesawat tebang to Banda Aceh?" I held up my right hand making the best charade of a plane that I could. The lady just looked at me, confused. I looked up airport. "Bandara?"

She shook her head and smiled. The thought of busing it another fifteen hours to Banda Aceh was too much for me. My head was hurting from all the beer. I thanked her and went looking for a bandara. Equipped with my new word I asked every Chinese grocer I could find. Please, I tried to communicate my desperation—I will pay a million dollars to fly to Banda Aceh! No bus! Please! But to no avail. Defeated, I returned to the guesthouse, packed up my bag and headed for the bus station to take the overnight bus into Banda Aceh.

I waited at the bus station for two hours drinking beer until I was drunk again— hoping I could numb myself from the long drive ahead of me. Passengers began boarding the big bus at six in the evening. Children walked down the aisle selling nuts, freshly cooked rice, swallows on skewers, banana chips and candy. I bought some rice, gado-gado, a roll of cookies and a bottle of water and settled in for my overnighter of 331 kilometers.

South East Asians equate freezing temperatures with wealth. I'm guessing that for people to feel like they are getting their money's worth they need the air-conditioning so low that you feel you are in the Gulag. What a horrific ride. I stumbled down the stairs the following morning at eight-thirty into the busy city of Banda Aceh with my backpack — and a cold.

From the bus terminal I walked about two miles to a quiet side street. I dropped my backpack and stood overlooking a sight that I had waited a lifetime (or maybe just four months) to see. The northern tip of Sumatra, where the Strait of Malacca and the Indian Ocean meet. Standing on the banks of the Sungai Aceh River I watched as plastic bags made their way out to sea. Banda Aceh. The doorway to Mecca. Poets and philosophers taught here, great sea battles with the Chinese, Portuguese and Dutch were fought here. I sneezed and blew my nose. I needed sleep. I knew how to get to Pulau Weh, I had read details for months on exactly how to get there from Banda Aceh. I just didn't have it in me right then to continue, no matter how close I was. So I flagged down a taxi and asked him to take me to a guesthouse near Malahayati harbor. The driver dropped me at Wisma Mesjid Baturrachman, a hotel named after the grand Mosque. This was a mouthful but I felt it was appropriate to be staying in a guesthouse named after the mosque that was built by the Dutch as a peace offering.

I found an ATM and withdrew three hundred dollars, a small fortune that would last me for a month. At the Internet café I finally wrote home.

Dearest parents, number five checking in safe and sound in the glorious port town of Banda Ache-Mom, please don't look it up on the internet, they are Muslim and have had some difficult transition years, but they are peace loving and accepting of blonde Americans traveling solo. Sorry it took so long to write, I've been stuck in some pretty small mountain villages. I am off to the island of Weh in the morning and not sure about Internet, so please don't worry and I will try and write soon. I miss you terribly and can't wait to show you pictures and tell you about seeing a Sumatran tiger in the forest...just kidding. Much Love, Mia

Banda Aceh is a big city complete with fully stocked grocery stores, easy transport and lots of people who speak English. I walked to the harbor and bought my ticket to Sabang. I chose to take the first ferry that left early the next morning. I found a market and bought a box of Thera-flu, throat lozenges, Kleenex and then made my way back to the guesthouse for an early night. I listened to the last call to pray around seven and fell into a medicated sleep with a fan blowing on my sweaty forehead.

Chapter Seven

My ferry was scheduled to leave Malahayati harbor at eight the next morning. I was already sitting at the dock at seven. I slept well and only had a slight cough and soar throat lingering from my overnight arctic bus ride. The ocean during the two-hour ferry ride to Weh was dead calm. We motored across the glassy green water. I looked over the rail and saw giant, crystal-clear jellyfish and brightly colored aquarium fish. The water became shallower and bluer as we got closer to Balohan port on the other side, until I could see brain coral rising up from the sandy bottom, hundreds of fish through the clearb water. Paradise found.

I knew I wasn't staying in Sabang, I had a place on the other side of the island picked out—the guidebook described it as a scuba Mecca with international travelers and cheap huts on the beach. I wanted to settle down there first before exploring the rest of the island and Sabang. The locals know when the ferry gets in from Banda Aceh and they wait with their pick-up trucks to whisk people getting off the ferry to all parts of Weh. I was a sitting duck and didn't even need to name my destination—the beach community I was headed for. A porter grabbed my bag and pointed to the back of a truck. I got in and held on to the roll bar as it sped through the jungle roads until, about forty minutes later, the driver stopped and pointed to a track leading into the jungle. "White Beach," he said with a huge smile. I paid the porter a dollar for the ride and watched as the pick-up truck zoomed away. Immediately, quiet settled in. My backpack was still sitting on the road where the porter left it. I looked up into the canopy above me. I heard insects, maybe a cicada, then something bigger in the trees, maybe a monkey or a snake. Birds were singing. I sneezed, slung my backpack on and followed the little dirt track toward White Beach.

The jungle opened up to a bay with dazzling white sand and aqua blue sea. Palm trees grew horizontally out from the sand, and coconuts littered the beach. The first hut complex I came to was called Mama's. I passed it because it looked full and I wanted something a bit smaller and less touristy. I kept walking. The path turned from dirt to sand. The next place had an Internet café, a scuba shop and a few western travelers drinking beers and listening to a Coldplay song. Pass. The path led away from the sand and up a steep hill back into the jungle for about ten minutes. I thought maybe I had passed all the hut complexes and I should turn around, but I kept walking, and the path turned down to the next bay. I was hoping I would find a quiet place with no scuba shops or bars. I passed about four more places and continued to check them off until I had to stop and have a Coke.

"Selamat siang," a man called out from his café. He was sweeping sand off the concrete floor. A sign carved from wood read, Welcome to Long Beach Resort & Restaurant.

"Apa kabar, Coca Cola?" I asked. He set his broom against the wall, took a cold Coke bottle out from his little red Coke fridge. He smiled, handed me the bottle with a straw.

"You return bottle here," he pointed down to a plastic crate filled with empties. He had taken the used straws out, cut the ends so he could use the straws again. Bees attracted by sweet dregs were landing on top of the empty bottles. I sat on a plastic chair and watched the ocean. Sweat trickled down my back, my nose was running and I was tired. The man returned to sweeping. I left my backpack on the concrete floor and walked down to the ocean. It was deliciously warm on my feet.

I turned and saw my hut—I knew it was going to be mine. It was plain, on a concrete slab with a thatched palm-frond roof. Two plastic chairs sat out front, the front door stood open with a cheap Made-in-China lock hanging on the hasp. I walked over and popped my head inside the hut. I saw two single beds flaunting matching Incredible Hulk sheets and mosquito nets tied in knots above each. A little window was cut into one side of the thatch. You reached the bathroom through an arch the led to an open-air mandi and squat toilet. I loved it.

I returned to the café. "How much for a bungalow per night?" I asked the man.

"Fifty thousand." He answered.

I raised my eyebrows and gasped, "Mahal!"—expensive! The bargaining process had begun. I took out my little calculator and pushed in 30,000 and showed it to him. He frowned and added that breakfast was included. We sat there for ten minutes, me in mock astonishment that he wanted $5.85 for each night and him pleading and slowly lowering his price, knowing that five of his eight huts were vacant. He tried to show me a better accommodation with a fan. No, I wasn't budging, and finally we came to an agreement. I would pay him cash in advance, for thirty days with no breakfast included for 768,600 Rupiah. Three bucks a day. I was happy and he was happy. I love bargaining. I gave him ninety dollars, shook hands and introduced myself, I'm Mia. I'm Hassis.

Hassis was married to Anna—they had a gorgeous little daughter named Aziza. It was Arabic for beloved, everyone called her Zizi. They had been living in Weh for six years. Hassis's five brothers all loaned money to build the resort and the couple were working hard to pay off their family investors. Anna cooked meals in the small restaurant making simple dishes for the guests, she also offered a laundry service to the tourists as well as keeping up with hand washing her own families clothes. Hassis repaired thatched walls and was the handyman for the complex. He went fishing early every morning, to provide food for his small family and helped raise Zizi. Darling Zizi had arrived four years earlier, unplanned but welcomed into their lives, a wondrous blessing from Allah.

I fell easily into a routine. I woke up early when the call to prayer was announced from the mosque and went for my morning swim. Then I walked over the hill. Some mornings I would treat myself to a pancake and coffee at a nicer resort, talk to the backpackers about their scuba dives, catch up on international news and gossip. Other mornings I went to the market, bought bananas, oranges, cookies and daily snacks. Resorts competed with each other by advertising different movies they would play in their restaurants each night, so I would walk by and read the chalkboards tempting me with pirated new releases. I returned over the hill back to Long Beach and my hut. Read for a couple of hours, napped on the beach, went for a snorkel. Every afternoon I took my newly adopted strays, Choco and Scar for a two-hour hour hike through the jungle. Many nights I took Zizi to the beach where we would watch the boys kick soccer balls. Back at home, I gave Zizi a mandi and chatted with Anna and Hassis. Other nights I walked back over the hill to watch a movie and have dinner at a resort complex.

I had found my Valhalla—a dream I scarcely imagined when I left Laguna.

One afternoon a guy walking by asked Anna for a Coke. She was doing laundry so I jumped up, grabbed the bottle from the fridge, stuck in a cut-off straw, asked him to leave it in the crate when he finished, took his money, and gave him change from the precious cash box. And that's how I started to work at the Long Beach resort on Pulau Weh. It wasn't a full-time job and Anna didn't expect me to show up for shifts! I just started taking orders from the travelers when Anna was busy. They trusted me to make change and talk to the backpackers. They didn't have a TV so couldn't show movies, so no one showed up to eat there at night. It was strictly a day gig. Anna couldn't afford fancy menus, the list of options were written on pieces of paper and taped to the tables. I promised Anna that when I got back to the States, I would send her laminated menus. I loved Zizi. Anna and Hassis were adorable with each other and hard workers. I helped them because I loved them. It made me happy and required no wage.

I'm unsure about its origins or history but Muslims generally don't like dogs. They think dogs are dirty. The Holy Koran emphasizes the importance of cleanliness and dogs are considered unclean. So, the mangy street dogs that roam and beg around the island are ill-treated. As an animal lover I felt sorry for the poor beasts. I met Choco and Scar on my second day at Long Beach. Anna and Hassis were disgusted by the idea of my feeding these dogs, but I fed them fried rice and leftover fish everyday. Talked to them, petted and loved them. After that first taste of compassion from a human, I had two loyal friends by my side during my long walks into the jungle each afternoon. They followed me everywhere and at night while I slept in my hut, they were stationed on my porch like round-the-clock bodyguards. I named Choco because he was the color of a Hershey bar and Scar had a healed gash along the entire length of his back where his fur didn't grow back. Anna and Hassis didn't allow the dogs anywhere near them or Zizi, but the dogs knew they had an ally in me, the woman living in hut number three.

If I didn't wake up to the morning call to prayer, the monkeys stealing my bananas would rouse me. Not sure exactly why the locals chose dogs to hate— monkeys were far more destructive and cheeky. Although I had only been on the island for a month I had found a measure of happiness that was much too great to leave behind. I decided to renegotiate my lease with Hassis and we agreed on another month at the same price.

I left my little world for the first time in four weeks to take a truck into Sabang where the closest ATM was located. I almost forgot about the entire reason I had been captivated by Pulau Weh. It was those glossy pages showing artists renditions of the famous Chinese fleet. Funny, I didn't care anymore. It was the week before Christmas and I walked around the streets of Sabang for an hour. The stores were decorated with red and green foil covered Christmas ornaments. 'Santa Claus is coming to town' blared forth from a Chinese gift shop. I bought Anna a new sarong, Hassis some fishing line and new lures. Little Zizi got a doll dressed in a hula skirt. I hailed a truck and headed back to White Beach. When they dropped me at the dirt track, Choco and Scar were waiting for me. I greeted my darlings giving them pieces of a hotdog I picked up for them in Sabang. We walked back home together. I couldn't have pictured this scene a month before when I was in bemo hell traipsing across volcanoes, but it was all worth it now. I paid Hassis the hundred dollar rent in cash and shook hands with him affirming another month in my hut.

Chapter Eight

The Chinese in town celebrate Christmas but the majority Muslims do not. Nevertheless, I gave my adopted family their gifts on Christmas morning then headed over the hill to write an e-mail to my parents. I received news from my mom that I had a new niece, born on December 21st. My sister Rose delivered her baby girl in a pool filled with warm water in her living room at six in the morning. Briana, her midwife, made the birthing process a beautiful ritual, candles flickering, music filled the air as a baby girl made her way into the world. Rosie called her baby Isla Pearl (after my grandma who had passed away earlier that year), bringing the Coffin grandkid tally up to twenty-nine. I felt sad that I wasn't there to share in the birth, but Rosie announced she was keeping the placenta in her freezer until I got home, so we could plant it under a tree. Thanks Rosie.

I guess I was on a mission to get drunk, maybe I was missing home, maybe it was a placenta in a fridge, who knows? But here it was, New Year's Eve, and I was feeling lonely. The English couple in the hut next to mine wanted to celebrate so we walked over the hill to Ring in the New Year at one of the dive shops that was playing very bad techno music. I ended up getting annihilated on arak (the clear licorice-tasting fiery liquid), dancing with an American named Jeff from Oregon. We ended up consummating our brief five-hour relationship by having sloppy sex on the beach. We hung out for the next week, but he broke down and confessed that he had a girlfriend waiting to marry him back in Portland. *Note to self: Travel romance never works.*

Ten days into January I began to regain a portion of my dignity and forgive myself for my misjudgment, clearly the result of alcohol and techno music. Two German guys staying in the hut next to me were both named Rolf. A few nights before, one of the Rolf's killed a giant gecko with a machete in his hut because it was making such a loud noise. I was incensed! Geckos are good. True, a gecko could be a foot long. A gecko is loud and could seem scary. However, they do no harm. They eat mosquitoes and cockroaches. So that morning I sat with them at breakfast, swatting flies and reminding this Rolf that the gecko probably would have eaten all these annoying pests. He half way apologized and said he thought the gecko would bite him while he slept. What an idiot.

I sat there with idiot Rolf at Anna's restaurant watching the waves crash while the sky threatened rain. I was scratching my itching ankles so badly they began to bleed. The sand fleas had feasted on my flesh at the beach the day before and the welts were incredibly painful. My scratching only exacerbated the pain and aided in spreading the poison down to my feet and up to my shins. Rolf explained to me with great seriousness that if I would make the sign of the cross with my fingernails through each welt, Jesus would help the pain subside. I was ready to try anything. In desperation, I actually scratched the Jesus crosses into my swollen red welts. It didn't work.

Searching for relief, I fled into the ocean, hoping the saltwater would sooth my festering bites. I wouldn't normally have gone swimming on such a rough day, but I was desperate to extinguish the fire in my ankles. The waves were forbidding, the wind was picking up—and what I saw before me was not welcoming. Should I go into that maelstrom? I put on fins, mask and snorkel and plunged into the water. I swam out under the waves. I swam hard. The pain had lessened on my ankles, but the waves were crashing down, so I kept swimming out past the protective reef. Out and out. Next thing I knew, I was being swept further out by a strong rip tide. Being a good California surfer girl, I knew that I couldn't fight the rip, so I just let it take me. I treaded water and waited for the rip to subside so I could return to shore. No problem, until I looked back towards the beach. It was gone.

Ocean surrounded me. The beach had disappeared. Faint tentacles of panic began to wrap around my thoughts. I forced the frightening breaths of panic away and reenacted the steps I had learned years ago at the YMCA pool for basic Survival Float. I hung my head down, I relaxed in the water, bobbing on my stomach with each wave. Conserve your energy Mia. I would lift my head up, take a quick breath, then close my eyes and dip my head back in the water, allowing my body to drift with the current—not fighting it—my heart rate began to slow down. I was a strong swimmer. When I came up for air, I would glance out hoping to glimpse land, and if I did, I would slowly make my way towards it. But there was no land to swim for. In which direction should I go? If I chose the wrong way I would be swimming straight into the middle of the Indian Ocean, next stop East Africa. Or Australia if I swim south for three thousand miles. More Survival Float. Then tears.

Ten, maybe twenty minutes passed—it started to rain.

At a moment when I looked up hoping for a glimpse of land, I spotted something else that would save me. A fishing boat! I took off one of my fluorescent green fins and stuck it out of the water as far as my arm would go. I was sure the fishermen saw me. I was saved! The boat slowed—I stopped waving my fin. I put it back on my foot and started to swim for the boat. My heart was racing. The boat was still 500 meters away. I swam as hard as I could. I gulped water. I looked up. The boat was turning away! The boat was leaving! The motor roared and it sped off. It hadn't seen me. It was gone. I floated and waited to be eaten by a shark. I had had a good life. I had a great family—I was educated, well read, well traveled, and loved. I had never been married or had the experience of childbirth. I should have married my last boyfriend when he asked, just so now— as I was floating out to my death in the Indian Ocean—that I had at least been married once. I thought of how my parents would find out how their fifth daughter had perished. They wouldn't start worrying for a month. I had convinced them not to worry if they didn't hear from me for a few weeks. Would a representative from the State Department come to their door? Or would they hear on CNN that a young American woman who went swimming off the coast of Sumatra had tragically drowned. I wondered how many people would come to my funeral. I was crying, and getting colder by the minute. I was losing critical energy. Panic had won. Overtaken by fatigue and hopelessness and despair, I felt myself sinking, with no energy to resist. Fight, Mia! Float! I urged myself forward! Don't give up!

Just at the moment when I had wearily lifted my face out of the water one last time to see the world I loved much, I saw it! Another boat! This was it. I couldn't miss this chance to be saved. With an energy I didn't think I could draw on, I took both fins off and wildly waved them above my head while treading water. I yelled, "HELP!" I screamed again, "HELP!" My head went under. My hands stayed above me with my fins waving while my face stayed under the water. I bobbed up briefly taking a huge gulp of seawater. I coughed and gagged but kept waving my fins. I watched as the boat turned and headed towards me. This time I wasn't fooled. I kept yelling for help and waving my fins until the boat was closing in and I could see the dive tanks and the three people on board.

I put my fins back on and began to swim for the dive boat with every last ounce of energy I had in my body. The driver cut the engine and swung the boat around only yards from where I was treading water. I swam to the stern and held onto the back step. A Western couple in wet suits, and the Indonesian driver were staring down at me, hanging onto the back of their boat. I was suddenly embarrassed. What do I say? Hey, how was your dive? I unexpectedly wretched salt water and bananas onto the step bobbing up and down with the swell, I looked up to catch the woman cringe with disgust.

"Sorry about the barf on your boat, can I get a lift back to the island?"

"Of course!" it was the guy who finally spoke and reached out to help me out of the ocean. He took my arm and actually lifted my entire body onto the step. I started crying and was racked with shivers. The woman handed me a towel. I blew my nose into it, then draped it over my shoulders.

"Where in hell have you come from?" The woman.

"Just let her breathe a while, darling." The man.

"OK, we go now." The driver.

I sat on a cushion, wrapped in a plush towel and said nothing. The couple smiled at me, the driver glanced back several times during the thirty-minute ride back to a dive shop on Weh. My ankles didn't itch any more.

The man's name was Iztok—he and his wife Danica were from Croatia on a dive holiday. We pulled up to one of the uber expensive resorts I had never been to. Iztok walked me to a restaurant connected to the dive shop, ordered me a beer and a shot of arak, and told me to stay. I was in shock. Lucky to be alive. I stayed. I watched them unload the boat, rinse their gear, and peel their wetsuits off. They were in their late forties, he was tall and handsome, dark hair, tanned, with a body that looked like he spent hours lifting weights in a gym. She too had a ripped body, was taller than me with a short brown bob and a splash of gold highlights dyed into her chopped bangs, enhancing her green eyes. I saw each of them shake hands with the boat driver and Iztok tipped him some cash. Then heard them speaking to each other in a Slavic language while walking toward me. Still wrapped in their towel, my head feeling dizzy after the shot of arak, and guzzling a large Bintang— I gazed over the now calm Indian Ocean and waited for my saviors to join me.

"How are you feeling, little one," Iztok asked me with compassion in his voice. Danica came behind me and touched my shoulders. "Are you OK?" They both sat down at the shiny teak table. Instantly a waiter in a starched white coat welcomed them by name and offered them a drink. Iztok ordered another round of beers and three shots of arak. All this decadence just a few coves over from my humble hut.

"Yeah," I mumble, "I'm fine now. I just went snorkeling, and a rip took me out."

"How long were you in the water?"

"Maybe an hour. A fishing boat passed but didn't see me. I was getting panicky by the time I saw your boat. Thank God you saw me!" At this point I'm thinking, I've got to get back to Long Beach. "I think I should get back to my place," I murmur apologetically. "I'm so grateful to you guys for picking me up and saving my life! But, I've gotta go now." I started to gather my fins and mask.

"No sweetheart, you must be our guest for the afternoon—you have been through a fright! You just relax now and have a drink," Iztok insisted. I had had enough to drink. I was in shock. An hour before I had been drowning in the Indian Ocean! I started to laugh. I was nervous—it was like an out-of-body experience. They laughed with me. The waiter returned with three big bottles of Bintang, three frosty glasses and three amber shots of arak.

"It's all over now, sweet girl—just have a drink and relax."

"Thanks, so much, you guys are so nice. I'm not sure what would have happened to me if you hadn't come along." Exhaustion and alcohol had affected my mood. I wasn't thinking straight. Part of me just wanted to walk over the hill, back to my hut and see Anna, Hassis, Choco and Scar. But these people had saved my life! I had to be polite and accept their invitation to stay on, drinking and cracking jokes—and feeling relieved my parents didn't have to see the news of my death on CNN.

Iztok raised his shot glass, "Cheers to fate and plucking our beautiful little sea nymph from the ocean." We all chinked glasses, smiled at each other, then tilted our chins back while the white liquid burned down our throats. I sat for two hours with them, drinking and talking about myself, where I was from, why I was traveling alone, all the places I'd been, my family. It was getting dark, we were drunk and hungry. They begged me to join them for dinner, so I followed them back to their room. There was an Indonesian boy about seventeen standing on the front porch of their bungalow who greeted them by name and opened the door for us. "Good evening, madam." He said to me lowering his eyes to the ground. "Selamat Malam," I wished him in return. Cold air welcomed us into one of the most elegant hotel rooms I'd ever seen.

"Who was that boy?" I asked Iztok.

"Oh, Suparno is our houseboy. He is at our beck and call 24 hours a day. He even went to get Danica ice cream when she wanted one in the middle of the night."
Pretty sure 'houseboy' went out with civil rights, but I went with it. "What a beautiful place, how much does this cost you a night?"

"Isn't it lovely? And only eight hundred per night."

"Dollars?" Trying not to sound surprised.

"Oh, Mia you are so adorable. Here put this on and let's go have dinner."

Danica gave me one of her shirts and a pair of loose fitting linen trousers. I put them on over my bathing suit. They smelled like perfume. Their room was fantastic. Polished teak floors, a huge bed with starched white sheets and a fluffy duvet—six wood fans slowly circulated the air-conditioned air, three huge flower arrangements stuffed with fresh white orchids sat atop polished tables, plus a desk and a huge armoire. The bathroom floor was white marble with a giant glass shower and western-style toilet. For a moment I was jealous of the luxury they enjoyed, while over the hill I slept on old Incredible Hulk sheets, sweating my butt off every night under a mosquito net in a room with no electricity. I checked myself quickly though, the same way when I'm home and start to covet BMW's and fancy clothes–

– it's just not me and I'd rather travel the world than spend my money on excess. I followed them out and into the hotel restaurant. Suparno greeted us again and walked us over the concrete path to the hostess. "Please enjoy your dinner." He left and stood at the front door, waiting to walk us back to the room after we ate. Weird.

The menu was extravagantly expensive. But I ate to my heart's content. Iztok kept ordering dishes even after we were all full. The waiters were all handsomely attired in white jackets and traditional sarongs. The service was impeccable with at least ten waiters to each guest. There were several other groups dining upstairs with us, enjoying spectacular views looking out over the moonlit bay. We finished off a New Zealand Sauvignon Blanc, then a Napa Valley Cabernet. Then dessert.

"How is such a beautiful girl like you not married yet?" Danica asked me while taking a strand of my hair and tucking it gently behind my ear. I looked at Iztok and thought I saw him wink at me. I was very drunk and full and tired. I felt uncomfortable, but I ignored my unease and tried to be a grateful guest.

"Well, I keep running away on my trips around the world and no one has caught me yet." Hoping that would appease them. I laughed a lot and finally admitted defeat and exhaustion. Suparno met us at the entrance to walk us the two minutes back to the room, opened the door and wished us a good sleep, adding that he would be outside if we needed anything. I felt more at ease with Suparno, the houseboy, than I did with these two. I'm a waitress, I'm a worker, I sympathize with the underprivileged. What was I doing rubbing shoulders with these rich people.

I saw a cot had been set up while we were at dinner. "This is where you will sleep tonight Mia, unless you want Iztok to sleep there and we can share the bed." Danica laughed while throwing her arms around my shoulders and giving me a hug. I felt like a child. She turned on her Ipod and a sexy Euro beat instantly filled the room.

"Thank you so much, this will be perfect for me." I desperately wanted to be back in my hut. Iztok was sitting at the desk rolling a joint. "Mia, please join us, this is marijuana and tobacco mixed, it will settle your stomach and help you sleep."

Don't these people stop?

"No, thanks, Iztok, I'm sure I will sleep fine in this air conditioning and these sheets are like butter! I'm pretty sure they'll hang you for smoking weed in Indonesia." I was sitting on my cot a bit nervous and drunk.

"Oh, Sweet Mia you are so precious!" Iztok lit his joint and started dancing to the horrible music. I pulled the duvet to my chin and propped my head up with two pillows. I watched as the couple shared puffs and kisses. They danced, letting their heads roll around, their eyes were closed. I hoped they didn't start having sex right in front of me. I pretended not to see them. I needed this day to end, so I turned my back to them and closed my eyes. My head was spinning.

Surrounded by all the physical comforts that I ordinarily missed, I should have slept well. I didn't! I was cold and uncomfortable. I had waitress dreams. I heard the distant call of morning prayer, making it about ten till five in the morning. The room was still dark. I stared up at the fans until I couldn't stand it a second longer. I had to pee, but I held it. I didn't want to wake Iztok and Danica by flushing the toilet, so I quietly slipped out from the plush white covers. The curtains were drawn over the huge glass windows. My eyes adjusted and I saw the couple sleeping under a thin white sheet. They were spooning, Iztok's naked ass was uncovered. Gross. As quietly as possible I turned the knob of the front door and slowly opened the slab of polished teak. Indonesian humidity greeted me, then Suparno, looking like he hadn't closed his eyes all night. "Good morning Mia, my hope is that you slept well." He startled me.

"Oh! Good morning." I said in a raspy voice. The mixture of salt water, alcohol and air conditioning had damaged my throat. How the hell did this kid know my name? I smiled and added, "Please tell Miss Danica that I will return her clothes later today. Thanks for your help." I didn't wait for the robotic boy to answer, I walked away barefoot, carrying my fins and mask, back over the hill to Long Beach Resort.

Chapter Nine

I passed a few local men on their way to the mosque for morning prayer. It was still early, about five thirty when I got back to my little hut. The door stood open. Choco and Scar were not there. I went straight back to my toilet, squatted down and peed. I had a headache and kept going over what happened the day before. It felt like a dream. I walked to my little bed and lay down on my back. Tears slipped from my eyes down into my ears. I wept with relief, anger, frustration, guilt and loneliness. I wanted to go home.

My eyes closed and I fell asleep. About an hour later I thought I heard something, I opened my eyes and saw Zizi standing a foot from my head staring at me. I heard Anna calling her. "Zizi!" Little Zizi ran out. Anna and Hassis came busting through the door a minute later. "Mia, you cannot do that to us! We called the police. We thought you were dead!" They interrupted each other taking turns yelling at me. I stood up and tried to hug Anna, she pushed me back, "No! You cannot just leave and not come home. The Germans said you went swimming and we waited for you to come out of the ocean." She was furious. Hassis was so angry Zizi started to wail.

"Shhhhhhhh, Zizi. Don't cry. I'm sorry, Anna. I'm here, I'm safe. Please forgive me. I didn't know you were waiting for me." I tried to soothe little Zizi but she was clinging to her father. The gecko-killers came over from next door.
"Wow, we thought you were dead!"

"Listen, I'm very sorry everybody. I am fine now. Listen to me. When I went into the water yesterday, I got caught in a riptide! It was terrifying! I didn't know how to get back to shore."

"So what happened?" Hassis was impatient.

"Luckily, a boat saw me and picked me up. The two divers, a man and his wife, took me back to where they were staying. They saved my life! I spent the night on the other side of the hill where they were staying. I was exhausted and almost sick from the seawater I'd swallowed, beyond thinking straight. No way to let you know anything."

"Well, you should have done something! We waited until it got dark, and finally after the last prayer we called the police and reported you missing! Anna and Zizi were so upset and worried Mia!"

"Well," I blubbered. "I'm so sorry! I'm home now, please don't be angry with me." I tried my best to reassure the six people now standing in my tiny hut. Anna took Zizi from Hassis and walked out with a hissing noise. Hassis caught my eye, shook his head, and then followed his wife. The two Rolfs stood there for a second until I said, "I need to sleep, I'm so sorry for worrying everyone." They left too.

I didn't talk to anyone the rest of the morning. I washed Danica's top and pants in a bucket and hung them up to dry on a line. Then I went down to the beach. Yesterdays disastrous events came rushing back to me but as I gazed out to the ocean, there it was, quietly lapping the shore, no giant waves, no rain, no whipping winds. I calmly spread out my sarong, sat down on it, and read my book. It took me until I was dripping with sweat, but I knew I had to go back into the ocean. I didn't go deep. I put my head under the warm water and wadded in the clear ocean while not letting the land out of my sight. From my warm pool I saw Iztok and Danica walking along the path. I didn't want to get out and talk to them but they saw me and came down to the sand. "Hey Mia, we missed you at breakfast this morning," Iztok said, reaching out to pat me on the head.

"Yeah, I'm sorry, I had to get home." I subtly pulled away. "I washed your clothes, Danica, they should be dry by now."

"Precious girl, you didn't have to do that, we have a laundry service. Then she handed me a wrapped gift that she had in her hand. "We have a present for you, open it." I took the box and thanked her.

I walked up to my hut and the couple followed. "So this is my palatial abode." I joked as I took Danica's clothes off the line and handed them to her.

"Please open your present." Iztok urged. I unwrapped the paper—inside was a white dress with a gold necklace and matching earrings.

"Thank you so much, you guys are so thoughtful." I hated it.

"Try it on, we'll take you to lunch." I didn't want to, but I agreed. I pulled the dress over my bathing suit but left the jewelry on my bed. We went to another hut complex on my side of the hill and had spaghetti and beer.

Danica started, "Will you have dinner with us again tonight? The restaurant has a gorgeous chardonnay chilling for us." I declined, apologizing that I really pissed off Anna and Hassis and thought I should stay home tonight.

Then Iztok began, "Listen Mia, we are leaving for Bali in the morning and would like to invite you to stay with us there for the week. We have an absolutely amazing hotel booked, you could have your own room if you want, we are going on a dive, we have a guide to show us around the island, we've booked a trip up to the waterfalls and into Ubud. There is a full moon party on the beach, we have ecstasy to take and make love under the moon." Did he just say make love? Holy shitcakes, I knew it! These people wanted to have sex with me! "We won't take no for an answer Mia, we like you and want you to join us for our last week on holiday."

"I can't afford…"

"Don't even think of money, we will be delighted to pay for anything you need." Iztok interrupted my poverty excuse. I sat over my bowl of spaghetti and sighed, "Listen you guys, I really like you. I am grateful that you saved me yesterday. I had a super fun night with you at dinner, but I can't meet you in Bali. I need to stay here and finish my own trip." They looked disappointed, but Iztok was unrelenting. "Don't decide just now, Mia, we will buy a airline ticket for you and if you change your mind, all you need do is pick up your ticket at our hotel."

I rolled my eyes and smiled. These people were nuts! "OK, it's an official maybe."

I would *never* go to Bali with these people.

"Great, then it's settled. We will see you in Bali." Iztok raised his beer glass to me. We chinked glasses and I added, "Maybe."

Never would I actually go out of my way to hang out with these nightmarish swingers.

We walked back to my hut along the path, I said good-bye and thanked them again for my gift and their generous offer. They continued over the hill probably excited at the prospect of having sex with me in Bali.

The next week was strained with Anna and Hassis. I offered to work in the restaurant but Anna said no. I went on long walks through the jungle with Choco and Scar but things felt different. I knew I gave Anna and Hassis a scare, but maybe that wasn't it. Maybe I had overstayed my welcome. I had spent nearly two months in my little hut in Pulau Weh, and another month had been spent getting here. A total of three months in Indonesia. My trip was over and it was time to go home. I was actually looking forward to working, making money, interacting with my own people and maybe taking a class or two. I had missed another birth and longed to see my family. I booked my ticket online from Banda Aceh to Jakarta to depart on the twenty-seventh of January.

I thanked Anna and Hassis as best I could. I gave them a note, written in Indonesian with the help of Suparno (whom I realized was just a nice guy and had to act like a robot at the hotel, or would get fired). I put the note, an extra hundred dollars and the ugly gold jewelry Danica gave me in an envelope. In closing, I invited them to come to California anytime and told them how much I love them, so kind and generous to me—and I sent my kisses to Zizi.

It was bittersweet, because I knew they would never have the money to come out and I probably would not see them again. I had slowly converted Zizi into being a dog lover and finally convinced her to feed Choco and Scar and be kind to them. She agreed after I promised to send her a Cinderella dress from Disneyland. Seemed like a fair trade.

I took a pickup truck, a ferry, and finally a taxi to get me to the Band Aceh airport and was soon winging my way to Jakarta. I cozied up to my window and watched Sumatra pass below me, remembering all those crazy bemo rides and harrowing experiences, none of which would have happened to me had I not been willing to sit in a broken-down minivan for days at a time. I landed in Jakarta within two hours, treated myself to a hotel near the airport with Internet and air conditioning to stay for one night before my flight home. Thirty-four hours later I landed at LAX. My parents, sister Rose and little Isla Pearl were there waiting for me in the arrivals hall holding a big sign, WELCOME HOME, MIA!

Chapter Ten

The first thing I did when I got home was send a care package to Indonesia, for Anna, Hassis and Zizi. I created a menu on my computer, had an artist friend illustrate it with charming designs then had Kinko's print out twelve copies. I had promised it to Anna for her restaurant. I packed the menus, a Cinderella dress, some children's books and a bag of dog treats for Choco and Scar then sent it off to Pulau Weh.

The months have passed quickly. I bought a new car with the help of my brother-in-law Jon who agreed to co-sign with me. I got my job back waiting tables three nights a week. I was accepted into a post-grad program and will be taking classes to earn my masters in Anthropology. My little sister had hijacked my room at my parents' house, so I was forced to cut the umbilical cord and rent a place of my own. I found a roommate to share a two-bedroom, and I got a cat —my mom thinks it's a good first step in finding a husband. I still devour my National Geographic's each month.

On a Sunday morning, eleven months after I had left Indonesia a 9.1 magnitude earthquake rocked Sumatra, its epicenter only miles from Pulau Weh. The subsequent tsunami ripped through the streets of Banda Aceh devastating the area killing tens of thousands. I've sent Anna and Hassis letters and tried to call the resort on the other side of the hill from their bungalows, but haven't heard from anyone.

I take long walks up the sage-covered hills in Laguna Beach and look out over the Pacific Ocean thinking about my beloved Anna, Hassis, Zizi, Choco, and Scar and continue to hope they are all well.

Me sitting outside my hut on PulauWeh

Promises
Tanzania

Chapter Eleven

Everyone is going to die at some point. I had hoped that I would meet my end in a more exotic way than a mere car accident or a cancer tumor, but I had no idea that my death would be as fierce as being plucked out of the back of a pickup truck and killed by an angry bull elephant in Africa. However unique it sounds, at the moment that I was eye to eye with that giant beast, I changed my wish and thought how much quicker and less painful a head on collision would have been. It's crazy how each decision during a day can lead to your demise. I could have easily chosen not to be in the back of that pickup. In fact, it was just at the last second that I changed my plans and went for a ride with Frankie and Sophie. Poachers had cut through a wire fence on the outer perimeter of the farm. Frankie and Sophie were headed out to survey the damage and see if they could fix the fence. I had been studying my African bird book on the veranda when Sophie asked if I wanted to join them.

"No thanks, I am going to quiz myself on the Kilimanjaro Weaver and then have lunch."

"We're going to drive right by a few Weavers nests if you want to see them up close and personal, Mia," Sophie tempted. "We won't be long and we can all have lunch together when we return. Come on Mia, you need to see these nests." I heard Frankie honk the horn in the driveway. "Okay, I'll come, let me grab my binos," I yelled back to Sophie who was already running out the front door. I jumped into the back of the Land Cruiser while Sophie rode shotgun and Frankie drove down the dusty road. Two local women were walking barefoot on the side of the dirt road with large plastic water cans on their heads. I waved to them as we passed; they flashed their beautiful smiles back at me. I hung onto the roll bar as Frankie whizzed by brush. "Mind the thorn trees, Mia!" he yelled back to me. I ducked behind the safety of the rear window, avoiding being whipped in the face by the branches. Finally, Frankie slowed a bit and stuck his head out the driver side, "Keep your eye out for a cut fence—it should be up here somewhere." All I saw was thick jungle. Frankie came to a sudden stop. Sophie got out of the pickup and walked into the bush. Frankie got out and asked if I was OK, "Yeah, I'm good, where's Sophie going?"

"She's checking to see if she can locate the fence that she remembers along this road. It's been years since they've had poachers."

"What are they poaching?"

"Game meat—kudu, impala, eland—whatever they can get."

"Are the poachers hungry?"

"No, they sell it."

Sophie walked back to the truck, "I can't find the fence, let's keep driving, slowly." Another few minutes of driving and Frankie stopped again. This time neither of them got out. I sat in the back with my binos hanging from my neck. A movement came from the bush but I couldn't see anything along the road. I thought this may be where the Weavers nests were, but just as I was going to knock on the window separating me from the couple, I caught a glimpse of grey. "Elephant." I heard Sophie say from the cab. I looked left and saw the massive animal just 100 yards from the truck. I took my cheap disposable camera from my pocket and snapped a picture. I watched the large beast from the safety of the vehicle. The elephant lifted up his head while his trunk found a branch high up on a tree. He cracked the heavy limb like a toothpick and dropped it to the ground with a loud thud. Was he demonstrating his strength to me? No need, my huge strong friend. I know you are king of the jungle. Then suddenly his ears billowed forward and swung straight out to each side making his head twice as big. He trumpeted a sound that would forever ring in my mind, a shrill cry as loud as a bulldozer engine and charged the truck. "Go!" I managed to yelp, but the engine was not turned on, and the truck did not move. My body was paralyzed. I couldn't jump out and run or defend myself.

I sat frozen, staring at this seven-ton animal running towards me. Shocked by how fast his massive body could move. My grip was so tight to the roll bar my fingers felt embedded into the metal. The elephant abruptly stopped ten feet from the truck. His yellow eyes were looking straight at me. I was silent. My mouth was stuck open but no sound came from my throat. My heart pounded in my ears. Then I heard a noise. It was Sophie and Frankie laughing. They were laughing at me! I couldn't take my eyes off of the huge animal that was still only ten feet from me, so without looking at the evil couple, I yelled to the window dividing us, "Drive Frankie!" The sound of the engine turning over was the happiest noise I have ever heard. With a lurch, we were off, leaving the angry elephant behind.

I took my first breath. My exhale came with a flood of tears. Sophie looked back at me through the window and must have told Frankie to stop the truck. "What's wrong, Mia?" Frankie jumped out of the cab and came around to the back.

"What's wrong?! What's wrong?!" What the hell do you think is wrong, Frankie? I was almost killed by an elephant, that's what's wrong! You're an ass, Frankie!" I yelled at him while wiping my tears away. Sophie had come around to the back too. "Mia, I am so sorry that the elephant scared you. He was an immature bull just mock charging." Perfect. And a beach girl from California would be privy to this information? How? "Mia, I would never put you in danger, you should know that." Frankie added trying to hug me.

"Stay away from me."

"Come on Mia, I'm sorry." Frank said mischievously.

There was true concern and remorse on the faces of both Frankie and Sophie. So I let out a sigh and said, "Promise never to do that to me again."

"I promise." Frankie said.

"Sorry my darling girl, he was just a juvenile showing off." Sophie added.

"Frankie or the elephant?" I asked.

"Come here." Frankie enveloped me in his arms.

"Sorry Mia." he whispered in my ear.

I sat in the cab behind Frankie on the way back to the ranch while Sophie schooled me on how to recognize the difference between an elephant's true charge and a mock charge. She told me that this young bull elephant was out there on his own, practically harmless. Typically, male elephants have nothing to do with the close family unit of cows, calves and baby elephants. It's a matrilineal system led by an old female. The bulls live separate from the herd, traveling alone and foraging for food until the females go into estrous, then they join the group to mate. Young solitary bulls display their powers with pretend charges every chance they get. They are immature, cocky, juveniles. Sophie explained that this bull was small compared to a full grown male—that when I ran into a bull with sizeable tusks, I could start worrying. Serious charges happen only after all attempts to intimidate have failed. So when the bull is pushing out his ears, trumpeting, throwing up dust and making a scene, no worries. However, when he pins his ears back, is quiet and puts his head down to run. Worry.

I still have the photo of that elephant on a wall at my parent's house. Everyone is so impressed with my telephoto lens that took such a close shot. I don't correct them. I just thank my lucky stars that I didn't actually die that afternoon, however unique a death.

Chapter Twelve

I met Frankie Navaro in High School. We were fast friends, always dreaming about leaving Laguna Beach, California to see the world. When I graduated early and went to Paris, Frankie sent me a letter every week. And after, as it happened, when we were both world-class backpackers, we began competing, sending each other letters and post cards from the coolest places on earth, a game of one-upmanship.

Years later, whenever I returned home from a trip I would go through the shoe box of mail my mom had saved for me, searching through the bank statements and credit card offers to find Frankie's post cards from places like Sri Lanka, Vietnam, Berlin, Caracas…always with a taunting *'Wish you were here. Love, Frankie'* at the bottom of each card. And I would write to Frankie wherever I traveled— trying to out-cool his destinations with my own exotic destinations— Sumatra, Mongolia, Denmark, Egypt.

Our competition went on for ten years. Then something changed, Frankie had sent me letters and post cards from Tanzania for over a year. It must be a girl I thought. So I wrote to find out.

Dear Frankie, What's up buddy? Have you contracted malaria and are too sick to leave Tanzania? Lost your passport? If you quit traveling who am I going to write post cards to? Is she pretty? She must be for you to post up for this long! Give me the scoop. I'm off to Brazil for a month, but when I get home I'll look forward to the excuse for your stagnant life! KIT-Mia

Two months later I returned home to find several letters in the shoebox from Frankie.

Dear Mia, Stagnant? I've never been so active! I am working my ass off and I've traveled this country from top to bottom more times than I can remember now. Yeah, she's pretty, and smart and I think she's 'the one'. Please call me when you get home from Brazil, I have to talk to you about an amazing job opportunity...this one will keep you traveling for years without having to be a waitress! Call me 011-867-9335. Wish you were here. Love, Frankie.

    I had only been back in the states for two days when I got his letter, but I was so curious and excited to talk to Frankie, I called him that night. The ringing sounded foreign on the telephone. There are two rings, then a wait, instead of one ring, then a wait like in the States.

    "Frank speaking."

    "Frankie, it's Mia. I got your letter today and I had to call and see what's going on."

    "Mia, it's so good to hear your voice. Listen, I have so much to tell you. I got your post card from Rio, how was that?"

    "It was awesome, but I don't want to waste money chatting over the phone about Brazil, I want to hear your pitch!"

    "All right, so I came out here, shit, it's been eighteen months now, and I met a girl, Sophie Cogswell. Her great-grandfather came out with the National Geographic Society from London in 1870 and never went back. Her family owns a huge part of Tanzania where they specialize in safaris and migration tours. It's amazing, Mia. I've been working with Sophie's family for a year now, and there is a job opportunity for you. If you can get your butt out here I can guarantee you some great money. You don't have to pay for anything, just your plane ticket. We need you out here in a month though. The migration tourists show up the first week in June and we have a booking for a seventeen-day safari on June 3rd. We need you out here from May until October. You can meet Sophie and her family and you will have a ball. Can you come?"

    "Can I come? You bet I can come! I can't wait. Thanks, Frankie, for thinking of me and giving me this opportunity. How did I get so lucky to have you as my best friend?"

"Mia, don't forget you'll be working out here, its not a vacation, you know."

"I know, don't worry, I'm a hard worker."

"Awesome Mia. I knew you'd come through, e-mail me your flight info and I'll pick you up in Arusha." I thanked him again and hung up. I was so excited. Africa! I have always wanted to go to Africa and now I had the chance of a lifetime.

I only had four weeks to prepare. Frankie gave me a website to look up with all the detailed information about the Cogswell family and their safari business. I was told by Frankie to bring a good pair of binoculars and an east African bird book. I was to be hired as the resident ornithologist. I spent the next few weeks in the hills of Laguna Beach becoming an expert birder.

My family wasn't surprised that I was off so soon after my South American trip. My mom was of course frightened at the prospect of her daughter going to Africa for five months, but as I always did, I printed up a map and a brief history of the place complete with pictures of tall buildings and cars to reassure her that it was "civilized." I was going to miss the birth of another baby, but with eight grown-up siblings it is bound to happen. I promised my pregnant sister I'd bring home a black doll for her new baby, hoping to teach my nieces and nephews there is diversity outside the homogenous world of Laguna Beach.

My whole family congregated at my parents' house the night before my departure. My sisters teased me that if Frankie had found someone to love, that perhaps I could too. I rolled my eyes and joked with them that my standards were far too high to find a man of my equal. My brother Martin reminded me that I would miss my favorite time— summer in Laguna. True, but I won't be waiting tables either! "What exactly *will* you be doing?" my dad asked. I answered with an

English accent, "Pardon me sir, but I am a professional birder specializing on the Kilimanjaro Weaver, endemic to East Africa." My dad, along with a few other members of my crazy loud family burst into laughter. "Good luck trying to fool them over there Mia!"

My mom and little sister dropped me off at LAX on May 15th for my flight to Dar es Salaam, connecting through Atlanta and Johannesburg. The flight was scheduled to land in Dar at 10 a.m. and Frankie told me to take a flight directly to Arusha where he'd pick me up. My mom had downloaded an Oprah book for me on my iPod, I had my bird book, Lonely Planet Tanzania, and the Cogswell family history to read for the next thirty hours.

People ask why I travel so often and to such "foreign" places. I think PaulTheroux says it best, "The traveler's conceit is that he is heading into the unknown. The best travel is a leap in the dark. If the destination were familiar and friendly, what would be the point of going there?" It describes me perfectly. I was so excited to spend the next five months in Africa learning to speak Swahili, a new language and history and culture.

Certainly unknown to me, this adventure would change who I was—forever.

Chapter Thirteen

I was exhausted when I arrived in Dar es Salaam. I just wanted to find a hotel, clean up and sleep before presenting myself to Frankie and Sophie. But I stuck with the plan and went to the domestic counter at the airport to find a flight to Arusha. The most beautiful woman in a smart red jacket and crisp white oxford shirt smiled at me from behind her desk, Sun Airlines splashed above her head in Red and yellow letters.
"Good morning, how may I help you?" her teeth looked like a fluorescent bulb they were so clean and bright. I thought of mentioning to her that she could make millions staring in Crest White Strips ads in the US.

"Good morning, I need to purchase a ticket to Arusha leaving as soon as possible." She started clicking the keys on her computer and began speaking to me in her accented English without looking up, "Let's see, we have a flight departing here in an hour that will arrive in Arusha at one o'clock."

"Perfect." The thought of waiting, boarding and flying on another aircraft was horrific.

"Is that one way or return?"

"Just one way, thanks."

"How many passengers?"

"One, please."

The domestic terminal was quite different from the international terminal where I had just landed. Large ceiling fans mixed up the warm air while in the international terminal it was ice cold with air conditioning. There were no security lines, metal detectors or electronic signs announcing the gates or time of departure, just a hallway with various airline logos printed on paper pasted up above doorways to announce the waiting areas. I spotted a pay phone and called Frankie to let him know I'd be in Arusha in a couple of hours. He sounded as far away as when I spoke to him from the States, but he assured me that he and Sophie would be there to pick me up. I found the waiting area that had the Sun Airlines logo above it. There were twenty bright yellow plastic chairs set in four rows of five. I chose the chair closest to the door and settled in for my wait.

    I set the current time on my travel clock to ten hours ahead of California, and then set the alarm for forty minutes, just in case I fell asleep. Three other travelers joined me. They were speaking German. Then exactly forty minutes later the four of us were herded onto the tiny plane waiting on the tarmac, and we were off.

    I stared out the plane window throughout the entire 70-minute flight. I saw herds of elephant, pink flamingos flying over acacia trees, giraffe running in slow motion with their young. I swear I heard the Out of Africa soundtrack. I wished that a young Robert Redford was sitting behind me holding my hand. I felt tears fill my eyes and an itch in my nose. It could have been my total exhaustion, but I was so moved by the scenery and the realization that I was in Africa. *Africa!* I kept saying in my head. *I'm in Africa!*

    Arusha airport is literally one dirt runway and a small concrete building. There is no baggage carousel, security or customs, just a few posters taped on a cement wall of a leopard lounging in a tree, a lion yawning baring his huge canines. About ten young Masai kids selling beads and masks set up on a blanket on the red dirt outside the terminal shouted, "Hello Misses, beautiful necklace for you, souvenirs, come look Misses!" I immediately spotted Frankie and Sophie driving up in a dusty white Land Cruiser. There was a black guy wearing olive green overalls sitting on a cushioned bench behind the driver's seat, hanging onto a roll bar.

    Frankie and Sophie parked and jumped out to greet me. "Mia! Welcome to Tanzania! I am so pleased you could come." Frankie let me go from a bear hug and put his hand on Sophie's shoulder. "This is the love of my life, Sophie

Cogswell. Please meet Mia Coffin, world traveler extraordinaire." I held my hand out to shake, but Sophie ignored my hand and enveloped me in another hug. "Oh Mia, it's so nice to finally meet you, I feel I know you with how much Frank speaks of you. I am so happy you are here. We need your help desperately this season. You must be knackered, my poor darling. Please, let's get you home and have a cup of tea." Frankie smiled at me as he grabbed my backpack. "Let's go my *poor darling*!" he teased.

Frankie handed my bag to the guy sitting in the back of the Land Cruiser. "Lucca, this is Mia from America." Frankie said to him.

"Jambo, Madame," Lucca said to me with a huge grin. I saw he was missing one of his front teeth.

"Jambo, Lucca," I said back. Frankie asked if I had learned any Swahili while I was studying the bird life in east Africa.

"Not so much Frankie, I had like a minute to prepare and all I've been doing is staring at birds.

"Good, you'll need to be an expert in two weeks," Frankie joked as he got into the driver's seat. Sophie sat on his left while I got into the back behind Frankie. Sophie handed me a bottle of cold water with a wink, "You must be parched my poor dear, we'll be at the ranch in a jiffy, my aunt Hilda has a room prepared for you, just sit back, no more traveling for you for a few days." No wonder Frankie adored this girl— she was naturally beautiful with her bright red hair, green eyes, freckled nose, and straight white teeth. She wore long khaki trousers with an ironed crease down the front and a perfectly starched white blouse with a green cotton hat hung around her neck with a nylon cord. She looked like an Abercrombie advertisement.

We drove along a road paved right through quintessential Africa. The exact scenery I imagined when I thought of cliché East Africa, big white puffy clouds against a painfully baby blue sky, green acacia trees with their classic flat table tops, yellow bush for miles. After thirty minutes of paved road Frankie turned onto a dirt track. Where a small shack sat. A skinny black guy manning the entrance to the road saw Frankie, smiled and lifted the red and white-stripped boom so we could proceed. "We are officially on Cogswell land now." Frankie reported to me.

Impalas leaped across the road startled by the vehicle. Warthog families ran along side us and into the bush. After a rough two-hour drive to the Cogswell compound we pulled off the dusty road and into a lush grass paradise. Peacocks ran in front of the truck as Frankie cursed at them. "Out of the way, stupid birds!" We came to an iron gate with the words *Uhuru Shamba 1906* welded into the top potion with the outline of a baobab tree exquisitely sculpted into the metal. Sophie looked back to make sure I was awake. Apparently, I had nodded off several times during the long ride. "Uhuru Shamba means Freedom Ranch in Swahili," She explained to me as we idled in front of the massive gate.

A very dark-skinned black man dressed in the same green overalls as Lucca appeared and began swinging open the two sides of the gate. "Habari, Stephen?" Frank asked the man.

"Good afternoon, Meestah Frank," Stephen stepped back from the gates and Frankie drove through onto a perfectly manicured grass lawn, under blooming purple jacaranda trees to a huge ranch style home. Four sleek Rhodesian Ridgebacks ran to meet the car. I looked back to see Stephen closing the gate behind us.

I guess Lucca got out at the gate because he wasn't in the back as he had been the entire way from Arusha. Sophie, Frankie and I walked through the open door into a big living area with comfortable furniture, a huge picture window and French doors that led to an English garden and swimming pool. There was another black man dressed in a green jumpsuit and rain boots using a net to skim leaves from the pool.

"Hilda? Hiiiildaaaa?" Sophie called out.

"Yes, in here, my darlings."

They spoke like English royalty. Hilda appeared from a back room wearing a pink dress and perfect pink lipstick. With short blond hair, she looked like a Barbie doll with a haircut. Sophie introduced me as Frankie's friend from California. "Welcome, my darling girl, you must be exhausted. I just put the kettle on." At that moment, another girl came in from the kitchen and introduced herself as Belinda, Hilda's youngest daughter. She was visiting from school in Australia.

"Come now my poppets, let Mia have a bath, then we shall have our supper on the veranda." I had no idea who these very well bred people were, I just knew I was tired and hungry and thankful to be here in this gorgeous home with these very accommodating folks. Hilda shooed me into a bedroom, pointed out my bed and bathroom and added that I should take my time and get cleaned up after my long trip from America. "Supper will be ready whenever you are, my poor darling," she added as she walked out and left me in an exquisite bedroom with shiny wood floors, a perfectly made bed with embroidered white cotton covers and matching pillowcases. Hilda closed the door behind me and I went directly over to the big bed and lay down. My head dented the pillow and I thought how lucky I was to be here. The very thought of having to make conversation made me tired, but I was hungry and I had to eat and be a little social to these people who took me into their home. I started the bath and searched through my backpack for a clean top and shorts.

I joined the group on the veranda twenty minutes later feeling cleaner but still hungry and tired. Everyone stood up when I arrived making me feel like a dignitary, "Please sit down, my darling girl," Hilda cooed. The table was set with a white linen cloth, crystal glasses and a huge bouquet of fresh lilies. We had a lovely dinner of fresh salad, home baked bread rolls and Kudu steaks paired with a Syrah from

Stellenbosch. Belinda told us stories of her school in Australia, her riding lessons and her stopover to see her brother in London. Hilda filled us in on life on the ranch. Sophie's family owned and operated the largest safari concession in Tanzania. Everyone referred to it as "the ranch" but I, for one, considered this place an estate.

Belinda asked me about California, she had never been to the States, and was so impressed to meet an American. I talked about my family and my latest trip to Brazil. I had the group in tears laughing about my latest shenanigan—spending the night in a Brazilian jail. I was crossing the border into Uruguay when the Brazilian border guard caught that I had overstayed my visa by three days. I thought he said, "go now." So I started to go through the doors into the Uruguayan border crossing. Apparently I need to brush up on my Portuguese because the guard said, "no," which sounds a lot like now in Portuguese. Anyway, a small misunderstanding evolved into a larger one and I ended up being detained at the border for questioning over night. Funny now, but not so much at the time.

The four dogs lounged under the table, I used one of them as a footrest through dinner. Sophie scolded one of them when he begged for food then complimented Hilda for training them so well and explained to me they were all champion ridgebacks, great hunting dogs from Zimbabwe.

Hilda picked up a little bell and rang it when we were finished eating. Another black man emerged from the kitchen wearing light khaki trousers, a starched white shirt and a white apron around his waist. While he cleared the table, Hilda addressed him, "Thank you, Friday, we will have tea and your yummy pudding now." What the hell kind of place was this, Mississippi 1950? A white lady rings a bell and a uniformed black guy comes running? This was crazy weird and a little wrong. Thankfully, I didn't say anything while my anthropological instincts kicked in reminding me not to judge another culture by my own standards. I certainly have never had a servant before but I sat there and pretended like all this was normal. I glanced up at Frankie and met his eyes in question. He looked back at me with a look that said *don't say a word, Mia*.

Friday returned with a tray of tea, five china cups, and saucers, silver spoons, pressed linen napkins and freshly baked custard with homemade whipped cream. When we finished, Hilda rang the bell. Friday came from the kitchen to clear our plates. The warm evening was delightful, the sky was turning from light blue to pink, and the lights in the pool glimmered like diamonds. Cicadas hummed and for a moment no one spoke. The five of us sat quietly enjoying the beauty of an African evening.

Bathed and fed, my eyes began to sting with the pain of jet lag. I thanked Hilda and Belinda for dinner and their kind reception and excused myself for bed. Frankie and Sophie walked me to my room and let me know they would be flying up to Lake Victoria in the morning to check on a camp, then fly down to Selous game reserve in the south to prepare the staff for the arrival of clients in a few weeks time. They would be away for three days and urged me to enjoy the ranch, relax and enjoy Friday's cooking.

"Do you guys have a private pilot too?" I asked Frankie. Frankie started to giggle and looked at Sophie, "Yeah, and she's great in bed too." Sophie punched him in the arm and said, "I have my pilots license and just bought a little Cessna last season to fly clients around." Frankie hit the jackpot, I thought to myself.

I quickly fell into a deep sleep and dreamed that I was walking around completely naked in London with my cat Fiona. Weird. It was four in the morning when I opened my eyes and couldn't get back to sleep. I fight jet lag like a trooper, but when you fly half way around the world in a day, it's bound to mess you up. I walked into the kitchen and put the kettle on. Poured myself a cup of tea and found a roll of biscuits in the pantry. Then sat at the outside table where we had dinner earlier. I listened to the sounds of the night and sipped my tea. How the hell did I go from worrying about the next restaurant I was going to schlep in to living on an incredible estate in Africa. I was a bit nervous that in a few weeks I was supposed to be an expert birder, and guide tourists around with a pair of binoculars, describing migration paths and mating rituals of the local bird life. But Frankie had faith in me. I *am* a born actor. The fifth daughter of nine children—I know how to play a role when it is required!

I saw the kitchen light go on then Hilda walked outside in bare feet, wearing a cotton robe, "Good morning, my darling girl, couldn't you sleep?"

"Oh, yes, I slept very well, I am just fighting a little jet lag and thought I'd watch the sun rise." I hoped I wasn't being an albatross—it was sort of an awkward moment for me. Hilda read my thoughts and responded to me, "Mia, please consider this your home, I want you to be comfortable like you would be in your own home. Help yourself to anything in the kitchen, sit by the pool, go for walks, wander through the garden, ask Friday to make you anything you want. I am not much of a hostess, I shall do my daily chores and if you'd like to join me, please do and if not, you certainly do not have any obligations, my dear, that is, of course, until you are taking clients out on a game drive to point out the local bird life." I smiled and thanked her for making me feel welcome.

We sat sipping our tea and talked for an hour about Africa, about the ranch and how she joined the Cogswell family. "You know what this time of the morning is called?" Hilda asked me, while looking out into the sky. "I guess I would call it the crepuscular hour, right before the sun rises," I answered.

"Mashambanzou," Hilda let this exotic word slide off her tongue with love. "It means the time when the elephants bathe, in Shona, the language the local people speak where I was raised," Hilda said still looking out at the lavender sky with deep nostalgia.

Hilda explained that she was born in Rhodesia, her father was a tobacco farmer. She and her three sisters learned the language of the Shona people who worked on her father's farm. "This was, of course, before independence—now they call the country Zimbabwe. It is a beautiful place, much more lush than Tanzania, you should get Sophie to fly you down if you have time." While Hilda and I watched the sky go from mauve to grey-blue, she told me stories about meeting Sophie's dad's brother, falling in love and moving up to Tanzania to raise her children on the ranch. Hilda recounted the bloody history of her country, then corrected herself, "This will never be my country, me and my family are merely visitors in Africa. Africa belongs to the Africans. Safari means journey in Swahili, and that's exactly what we are on, a journey in this radiant land." Hilda was insightful, articulate and clearly loved Africa.

I spent the next few days following Hilda's suggestions. I lay by the pool, took long naps, ate Friday's delicious goodies and took leisurely walks through Hilda's vegetable and flower garden. I was introduced to so many family members I forgot who most of them were and where they fit into the Cogswell family tree. Sophie's father had two brothers and three sisters who were married and had children. They lived on the sprawling acres of Uhuru Shamba and were all in the family business of safaris and tourism. I overheard them speaking to Hilda about dates, clients and the huge job of detailing itineraries and preparing the accommodations at the various sights. They owned eighteen camps in most of the game reserves all over the country. I was excited to be part of the family business for the season.

Frankie and Sophie returned after four days. We sat around the table to talk business. Frankie and Sophie explained to me what exactly was in store for me along with a little history of their Safari outfit. Frankie began, " This may seem like Shangri-La to you Mia, and that's exactly how it should feel. But there is a lot of work that goes into making it *look* so simple. The Cogswell's are not as royal as you think. They are very hard workers and are certainly not afraid to get their hands dirty. They are whatever they need to be at the time, whether it's fixing a refrigerator, a generator, or the transmission on a Cruiser. They have to know where the animals are, serve drinks, make conversation, and there is no sleeping until each camp is secured. Every year Safari companies pop up with better equipment, finer wine, posh accommodations, expert guides, and we need to be competitive. Just because the Cogswell family is the oldest, most established Safari company in East Africa doesn't mean it's going to succeed." He finished his lecture and searched my eyes for my response. I had none. I knew the Cogswell family was a very hard working and established family business. "How was your trip?" I asked half joking, knowing Frankie was stressed out. "It was crap!" Frankie finally let his guard down and sighed, "Sorry, Mia, I only want to establish how important this season is going to be—there is so much competition and we need to impress our clients more than ever." Sophie spoke up between sips of white wine. "Mia, we are so pleased that you decided to join us this season, we truly need your help, don't listen to Frank, he's just a worry wart, we are going to have a great season, you'll see!" Sophie raised her glass and added, "Cheers to a fun, profitable and memorable season with Mia, our expert birder." We all clicked glasses, and Frankie finally seemed to relax. Every time I heard myself referred to as an expert birder, I gulped!

Chapter Fourteen

The first clients of the season arrived two weeks later. Frankie and I drove down to Arusha airport to pick them up. Lucca rode in the back, hanging onto the roll bar. We spotted the two middle-aged couples at the curb. They were decked out in safari wear complete with camouflage suitcases. "Wow, these people are serious!" I joked to Frankie. "Mia, this is a dream come true for these people, they have probably seen The African Queen a million times," Frankie said under his breath to me, while we approached the four Americans.

"Jambo, and welcome to Tanzania!" Frankie greeted the two couples. I was laughing inside to see Frankie go from the dorky teenager I met years ago, to a competent and professional safari director. And there I stood, the expert ornithologist. I was nervous. How was I going to pull this off? But all of the sudden I heard myself speaking to the clients, welcoming them to Africa, introducing myself, then taking their bags and heading to the Cruiser like it was quite natural.

Frankie drove to Uhuru Shamba, I stood in the back with Lucca, holding onto the roll bar, reveling in the scenery and the experience. When we arrived at the ranch Hilda had a cheese plate ready with white wine chilled. This is what the Cogswell's did— they entertained. Friday made an incredible meal of impala steaks, fingerling potatoes, sautéed spinach with a passion fruit béarnaise sauce. We sat on the veranda around an elegantly set table, a quiet classical jazz CD played in the background, the pool was lit, the cicadas sung like they were directed, the set of Africa was on. Frankie detailed their itinerary with the clients during dessert. They would begin their seventeen-day safari in the morning.

That is how it went for the next five months. My work became routine to me, but I always kept in mind that these people were on a trip of a lifetime. I greeted them at the airport with a big smile and, "Jambo!" Drove them up to the ranch, had dinner in Hilda's grand home entertaining and answering their questions. Most clients booked for a week, some only four days, while others up to seventeen nights. No matter who the client, we wowed them with surprisingly comfortable accommodations in the bush, decadent meals and first-rate information on the migration and specific animal habits, traits and characteristics. I surprised myself with my birding knowledge. Even though recently acquired, my proficiency had grown exponentially now that I was watching these colorful flying objects burst forth from trees and underbrush everyday. I had become an expert at recognizing species. At first just winging it, but soon, finding myself spotting a strange bird whose name I found I knew as well as its song.

The first day of October dawned oppressively hot. The tourist season was over and no more clients were arriving until next June. We had worked solid for the past twenty weeks and guided over seventy clients into the bush. Sophie flew Frankie and me down to Zimbabwe for a much needed three-week holiday. Zimbabwe is an amazing mix of friendly people, diverse landscape and untamed bush. And you still feel the tenor of its colonial English past—high tea served with scones anyone? We stayed at the Victoria Falls hotel, named after David Livingstone's famed discovery in 1855 of this natural wonder. The local Shona people call the falls Mosi oa Tunya, the smoke that thunders. A brass plaque affixed to the base of a marble statue of Livingstone reads that— although Livingstone was credited by the British for discovering the falls, the local people had inhabited the region for over 2000 years and were well aware of the greatness of their water source.

Throughout my travels in Zimbabwe formerly Rhodesia, the struggle between the British settlers and the original inhabitants was evident. Maps included two different names for each destination. Wankie Park and Hwange Park,

Fort Victoria to Masvingo, Hartley became Chegutu. Salisbury was now Harare. History had been written and rewritten. With its fertile soil, abundant resources and vast size, its borders had been disputed long before England's bid. Wars raged and blood spilled as the original inhabitants fought to remain the keepers of their magnificent land. In the endless struggle for power, the Shona people had prevailed—at least for now.

    We stayed with Hilda's sister Janet on the family farm where she still grew tobacco. Her father had toiled over every plant still harvested today on the farm. As I traveled further in the south of the country where the Save river crossed into Mozambique, I got to experience a different Africa, where lions are scared of people instead of lounging on the hoods of Cruisers. The animals seemed more wild, the bush seemed more dense, the land rugged, native and untouched. Zimbabwe was a taste of the wild Africa that Tanzania had tamed. Three weeks flew by and when we returned to the ranch, I knew I had to start planning for my return to the States. I needed to leave *just now*.

    Zimbabweans have three times— now, just now and now now. *Now* could mean any time from three weeks to a year or two. *Just now* encompasses two weeks through nine months. *Now now* could mean any time from a minute to a week. I was completely and undeniable on Africa time and my departure had been relegated to *just now*. "When are you going back to the States?" some one would ask me, and my answer on November 20th was, "just now."

    I knew it was time to be getting a bit more aggressive, like actually calling British Airways and booking my flight. I missed my family and I had a new nephew to meet. Frankie and Sophie were headed off to London, New York, Montreal and Reno for the next two months to sell safaris on the convention circuit. They were leaving on the fifth of December, so I booked my ticket to fly with them the hour from Arusha to Dar es Salaam. They would head directly to

Nairobi and London and I would stay on a few days in Dar. If I were going to be in Dar es Salaam anyway, I thought I might as well go see Zinj.

Our farewell dinner was extravagant, no surprise for the Cogswell clan. About forty of us drove down to the river. We enjoyed sundowners and a huge brai on the sandy bank. The guys started an impromptu soccer game, then jumped into the water to cool off. The river was, of course, filled with hidden man-eating crocodiles. But, that didn't stop us from taking a dip too. Carefully. I felt happy. Just like a member of the Cogswell family. I thanked Sophie's father, uncles and aunts for taking me in and being so kind to me during the illuminating seven months. They gave me hugs and cheers— and invited me back whenever I needed a job. Hilda made a point of correcting her brother— I was always welcome as an employee or a family member.

Lucca drove Sophie, Frankie and me to Arusha airport the next morning where we took a puddle jumper back to Dar. My adventure was over, I felt melancholy but excited to get home and back to my life in the States. Frankie and Sophie were catching a flight directly to Nairobi while I was staying in Dar es Salaam for a few days before returning to California. I tried not to cry at our parting—Sophie was brushing back her tears and whispered in my ear as we embraced, "Thanks, my darling girl, we will miss you." Then a quick hug from Frankie, "We'll see you in Laguna around March."

"Thanks for everything you guys, I'll see you soon, love you!" I called back as they walked off hand-in-hand toward their gate. I hailed a taxi and headed to the YMCA in downtown Dar es Salaam.

Chapter Fifteen

Most people go to Dar es Salaam for the beaches, the nightlife, the history— I went because I wanted to see an ancient skull. I didn't know when I was ever going to be in East Africa again, maybe never, and I just *had* to see Zinj. As an anthropology student I had romanticized Zinjanthropus (or Zinj, as insiders say) ever since my first biological anthropology class years ago. Zinj was discovered by Mary Leaky in 1959. Originally called Zinjanthropus boisei, it was an early homini and described as the largest of the paranthropus species. Zinj lived from 2.6 until about 1.2 million years ago during the Pliocene and Pleistocene epochs in eastern Africa and is now housed in the National Museum in Dar es Salaam, Tanzania.

I was totally unprepared for Dar. I had lived and traveled through southern Africa for seven months, this had given me a confidence that inhibited reality. The reality is—I am a single, white, American girl in Africa. I was not in the bush describing Weaver nests to rich tourists anymore, I was in a city, a big boisterous African city. My guard was down. I was usually primed and wary of taxi drivers on the lookout for victims. Usually isn't always. I walked right into the arms of a smiling driver who then charged me triple the regular fare.

Fortunately, the receptionist at the YMCA was an honest guy. When he found out how much the driver ripped me off, he ran out to see if he could recover my loss. The taxi was gone. He told me the correct fare for distances, warned me not to walk alone at night, and to bargain for everything on the street, even a soda. My room was simple dorm style. The shower and toilet were down the hall. Ten US dollars a night, fine with me.

The steel grey sky promised rain. It was hot. I wandered around the city looking for the museum where Zinj lived. I bought Kangas, a brightly colored cloth the local women wear as skirts, shawls and headscarves. I made friends with several bootleggers who sell Gucci purses and Mariah Carey CD's. I bought a wood carving of an elephant, marble rhino bookends, and a Masai bead necklace, all the must-haves for a tourist in East Africa.

I found the museum at around four o'clock in the afternoon— it was closed. I understand that this museum isn't the Louvre, but their opening hours are eleven in the morning to one in the afternoon. They close one to two for lunch and reopen from two to four. So the National Museum is open for a whole four hours, five days a week. Really? That is so Africa! I started reconstructing post-colonial Africa in my head, changing all the crazy bureaucratic nonsense, but stopped myself, realizing I had just two days left on this curious continent. I would be back in the morning to see Zinj.

I walked back to the YMCA before dark, as instructed. A cook ladled out a bowl of oxtail soup for me at the cafeteria. I shared my table with a priest from Nigeria and a Swedish couple who were driving their Volvo combie from Stockholm to Cape Town and back. The wife's arm hung in a sling—she broke it when their raft capsized on the Zambezi river rapids. The husband told me they could write a book with all the outlandish things that had happened to them during the past year of driving. The priest and I just sat and listened to the couples' stories and laughed.

The last call to prayer pierced the dusk with its mourning song. It was the holy month of Ramadan and the faithful were about to break their long fast. I showered the sweaty day off my tired body and lay down on the bed watching a fan spin above my head. On safari I could identify birds by their call. The city noises drowned out any night birds— car horns, idling diesels, high-pitched motorcycle engines changing gears, and sirens choked the air.

From eight until ten the next morning, I sat with a man named Joshua who was a refugee from The Democratic

Republic of Congo. We talked over tea, toast and oatmeal-like gruel in the YMCA cafeteria as he recounted his unbelievable story of survival, war, famine and luck. I listened to him with shock and humility—I couldn't begin to relate to this poor man. I asked him why he thought the United States did not intervene in the genocide he described.

"There is no oil there, my friend." He answered, with his big, beautiful, sad smile. Joshua was on his way to Durban, South Africa where his brother had settled, and had found him a job driving a bus. I wished him luck and felt thankful for my family—and my country—at that moment.

I walked the six blocks to the museum. The day was hot. I wore long slacks, a long sleeved shirt, and covered my hair with a kanga, my way of being respectful in this Muslim city. In New York, I would have worn a tank top and a mini skirt.

"One, please," I told the woman at the museum entrance kiosk.

"Six thousand shillings," she replied—and I was in.

Except for several workers in the courtyard cleaning a display case with a hose, the place was empty. I walked through the old colonial building past display cases with taxidermied impala. *Ethnography Hall,* written on poster board, was taped above a room entrance. *Our Relatives,* another poster board read, with several framed pictures of different monkey species hanging on the wall. The descriptive labels, simple pieces of paper with typed-out Swahili and English notes, were glued or pinned to the wood partitions.

And there he was. The giant skull of Zinj, sitting on a box. He was not under a glass case. No security guard or infrared laser protected him. Just a naked skull sitting on a platform with a typed description taped to the wall behind him. I read the short paragraph, gazed at him long enough to satisfy any questions—Yep, that's Zinj. I felt like I should stay longer. I read the words again. Then again. But I hadn't missed anything. *This* is what my anthropology teachers got me so excited about? I know it wasn't the actual skull they were so thrilled about, it was what it represented of course. A link to modern humans, a bipedal hominid that may have shared a common ancestor. So I stared at Zinj until he came alive, his hairy body, his huge jaw and tiny brain jam packed with new discoveries—*hey guys look at me, I can take this stick and jam it into the ant hole and eat all the ants I want! All his friends cheer...*

It was underwhelming, I admit, since I had created a huge drama around my trip to see this skull! Not that I was disappointed. It was just too quiet. I wanted a fanfare, confetti and a parade. Welcome Ladies and Gentlemen! Children of all ages! Introducing...drum roll please....ZINJ! And the crowd goes wild...! Maybe a bit much but it seemed like a big nothing. Way out of my way—and not worth it. Like the Mona Lisa. And now that I came and checked that one off my list of things to see before I die, I want to go home as quickly as possible. I headed back to the YMCA looking for a travel agent. British Airway's flies four times a week from Dar to London so I was confident that I could get a seat on a plane leaving that evening. And be home telling my family my Zinj story the next day.

"The soonest we can get you on the flight is January sixth," the gentleman working at Arusha Travel and Safari informed me. What? That was over a month away! I wanted to leave tonight! I must have looked dumbfounded because he added quickly, "It's holiday time."

"You don't understand, sir, I've been in Africa for nearly a year. I have to get home now to see my mom!"

"Well, I can call BA and see if any stand-by flights are available. He punched in a number on his phone and sat back, smiling, as if trying to assure me. I looked like I might start crying. To distract myself from weeping hysterically, I looked around his office at posters of snow-capped Kilimanjaro, tourists sitting in a Land Rover watching a lion groom himself on the hood, gorillas in a jungle, a perfect white beach with crystal clear blue water.

"Yes, she would like to be put on the waiting list for the soonest departure. C O F F I N, M A L I A, middle name F R A N C I S yes, just one passenger ma'am, her ticket information is, hotel whiskey niner niner zero lima four two. Yes, I'll hold." He looked at me and held his hand over the receiver, "We are doing all that we can for you to see your mum."

Thanks pal.

He didn't realize that if he *didn't* get me home to see my mum, I would be forced to smash his phone, kick him in the shin, rip those posters off the walls and scream bloody murder! I leaned forward in my chair and glared at him.

His brow furrowed and he blinked at me warily. Good, he was scared.

"Is that the first available?" He said into the phone, his voice breaking in the middle of the sentence. "Yes, yes, I understand, it's holiday time, please book her for that flight's waiting list, thank you." He smiled at me hugely as if he were about to make my day. "OK, we've got you on a list departing Dar es Salaam on the twenty-fifth December at eight a m.

I waited for the 'just kidding!' but it didn't come. "Nineteen days away? On Christmas Day?" I gasped. The man winced and I realized that I had yelled at him, loudly. But I didn't care. What the hell was I going to do in Dar es Salaam for three more weeks? I barley filled one afternoon with out getting bored.

Looking a bit scared of me, the travel agent went into salesman mode and started selling me a safari on the Serengeti Plain.

"You are guaranteed to see the big five." I had already seen the big five—lion, leopard, elephant, rhino, buffalo.

"Listen man, I just came from living in the bush for seven months, I'm done with animals, safaris and Africa. I need a beach with no elephants and no lions."
His face lit up. He had just the beach! Zanzibar, a small island off the coast of Dar, just a thirty minute flight away.

Chapter Sixteen

I gave up. I broke down. I had no fight left in me. I crumbled. Those posters on the wall were safe. I didn't even cry. Was I going to sit in Dar for nineteen days, not a chance. The guy convinced me and I bought a ticket for Zanzibar scheduled to leave that same afternoon. I bargained for a taxi to take me to the YMCA, wait ten minutes for me to grab my stuff, then drive me to the airport. Unlike the naive girl I was just two days earlier, I now knew the price of a taxi ride. It made all the difference.

Back at the domestic terminal at Dar, no air conditioning or electronic screens announced flight arrivals and departures. I rested on a hard wooden bench in a muggy room with four other people and a broken ceiling fan. A plane sat on the sizzling tarmac just outside the open door of our waiting room. The aircraft outside looked like those planes on the old Pan AM posters going to Hawaii. I thought maybe there was a vintage airplane museum nearby. Wrong again, Mia. A man about forty, looking more Arab than black, wearing a pilot uniform walked into the small room and announced to the five of us that he was ready to fly to Stone Town. Everyone got up and followed him outside to the antique flying machine.

"Excuse me sir, but I'm going to Zanzibar." I questioned the pilot.

"Welcome aboard, then." He smiled and gestured to the staircase that led up to an ancient door on the side of an ancient plane. I've heard people talk about having an overwhelming feeling that they should walk away from their scheduled flight. Then the plane crashes, and they inevitably say, 'I just had this feeling that I shouldn't get on that plane.'

I had that feeling.

I fought it though and tried to focus on the statistics about how much safer flying in an airplane is than driving in a car. There was a better chance of being struck by lightning than dying in a plane crash, right? I smiled back at the pilot, though I'm not sure I pulled it off, more like a frightened sneer. The staircase wobbled under my weight as I forced myself to board. I found a window seat and buckled up.

The four other passengers looked comfortable and calm—that helped. I watched out the window. The pilot was under the plane's wing. He was shouting at the mechanic and pointing to a valve, which he then pushed forward, shaking his head. The mechanic angrily threw his hands up, abruptly turned and stormed away into the office. The pilot yelled something back to the mechanic, turned to the stairs and boarded.

"Welcome aboard flight nineteen to Stone Town, may I see your tickets please?" Maybe the flight attendants were on strike. The pilot visited each of his five passengers, checked our tickets then turned back down the stairs. I was transfixed—he removed the blocks from both tires, ran up to the front propeller, reached up to one of the silver blades and pulled downward with all of his might. He did this three times. Finally, the engine caught and the propeller whirred into full swing. He gave a big thumbs-up to the mechanic who was watching from inside the office. As if maybe it didn't always happen? Yikes!

Once again the pilot ran up the stairs, this time hefting the door closed and locking it with a big metal arm in a downward motion. He was drenched with sweat. He sat down in the cockpit, pulled a safety belt over his head and fastened it, put on a pair of headphones with a small microphone attached. "Hotel, november, one, niner ready for takeoff," He said into his mouthpiece with authority.

Holy shit, this guy was the baggage handler, the ticket taker, the mechanic, the flight attendant and, it seemed, the sole pilot of a prehistoric plane. And I was strapped into this death machine about to fly over the Indian Ocean to a remote island off the coast of Africa—I should have e-mailed my mom.

Twenty-eight minutes later, our very resourceful pilot landed in Stone Town, on the island of Unguja which together with Pemba forms the archipelago of Zanzibar. The in-flight magazine told me everything I needed to know. I read about the flora, fauna and history of the islands. It listed several hotels. And a lengthy article described the Arab influence in Zanzibar. Three hundred years ago Arabs ran the slave trade. Now Arab leaders are the ones responsible for having Stone Town added as a UNESCO world heritage site. Reading had calmed my nerves and educated me on a place I knew nothing about.

When I walked from the runway into the tiny arrivals hall I found the customs agent asleep on a cot. A policeman was reading a paper and smoking a cigarette. Two taxis waited curbside, apparently unaware that the white zone was for the immediate loading and unloading of passengers only, no parking. The welcome desk was vacant so I picked up a flyer with a photo of a white couple walking on a pristine beach. *Welcome to the spice island* was written in bright blue lettering across the orange sunset. I checked out the map inside and I saw the city center was only six kilometers from the airport.

It was almost evening, but it was still incredibly warm. I slung on my backpack and began to walk into town. The taxi drivers didn't even ask if I needed a ride. I loved this place already—anywhere else in the world, thirty different drivers would have already accosted me. Armed with my pamphlet, and the in-flight magazine, I followed the main road into Stone Town. Looking out at the ocean, I saw the famous dhows with their unique triangle white sails.

It was a picturesque setting for anyone but lost on me at that moment. I was on a forced vacation when all I wanted to do was be home. I was hungry and hot and tired and lonely. I stopped at a little grocery store and bought a bag of

Fritos and a Coke. I sat on a concrete wall outside the shop and thought of how I ended up here when I was supposed to be on a flight to London.

What are you doing, Mia? You have no money, no place to live, you dropped out of college to be a bird watcher. What are you doing sitting on this wall on an island off the coast of Africa, eating Fritos by yourself? One of my Marine father's favorite Vince Lombardi quotes popped into my head, "Fatigue makes cowards of us all." That's how I was feeling, like a coward. Stop feeling sorry for yourself, Mia. You just had an awesome seven months getting paid to go on safari. Now you are here on this tropical island, a virtual paradise—people save their whole lives to visit an island like this one, and to go on safari. Stop whining. Go find the silver lining.

I returned my empty to the crate and tossed the Frito bag. After another ten minutes of walking I saw a modern hotel, the Ali Baba. I went in to ask the cost of a room. A man in an impeccably tailored suit replied, "One hundred and sixty US dollars per night."

"Ouch." I smiled back at him. "Do you know of another hotel that is less expensive?"

"Absolutely, madam. There is the Marco Polo just down the road to your right." I was surprised at how kind he was to me, when obviously I had walked from the airport and couldn't afford such an opulent hotel. Like the pilot earlier, this guy wasn't black but a mix of something very exotic. I asked him where he was from. He laughed and said he was a proud seventh-generation Zanzibarian.

He explained that Zanzibar was a unique place in the world, a place where Africans, Indians and Arabs met, intermarried, and lived in harmony. He added that as time went by these different cultures began to live peacefully together. I bought his explanation for now, but I'd have to do my own investigative work on the multicultural-ness of this little island. First things first though, I had to e-mail my mom and let her know my dilemma. I asked my new Zanzibarian friend if there was a business center where I could send an e-mail.

Jambo Family, My stop in Dar es Salaam has led to a small problem. I can't get a flight out until Christmas day! So I decided to come here, to Zanzibar and wait it out on the beach! I am super tired and scummy and have to go. But I wanted to let you know that I am 100% safe and happy and I will email you when I can. I am sorry mom, I didn't plan this, but I have to make the best of it! I love you and miss you so much. Mia P.S. Kisses to my new little nephew Owen!

The Marco Polo looked a little more my style—cheaper. There was a young black kid at reception. "I need a room for tonight," I said, hoping this place was in my budget because I was ready to put my backpack down and have a cool shower.

"How many?" The guy asked.

"One, please. How much is a room?"

"How many nights are you staying?"

"I don't know—how much is a room?"

"Well, rooms are thirty US dollars, but if you stay three nights I can make it twenty five, that includes breakfast."

"I don't need breakfast, I'll stay for three nights at twenty US dollars a night?"

The boy smiled at my brazen offer, his huge teeth were gleaming against his dark skin. "Where do you come from?"

"I came from Dar today." I knew what he meant but I wanted to mess with him and not admit my Americaness just yet.

"No, what country do you come from?"

"Do I get a discount if I'm from Germany?"

"You are a little crazy."

"I'm sorry, I'm just tired and need a place to stay... I'm from America."

"I have a nice room for you, and you can have it for twenty with no breakfast. Would you like to see it?"

"Sure, thanks. What is your name?"

"My name is Juma, and yours?"

"My name is Mia, very nice to meet you Juma."

"And you. Please follow me."

I followed Juma up the wooden stairs to the third floor. He opened room five and there was a clean double bed with a mosquito net hanging over the top. I popped my head in the bathroom—perfect, clean and simple with a tiny view of the harbor.

"Thanks Juma, this is perfect."

I filled out the register and gave Juma my passport. Taking a cold bottle of water from the fridge I asked him to add it to my bill, thanked him again and went upstairs to shower and lie down.

The captivating call to prayer sung from the minarets woke me up an hour later. I went downstairs and asked Juma where I should eat. He told me that near the harbor across from the mosque, vendors set up food stalls each evening. I went to check it out and first saw an old man pressing sugar cane through an old metal juicer— he cranked the handle and out the spout came fresh sugary liquid. I held up one finger, I had to try this. But he pointed to his watch then held up seven fingers and tapped his watch again. I was confused until the clock hit seven and men started flowing out of the mosque and across the street to eat. Ramadan, the holy month of fasting was in full swing, and even if you're an infidel, like me you have to fast too. However, from seven in the evening till 4 in the morning, it's a smorgasbord at the harbor! I hit about five different stalls until I was so full I could barely walk back to the Marco Polo. Juma greeted me, "Hello American Mia."

"Hold off on the American part, Juma, I have a Canadian flag on my backpack, I need to keep up appearances!" He laughed. I sat with him and had tea, I described the food I ate— fried banana, coconut curry over rice, barbecued chicken sticks, those fried roti-looking things with potato and mango stuffed inside, coconut milk straight from the nut and these cheesy crepe-like creations this guy was cooking in a huge wok. I confessed I wasn't sure of everything I ate, but it was delicious and cheap, as Juma had promised.

"Just wait until Eid al Fitr," Juma said, he explained that at the end of Ramadan there was a crazy party for three days of feasting and gift giving. Juma and I lingered in the reception area of the hotel talking into the night. He told me about his family, his dream of being accepted into an engineering program at Nairobi University and his hopes for his future. I talked about my family, my job as an ornithologist on safari and my plans to continue University, too, when I returned home. I expounded on my predicament–– that I was stuck in Zanzibar for nineteen days until I could get a flight home. He gave me a list of all the must-sees in Stone Town and Zanzibar and by the end of the night, I had my remaining days filled with spice tours, museums, caves, monkeys and markets.

Juma was right, I spent the next five days wandering the streets of Stone Town, shopping, going to museums, walking the quaint alleyways, and taking pictures of huge wooden doors. Zanzibarian doors are world famous. The greater the wealth and social position of the homeowner, the larger and more elaborately detailed his front door will be. I heard a rumor that the big brass knobs and spikes on these doors were there to keep elephants away. But since there are no elephants there, nor have there ever been any elephants on the island, this brass work is simply another beautiful ornament adorning these massive pieces of art. Like giant carved business cards they confer status to passerbys.

The architecture was an exotic mix of Indian, Arabic and Ottoman. Each evening I returned to the hotel and told Juma all about my adventures. We laughed and drank tea while he taught me the history of Zanzibar. I listened and learned about the slave trade, the Oman takeover, the spice trade, the Portuguese and English colonial rule, the wars against the Hindus, and the hierarchy that existed between Africans, Arabs, Asians and Indians and how the economy went from agriculture to tourism. "We all smile and live happily together while taking the money from the tourists." Juma laughed.

    Juma told me about his sister's death, three months earlier, giving birth to a son named Promise. Juma's sick grandmother takes care of the baby, but it is too difficult for her. I asked if there were another family member who could take the infant. Juma said he had a brother in Dar, but he and his wife already were parents of four sons and could not afford to take in another child. I felt sorry for Juma—his life was so different from mine. He was eighteen years old and supporting his grandmother and his nephew. I wished there were something I could do—but I was just one person, and I was on my way home soon.

I visited the slave museum and church the next afternoon. I paid a guide to take me through the underground tunnels. He told me the history of how the slaves were caught in the interior of the continent then walked sometimes hundreds of miles most times carrying heavy loads of ivory. Those who didn't perish en route, left to be eaten by hyena and vultures, made it to the coast. Then they were shipped to Zanzibar on small dhows—as many as 600 souls were forced under decks where there was not enough room to sit, or to kneel or to squat, just a crippling combination of all three sometimes for days. If they survived the journey to Zanzibar they were auctioned off to ship owners bound for Oman. I sat in the underground holding area where slaves were forced to wait until it was their turn to walk up to the auction block. The actual chains, leg irons and shackles were displayed on carved stone slave statues. Next my guide led me to a church. The altar had been carved out of the actual tree that the slaves had been chained to. Where they were whipped and then sold. Not the most upbeat tour I had ever been on. I left feeling drained and depressed at the cruelty of man, and embarrassed at the stain on humanity that is slavery.

    I left Stone Town the next morning to explore the rest of the island. I spent my last night with Juma talking about my family and how my sister had a baby boy while I was in Zimbabwe. Little Owen. I couldn't wait to hold him and smell him. I told Juma I had six sisters and two brothers just like an African family but, my father only had one wife. He was amazed that my mother could feed all of us, especially with my appetite. Juma advised me to speak as much Swahili as I could so I wouldn't get ripped off by locals. "They just see you as a tourist, Mia, you have to show them you are a Tanzanian." We said our good-byes, but I knew I had made a friend for life.

Chapter Seventeen

A dala dala is a converted pickup truck with two rows of wooden benches set in the back. Each dala dala has a different route around the island. To get a ride you just stand next to the road and wave your hand. People get on and off throughout the ride, so sometimes you have lots of room, and other times you are crammed in with ten other people. This local transport is cheap, fast, efficient—and probably a total death trap. But that's how I got to Nungwi. Nungwi is located on the north east coast of the island and is known for its white sand beaches, warm ocean water and cheap bungalows on the beach. It's where the backpackers congregate, so I fit right in.

I wasn't worried about finding accommodation. In fact when I got off the dala dala several young boys representing different bungalow complexes were competing to sell me a room. I agreed with one of the youngsters to go see his bungalow overlooking the ocean for twelve US dollars a night. It was basic, but exactly what I wanted, so I bargained him down to ten US dollars per night and promised to stay three nights.

The hut had a cement floor, a palm thatched roof and a bed with a mosquito net over it. It could be anywhere in the mosquito-infested world. The toilet and shower were down a sand path about 100 yards. Electricity was provided by a very loud generator from dusk until eleven every night. I spent my days walking the beach and collecting shells. I did some bird watching, but was unfamiliar with most of the sea birds. I threaded shells, coral and wood onto fishing-line, making arty mobiles which I hung in my hut. I traded my Ann Patchett for a Dean Koonz paperback, just to scare the crap out of myself before the generator quit and I was plunged into the darkness of my hut…alone.

The local women farmed seaweed in the shallow ocean— the wind blew their colorful kangas off their faces and heads, flying in the wind like colorful kites. I watched these woman walk into the sea—shallow for a mile. They would smile at me, their children would yell, "Hello, misses!" I swam and read and walked down the long beach during the days, then at night I would join other foreigners at the main building for dinner.

None of us were used to fasting all day so we were starving by seven. Finally, after prayers, we would enjoy delicious home-cooked curries and ice cold beers. We talked into the night. I became friends with Jaap, a Dutch guy whose parents were doctors in Moshi, and a French couple who lived in Paris. The French guy was an artist and had such a fondness for the local fishing boats, called dowhs, that he was determined to buy one of those canvas triangles to take home to Paris and make art from it.

He finally bought a sail from an old fisherman and spent the next two days scrubbing the life out of it, then drying it so he could wrap it up and take it on the plane back to France. I wondered what that fisherman thought of the crazy Frenchman who had purchased his crappy old sail. Whatever it was, the fisherman and his family lived for a month off that deal.

Jaap and I signed up for a snorkel adventure on my third day. It was like swimming in an aquarium. We had a going-away party for the French couple that night—one more wonderful going-away party, an oft recurring event when on the road. The next day Jaap left for Amsterdam. I was left alone again. I had four more days left until I had to be back in Dar for my flight on Christmas, so I headed back to Stone Town to see Juma.

"Jambo Kaka!" Juma recognized my greeting—Hello brother. He jumped from behind the desk and expecting a hug, I held out my arms. He completely ignored them and thrust out his hand for a very aggressive handshake.

I noticed that African men acted conservatively towards the foreign tourists, especially the women. I was never sure if it was a Muslim thing or just a foreign woman thing. I shook his hand. I was genuinely happy to see him. I told him all about my trip north and the things I did. I presented him with one of my shell mobiles. We talked into the night until it was time to sleep. I went up to my room while Juma manned the desk until dawn.

I spent the next morning at the Internet café and post office. I wrote a long e-mail to Frankie and Sophie explaining why I was still in Tanzania. Then I sent home a box of souvenirs I bought in the market. I also booked a room at the YMCA in Dar for the night before my flight. I called British Airways to confirm that I was on their waiting list and to find out the chances of getting on the flight. They told me I should show up early so I'd be first on the list in the event of a cancellation. Damn, I HAD to be on that flight!

When Juma got to work, I was waiting in the lobby for him.

"Jambo Kaka."

"Jambo Sista." Juma answered, clearly upset about something.

"What's wrong?" I asked, concerned.

"I spoke to my grandmother, she is very sick and cannot take care of Promise anymore. I cannot quit my job and we have no one to help. I spoke to my grandmother about you, Mia. About you taking Promise to give him a better life in America."

"What? But I..." I was pretty sure that I had misunderstood Juma's heavily accented English. At least, I hoped I had misunderstood him.

"Listen Mia, I have thought about this for a long time, I discussed it with my grandmother and my brother in Dar. We have all agreed that it would be the best decision for Promise, and I know you have told me that you want a baby and a family."

Well, I was certainly glad they were all in agreement on such an important decision.

"Yeah, I said that, but I meant *someday*, not now, and I definitely didn't mean I wanted to steal a child from Africa."

"Mia, we need your help."

"What are you talking about Juma! What the hell would I do with a baby—how would I get it home?"

"Please, do not swear Mia, I don't want to make you angry."

"I'm not angry, I'm very confused."

"Mia, there are things… circumstances… I did not tell you because I did not know you. My sister had the AIDS. She fell pregnant and did not know she was sick. When they cut the baby from her stomach she got an infection in her blood and that is how she died. The baby does not have the AIDS. The clinic where they cut my sister tested the baby and he came out negative for the AIDS. My country is very quiet about this— no one in my family will speak of this. No one wants this baby. My grandmother's neighbors tell her to kill this baby, that this baby has a bad spirit because it killed his mother."

I could barely comprehend what Juma was telling me. I felt sick and numb and horrified and scared and alone and confused.

"There is no one for this baby." Juma's voice broke and he started to cry.

"Juma, what can I do? I cannot take a baby!"

"Take the baby to America, give him a chance. You are a smart and rich woman. You can raise this baby as your own, teach him Swahili and teach him to love. You told me that the color of skin does not matter to you."

"It doesn't Juma, I just don't know how to tell you that I'm not rich in my country. I have nothing. I live with my parents and I just quit college. I don't have a boyfriend or a car…"

"You have a very big family, like an African family— they will help you and love you and take care of him. Mia, this baby sits inside the house all day. My grandmother

cannot pick him up, she is sick. I work all the night. This baby stays alone and cries for love that I cannot give. This boy needs a mother."
My lip started to tremble at the word *mother*.
Could I be a mother?

At home, when I would ask my mom which of her children was her favorite she would always say, "Mia, you are all my favorite. It may be hard for you to believe but, with each baby I had my heart opened up for another—I love each new baby just like I did my first."
My mom had nine kids. I could raise one, right?

I thought about my childhood and the circumstances surrounding my birth. I knew my parents were delighted to have their first daughter my oldest sister, Paige, then my next sister Bridgette came, Lindsay was their third daughter. When my older sister Emma was born, my father called his mother with the bad news that their fourth born, was again—a girl child.

That was when my mom and dad went on their first and only trip to Hawaii, I'm pretty sure they went to mourn their failure at not being able to produce a baby boy. They bundled up Emma, the newborn daughter and left her and the three other sisters with grandma. Then they fled to Hawaii to tan away their blues away on Waikiki beach. That's where my mom conceived me, daughter number five.

My parents were devastated. Another girl? Yes. Me. And I've been in therapy most of my adult life trying to figure out why I seek negative attention. To add insult to injury I got the only Hawaiian name in the family, Malia, which means calm and tranquil in Hawaiian. They wanted to make sure I felt different from my siblings. That I would be the unique one. It worked.

Then, it happened. The long-awaited, yearned for, prayed for golden boys were born. Eleven months after I was born, my mom gave birth to identical twin boys! What a prize! Martin and Michael had arrived. Boys! At last! Then my mom went on with the job she did so well—making girl children—two more girls followed, Rose and Tess.

I grew up with my six sisters and twin brothers. I couldn't help believing that I had been a big mistake. A disappointment. No one wanted me. The truth is my parents never said anything of the sort, they loved all of us the same. But I was the fifth daughter and that takes its toll.

I thought of that little baby Promise—no one wanted him. I had felt so unwanted at times. Maybe I could take him and love him. I was actually thinking about stealing an African baby and packing him off to Laguna Beach, California, the whitest place on earth.

"What about the father and his birth certificate Juma, I'm totally white."

"My brother lives in Dar and has access to fake papers. I will be listed as the father of Promise."

Lets get this straight. "So, I take this baby, get on a plane, go to Dar, meet your brother to get a forged birth certificate naming me his biological mother and you his father. Call British Airways to let them know I suddenly have a lap child I will be taking home with me, even though I entered Tanzania seven months ago without him."

"Yes."

Sure, right, no problem.

"Do you believe in God, Juma?"

"Yes, I do."

"What does God say to do?" I ask Juma sincerely.

"God made you come to me and let me see you and hear you and know you are a good woman and God wants you to take this baby and give him a happy life."

"Yes, Juma," I said then. "I will take Promise home and give him a good life." Of course, the whole time I am saying this, my mind was screaming at me—are you kidding, what the hell do you think you are saying?!

Both Juma and I cried with fear and relief. We stayed up the rest of the night making plans for tomorrow when I would meet Promise and his Grandmother.

In bed that night anxiety ripped through my body. My stomach was sick at the prospect of what I was doing. If I took Promise home, my life would be over. But how could I say no to a baby who would probably die if I didn't help him? I had no choice. What would any of my sisters do, or my mom?

I was taking this baby home and raising it. Every thought imaginable went through my head just then—what about his culture and his blackness, would people ask where I got this child, would I be arrested and put in some horrible prison in Africa? I felt scared and confused but sure of what I had to do. I prayed for the first time since I was a child, asking God what I should do. I lay awake waiting for him to answer me.

Chapter Eighteen

Morning prayer filled the dawn. That melodious invitation for the devoted to come and praise Allah. I went down to find Juma sleeping behind the desk on an army cot. I went back upstairs and let him sleep for another hour before he got off work.

"Habari za asubuhi, kaka."

"And a good morning to you, my sister."

We walked into the center of town together to catch a dala dala towards Juma's village. The truck followed the coast north with the Zanzibar channel to our left past the town of Bububu then east to Selem. Forty minutes later we got off and caught another truck from Selem, north to Mangapwani. Before the main town, Juma signaled the driver to stop. We got off in the middle of nowhere.

I searched Juma's face for an explanation as to why we got off before we arrived at the village. Juma smiled and motioned for me to follow him off the road onto a small dirt trail. We walked single file into the bush. Several women and children carrying jugs of water and sacks of corn passed us.

"There is no running water here, only a community well." Juma said without stopping. We arrived at a cluster of cement buildings with corrugated tin roofs. Chickens ran around, and several cats lay on the dirt sleeping in the sun.

"Please, welcome to my home," Juma said to me upon pushing open a wooden door painted bright blue. His concrete home was one room. A cot leaned against a wall on a clean cement floor. A calendar was the only adornment on the wall, sponsored by the 'pride of Tanzania,' Air Tanzania and Coca Cola. The infant lay sleeping on a woven mat, a cat was curled up under one of the baby's outstretched arms.

"Promise sleeps during the day and is awake all night my grandmother says. We feed him milk from the goat when he wakes up."

I walked over and saw the baby's face for the first time, an absolute cherub with a big round fat face and pouting lips. When I reached down to pick him up from the floor he woke up and started to cry. He was wearing a stained white shirt and no bottoms.

"Do you have a diaper for him?" I asked Juma.

"No, diapers are too expensive."

I rocked the infant and said "shshshshshsh." Promise fell back to sleep on my shoulder.

"Where is your grandmother?"

"She must be at the market."

She was at the market while a three-month-old baby was left alone sleeping on the floor with the cat?

"Okay, let's go to her." I said. I followed Juma down the dirt path with Promise sleeping in my arms. The market was actually just one small table set with four mangos, one bunch of bananas and about ten packs of chewing gum. The man behind the table said to me, "Jambo, maybe you like some chewing gum for the baby?" I guessed the guy needed a sale. There were women doing wash in huge plastic containers and children running around naked, teasing the chickens with sticks. An old woman sat on a crate in the shade of a banana tree. A cardboard box sat in front of her with several plastic bags filled with water and white blocks. The grandmother.

"She sells homemade cheese to help pay for the baby's clothes." Juma told me. I smiled at the woman and said, "Jambo." I extended my hand to her but she did not reach for it. Both of her eyes had cloudy cataracts in them. "She is blind." Juma said.

Seriously? A blind old woman selling goat cheese was taking care of an infant? That was it. I could definitely take this kid. I could give Promise a better chance than he would ever have here.

A blind old lady taking care of a newborn baby?

"You forgot to mention that Juma." I said, exasperated.

Juma's grandmother asked the bubblegum man to watch her cheese. She slowly got up and began to hobble down the path back to the house, her cane leading the way, the two of us following, me with Promise in my arms. She made tea and offered it up in plastic cups. Promise had woken up crying so Juma took him and gave him a bottle. Promise sucked the bottle dry. Juma spoke to his grandmother in Swahili— they spoke for about ten minutes before Juma asked me if I understood what they had said.

"No." I answered quietly.

"She wants to make sure that you will give this baby a good life in America."

"Tell her I'll try."

"No, you need to tell her you will."

"OK, yes, I will give this baby a good life in America." I nodded toward Juma's grandmother. She couldn't see me. She got up from the cot with the help of her cane, shuffled over to where I was standing and found my hand with hers. She turned my palm up, brought it to her mouth and kissed my palm. Then she turned from me, walked out and back down the dirt path.

There was nothing to gather for the child. He had no clothes or shoes or blankets or stuffed animals. He had one tiny shirt that he wore and one bottle. I put his empty bottle in my bag and left with Juma to go back to Stone Town. While we were sitting in the back of a dala dala I asked Juma, "Is there a supermarket on the island?" He said there's one in Selem so, we got off and made our way to the store. It wasn't exactly Safeway. But I stocked up on diapers, formula, baby shampoo, baby powder, a pacifier and new bottles. The week before I was buying suntan lotion and rounds of beers—what a difference a few days make. I didn't stop to think how Promise would change my whole life. I wasn't thinking at all.

I was on some rescue mission and the only thing that mattered was the little baby boy in my arms.

I left Promise with Juma at a park near the harbor back in Stone Town so I could shop around for baby clothes that Promise could wear on the plane. I returned forty-five minutes later to find Promise sleeping in Juma's arms.

"That kid sleeps a lot." I said. "Yeah, during the day." Juma raised his eyebrows at me. Implying that at night it's a different story.

"Look at all the cute stuff I got him." I pulled a onesie out of my shopping bag.

"You will be a good mum to him."

"I have no idea what I'm doing, Juma."

Juma held Promise as we walked to the Marco Polo— Juma's shift started in ten minutes. At the hotel entrance Juma carefully handed the sleeping baby to me. I carried him upstairs, laid him on my bed and stared at him. Tears streamed down my cheeks. I let out a breath and the floodgates opened. I wept. Fear and confusion swept through my body. I stared at this ethereal child on my bed and could not accept that he was mine.

This boy's life is in my hands? I can't even take care of myself!

I didn't have a job, an apartment, a car. Still, *something* in my heart made me feel calm as I watched him sleep. When he opened his eyes, he cried hysterically at the white woman standing over him. I suddenly knew what that *something* in my heart was. It was love.

Chapter Nineteen

I bathed Promise in the sink with his new shampoo—I put powder on his skin and zipped him up in a little pajama with built in feet. I made him a bottle and walked down stairs with him in my arms.

"Who is this handsome boy?" Juma asked

"This is my son, Promise." I said proudly. It was the first time I had referred to the child as *my son* my breath caught in my throat. My love for this baby was real. Juma and I sat in the lobby playing with Promise during my last night in Stone Town. We went over what was to happen the next day in Dar with his brother and the forged birth certificate. I described where Promise would live, where he would go to school, that he would grow up swimming in the ocean in California with his many cousins. I said goodbye to Juma around midnight. He gave me a hug for the first time and vowed to visit California—which we knew would probably never happen.

"I know God sent you to me." Juma was crying again.

"And God sent you to me, Juma."

I walked up the stairs with Promise sleeping in my arms. I lay him down on the bed and put my nose up against his little face to smell him. He was so innocent and sweet. I closed my eyes and fell asleep with my baby. An hour later we were up— a bottle, a lullaby and another hour of sleep. Awake again, a bottle, a walk around the room, a poop, a burp, another bath another lullaby, another bottle, another hour of sleep, then the call to prayer.
Holy shit, is this normal?
I packed my bag, scooped up Promise and headed down stairs. Juma had gone home two hours before and I recognized the man who worked the day shift at reception.

"Good Morning," he said.

"Good morning to you," I responded.

"And who is this gorgeous child?"

"This is my son." It was my first time saying it, to a stranger, my heart nearly pounded out of my chest.

"What a beautiful boy," he said with no question or accusation of kidnapping. My stomach was in knots. I kept rehearsing in my head my son's birthday, who the father was, when I got pregnant, where I had the baby. Any question that someone had for me, I had an answer. Still, my story was full of holes and if anyone did the slightest bit of detective work, the jig was up.

I *just* flew over from Arusha without a baby, then twenty-two days go by and I leave with a three-month old? Really? Yeah, I had every reason to be tense and I was. I hailed a taxi to the airport—I didn't bargain for the price for the first time in my life. The six kilometers cost me more than my hotel room. All my travel rules went out the window. I felt so defensive, like I was ready to pounce on anyone who questioned me.

Relax Mia, don't be so paranoid, no one knows you're stealing a baby…you're not stealing this baby, Mia! Juma was desperate and the baby would have died. Just stop. Stop thinking and act normal.

An hour later we boarded the flight to Dar. This time there were only three other passengers—all men. How did this airline make any money? It was the same pilot that flew me over nearly three weeks before… shit! I dug through my bag and pulled out my sunhat shoving it on my head and pulling the front down low over my eyes. I couldn't let him recognize me. If he did, he would ask me where I had picked up the kid. My pulse pounded so hard, I could see the vein in my wrist, I realized that I was acting worse than a paranoid pothead.

Fortunately, the pilot didn't even give me a second glance. Maybe lots of white college girls went to Zanzibar and had babies in mere days. The flight was easy— Promise sat on my lap and mauled a chew toy I bought the day before.

We took a taxi to the YMCA. However, when we pulled up in front of the Y I had another anxiety attack. I could barely breathe as I realized that this is where I stayed before. What if someone here recognized me? How would I explain the baby? I asked the driver if he knew a cheap hotel nearby.

Of course he did, and he drove another two blocks to the Hotel Livingstone. Apparently all the hotels in Tanzania are named after explorers. I asked the taxi driver to meet me right here at the same spot at five the next morning to drive me back to the airport. I kept repeating what time I needed the taxi driver, praying he would remember and would not leave me stranded. The driver looked at me and said, "yes, OK, I'll be here at five tomorrow morning." I repeated, "I'll see you tomorrow at five," about thirty times.

I was nervous. I could feel that Promise needed a diaper change. We walked into the Livingstone and paid for one night. I called Juma's brother, Nazir to let him know that we had arrived and to set up a meeting place and time to collect the birth certificate. He didn't answer his phone. I waited ten minutes and dialed again. No answer. Maybe I could take Promise through security without a birth certificate. I had two flights. The first left Dar es Salaam and landed in London, flight time was nine hours and forty minutes. The second left London and landed in Los Angeles, flight time eleven hours and twenty minutes. Maybe no one would notice a super white girl and a very black baby for twenty-one hours.

I called Nazir again.

"Hallo?"

"Hello, this is Mia, is this Nazir?"

"Yes, where are you calling from?"

"We are in Dar, we are staying at the Hotel Livingstone."

"I thought we were to meet you at the YMCA?"

"No, we are only a few blocks away, can you meet me here?"

"Yes, I will pick you up at five o'clock this afternoon on my way home from work."

"Is everything O.K. with the documents?"

"Yes, everything is in order. I will see you at five."

Promise was asleep on the bed. I took a shower and lay down next to him. I guessed I'd start sleeping during the day too. I woke up hungry two hours later. Promise was already awake, gurgling and staring at the ceiling. "Let's go find something to eat my little dumpling." The baby didn't weigh very much but he got heavy, so for the sake of my back, I bought a little stroller. I pushed Promise around the city for an hour buying snacks and spoiling him with a new blanket, clothes, books and toys. I bought a little bag to put all Promise's things in for the plane.

We got back to the hotel and waited for Nazir to arrive with the birth certificate. At five minutes after five the room phone rang. It was Nazir, he was downstairs. Sweat rolled down my back as I carried Promise down to the lobby.

"Nazir?"

"Hallo, Mia, it is very nice to meet you." He looked a bit like Juma but far older and more tired looking. He touched the baby's head and said "Hello, Promise." Promise did a head wobble and smiled.

"Please follow me, my car is just outside."

I sorta thought he was going to hand me an envelope with the forged birth certificate and go, like something out of a double o seven movie, but it didn't happen. I followed him outside. He unlocked his Honda Civic for us and I got in the passenger's seat with Promise. This had been my first car model when I was a senior in high school, same brown oxidized paint on the hood, same interior plastic seats, same smell. We sat in silence while he drove the forty minutes to his house. Promise fell asleep on my lap. I wanted to ask if I could see the birth certificate, but I didn't say a word and neither did he.

We parked in front of a fairly nice home by African standards, where they grew maize and tomatoes instead of a lawn. We entered through a side door to the kitchen. A woman greeted Nazir at the entrance. She was wearing the traditional Muslim head cover and a long dress over trousers. She was barefoot and I saw a pile of shoes at the door, so I took my shoes off and walked in. Nazir introduced me to his wife, Fatma. She was stunning—with a broad forehead and high cheekbones, she looked like a model.

Promise was sleeping in my arms and Fatma gazed at the baby with what I thought was contempt, maybe just fatigue. The kitchen smelled of cooking onions and I noticed several pots on the stove. Fatma turned her back to us without a word and continued making dinner. Nazir explained that Fatma didn't speak English well. Chaga was her native dialect. Maybe, but I got the feeling she didn't have anything good to say to me in any language. Nazir told me to put Promise down, so I followed him out of the kitchen through a short hallway into a room with a queen-size bed.

"This is the boys' room." Nazir said.

"Which boy?"

"All four share this bed."

I laid my sleeping baby down and followed Nazir back to the kitchen.

"I must go to the mosque for evening prayer, please make yourself comfortable and I will be back to join you for dinner. The boys are anxious to meet you and their new nephew. Nazir and Fatma spoke to each other in Chaga then, so I went back down the hall to find the boys and escape from being left alone with Fatma.

I stuck my head in to a room where I heard a T.V. Four little cuties sat there glued to the screen watching The Golden Girls. I heard Betty White complaining about a lost recipe, the laugh track roared and the boys followed suit, giggling. Two sat on a couch and two were on the carpeted floor. "Hello." I said. They turned as one, "Hello misses," one of the boys said to me. The smallest boy stared at me like I was a ghost, his eyes wide and scared. The older boy broke the silence. "My father told me you are from where Michael Jackson lives."

"Yes, I come from California and Michael Jackson lives near my house."

"Are you friends with Michael Jackson?"

"No, but I can do the moonwalk, wanna see?" Dancing was always an icebreaker in any culture. One time I danced the Macarena for some girls in Vietnam and they laughed for hours. The boys schooled me on my moonwalk technique telling me I looked like a robot. One of them actually had some smooth moves for a seven year old. They all told me their names and ages and what grade they were in, they spoke perfect English and explained to me what they wanted to be when they grew up. The twelve year old was going to be a rapper. I was so proud that my American culture had influenced this kid half way around the world to wear gold chains and call women bitches. Perfect.

The ten year old wanted to be a doctor so he could take care of his mom when she coughed. She had asthma and was always sick. The third boy was eight and was proud to announce that he was going to be a cricket player. The youngest was still scared of me, but told me he was going to be a policeman so he could ride a horse and have a gun—made sense to me. I talked to the boys for an hour then went to check on Promise. He was awake on the bed, just staring at the ceiling with a grin on his face. I picked him up, changed his diaper and went back to introduce the boys to their nephew.

When the boys told me they didn't know who Juma was, I understood it wasn't my place to explain family relations. For whatever reason, if they had never heard of their uncle then I was going to keep quiet about everything going on. I heard Nazir return and call us for dinner. The boys were not expected to keep the fast, but were praised if they skipped at least one meal. The boys seeking attention for their devotion had all skipped lunch and were starving.

We all sat around a large table in the kitchen and ate quietly until the ten year old spoke, "Mia can do the moon walk." And then the oldest, "Who is uncle Juma?"

I saw Fatma look at Nazir. "Boys, go to the TV room," she snapped. Obviously she was the disciplinarian because those boys jumped from their seats without one word of dissent. Her English was perfect, as I suspected she just chose not to speak to me.

I sat at the dinner table holding Promise and feeling very uncomfortable. All I wanted was to get that Birth Certificate and leave. I wanted to take my son and get out of there. Fatma began speaking Chaga to Nazir. I wasn't sure if I should join the boys or stay put. I really wanted to join the boys. Their conversation turned heated and in a few minutes Fatma was crying and slamming dishes in to the sink. Nazir sat there holding his head in his hands glancing up at me and Promise.

"I...is there something wrong?" I asked Nazir.

"Fatma and I have been arguing about taking Promise to live here with us and the boys."

"I am taking Promise with me tomorrow morning to California—all I need from you is the documentation that Juma arranged."

"Fatma does not think it's a good idea for you to take Promise."

"But Juma…"

"Juma is a child!" Nazir interrupted me. "And you are a white Christian woman saving an African baby—we don't need your saving!"

"No." I said crying, "I don't feel that way, I don't care about color or race or religion, I love Promise."

"We love Promise, we want him to grow up with his family, his people and his religion."

"But, Juma..." If you couldn't tell, I only earned a C minus in debate. But, repeating Juma was the extent of my skills, it seemed.

"Stop! Stop with Juma! He is a child who does not know the laws of Islam and is a spoiled boy—he does not know what family and loyalty mean. He is my father's son from a whore."

Fatma said something in Chaga to Nazir. They began to argue again but I couldn't understand. I sat there in total disbelief, horror. I couldn't lose my sweet baby now. No one had the right to take Promise from me, he was mine and I already loved him. I had plans—he was going to grow up in California with his twenty-nine cousins and be loved and taught that he can be anything he wants. I would not allow Fatma to take him from me. No fucking way! I took a deep breath, hoping I would say the right thing to convince them that Promise belonged to me. But Nazir spoke first, "Listen to me Mia. We have decided that we have to take this child. He is my family. We told Juma no when the child's mother died because we couldn't afford another baby. But now, circumstances are different and we are bound to this obligation."

"Obligation?" I felt a tear slip down my cheek. I didn't want Promise to be an obligation. I want him, I need him, I love him, he is not an obligation to me, he is a blessing to me. "Please. Please. Please. Understand that I have thought about this very hard and know it is the right choice for me and for you and your family and for the baby. I will give him a good life in America. I will raise him Muslim if you want. I will do whatever you want." I was grasping at anything that would persuade them to allow me to keep my Promise.

Chapter Twenty

"The decision has been made, by Allah. This child will be raised by me with the doctrine of Islam in his own country with his own people. I will take you to your hotel now." I pulled Promise closer to me, protecting him with my embrace. "Please, please reconsider, I already love him and have planned and bought him toys and..." Nazir told Fatma something in Chaga and she moved closer to me. She reached toward my baby. I was crying. Promise was crying. Fatma was crying and coughing. I looked down at the soft black baby hair on Promise's fragile little head.

No!

I gave her the child. I looked into Fatma's eyes—I knew she didn't want a fifth boy to raise.

No!

"Please take care of him," I whispered to her. She looked back at me and nodded, never having said one word to me. I felt broken. I followed Nazir out the kitchen door to the car. He drove me back to Dar in silence. When he stopped in front of the Hotel Livingston, I asked if he would wait for five minutes while I got something for Promise. He agreed and I ran up to the room and collected all of Promise's new things. I dragged the stroller, bags of diapers, toys, books and clothes that I had bought for Promise to the curb. I opened the hatchback of the Honda and loaded all of my sweet baby's things into the trunk then walked to the driver's side. I looked down at Nazir. "Did you have the birth certificate?"

"Yes, everything was complete for you to take him. I just couldn't let it happen. I am sorry. I wish you could understand." Nazir looked up at me with tired eyes.

I had been so close. "I do understand," I said, though I wasn't sure that I really did. "He's family." I added.

Nazir drove away leaving me alone.

I woke up every hour that night and yearned for Promise. At five the next morning, I stood at the curb where Nazir had left me. The taxi was there.

"Good morning, madam," the driver said.

"Habari za asubuhi," I said back.

"Now you go to airport, madam?"

"Yes, please."

"Where is your son?"

A huge lump rose in my throat, "He is not my son, he will stay here with his family in Tanzania." Each word hurt as if they were stinging bees, but the driver just shrugged. He didn't know what I had just been through. He didn't care. And why should he, I was just his first client at the start of a long day.

British Airways' grounds crew hadn't arrived for their shift yet, so I sat on the floor in front of the closed booking counter feeling numb. I was emotional and defensive. I was looking for a fight. Any excuse someone gave me, bring it. If anyone so much as looked at me the wrong way, I would take them down. Don't even *try* to say I was not getting on that plane. I was so ready to leave Africa.

I was first in line. I was the only person in line. I may have been the only person at the airport.

A young blonde woman with a red beret on her head looked over the counter to me on the floor and chirped in an English accent, "Good morning, and Merry Christmas, how may I help you?" I nearly ripped the pert beret off her and shoved it down her throat. Don't even begin to screw with me lady, you have no idea!

I stood slowly, giving myself time to breathe. "Yes, I am on the waiting list for the flight to London this morning and they told me to be early, that my chances would be better if I got here early, so I got here early." Did she get the part that I was here early? She took my passport and started clicking a computer keyboard, her face lit up green from the monitor. I glared at her, daring her to say I was stuck in Dar for another two months.

"The early bird gets the worm, right?" she giggled. A grown woman should not giggle. Actually, no one should ever say clichés and then giggle, it was all bad.

"You certainly did Miss Coffin, get your worm, I mean. I am pleased to tell you that we have a seat for you, would you like an aisle or a window?"

I was so ready for a confrontation that it didn't register with my brain for a second, "I have a seat?"

"And a connection to Los Angeles, departing London Heathrow at twenty-one hours and arriving Los Angeles at seven-fifty."

All my fight left me, my sadness about Promise came boiling to the surface and I began to cry. Huge tears rolled down my cheeks and snot immediately plugged my nose.

"Are you OK, Miss Coffin?" I tried to tell her yes, I'd be fine, what came from my mouth sounded like Mary Tyler Moore's wobbly high pitched helium voice.

"Take your time." The beret lady consoled watching me try to get it together. Then she added, "Time always helps."

She was right, with time, a lot of blessed time, I'd be better.

Zinj on display at the National Museum
in Dar es Salaam

Crazy
Lebanon

Chapter Twenty-One

I romanticize everything—relationships, jobs and especially travel destinations. I went to Tahiti once because I saw the cover of Conde Naste Traveler magazine at a Barnes and Noble with those little thatched-roofed bungalows perched atop crystal clear water. When I arrived in Papeete I searched for that picture but all I found was a cinder block hut with a communal toilet, a giant mango tree with its rotting fruit littering a path to a filthy black sand beach. I'm sure with better planning I would have discovered that those cabanas were on Bora Bora and go for about $1,600 a night. Well, I saved $1, 585 a day.

So when I decided to go to Lebanon for a month, I tried to keep my romantic notions in check. I went to the library to research Lebanon's history and did my best not to picture myself lounging under a date palm on the Mediterranean overlooking ancient Phoenician ruins as I sipped arak. Sitting in the library with books piled up high around me I began to picture myself walking along the famous Beirut Cornish, stopping into the stylish St. George's Hotel for a lunch of freshly made mezze of hummus, tabouli, sweet olives, warm bread, spicy lamb kebabs and a Bordeaux style Bekka valley wine. Right, so romanticizing is going to happen no matter if I hit myself over the head with huge tomes of history. Still my unromantic side realized that Beirut has just come out of a thirty-year civil war. I would probably be stepping over unexploded bombshells, walking by bullet-riddled buildings and dodging Israeli missiles as air raid sirens warned the city to take cover.

It's impossible to envision a place accurately, until you've seen it for yourself. And while it's best not to have *any* expectations, it's hard not to get excited about visiting one of the longest inhabited parts of the world. Every aspect of my research just re-enforced my desire to go. The history of Lebanon is incredible: the food is world famous, its politics are steeped in turmoil and heroism, different religions and traditions fuel its exotic ambience. This multicultural society has evolved over centuries into a tolerant, warm and welcoming place. As for natural beauty, perched on the warm Mediterranean sea Lebanon enjoys a glorious climate that makes it an agricultural paradise.

"Why in God's name would you ever want to go to Beirut!" was my father's reaction to the news of my next trip, pretty much exactly what I expected. So I was prepared to defend Lebanon, even though I hadn't been there yet. And neither had he.

"Dad, it's in the fertile crescent, the cradle of civilization!" I appealed to his love of culture.

"Yeah, Mia, so is Baghdad. Why don't you waltz on over to Iraq too?" He was fuming mad mostly because he was scared. He didn't understand why his fifth daughter had to go off to these crazy places when most of his friends' daughters went to Florida or Hawaii for vacation.

"I *would* go to Baghdad, except there's a war going on, dad. The war in Lebanon ended almost twenty years ago. They have rebuilt Beirut, it's a prosperous, safe and stable place now." Realizing no amount of reassuring him would work, I nevertheless kept trying to help him understand that I am very careful and always pack my common sense on my trips.

"Listen to me Mia, I am a Marine. Do you know when the last Prime Minister of Lebanon was assassinated? Well I do—and it was in 2005. The bastards used so much TNT, they blew a twenty-foot hole into the sidewalk in Beirut. Your uncle was there in 1958 and I can promise you, the Lebanese didn't welcome the US Marines with open arms. Your cousin was there in 1983 when a suicide bomber slammed his truck into the Marine barracks killing two hundred forty one Americans!"

"Dad, that was between Reagan and Iran, it was retaliation for…"

"Stop Mia! There is no justification! The Lebanese are our enemy! In 2008 Hezbollah was recognized as a political party. Their flag shows a hand holding an AK-47—they are a bunch of terrorists!" Well, clearly I wasn't going to calm my father down with talk of history and Mediterranean beaches. He was right, Lebanon does have a war-torn past, and nothing I could say to him would prove that Lebanon has changed for the better. Only going there and returning home safely would show him. Now I just need a ticket, and I had enough flight miles accumulated to fly business class non-stop the whole way with out spending a penny.

You know those corny e-mails that are forwarded to you from your mom and sappy friends? There's one that advises to wear your most expensive underwear or use your finest china rather than saving it for a special occasion—because you never know when you might get hit by a bus, never having enjoyed those luxuries. I have an addition to that list. Flight miles. Stop hoarding accumulated airline miles for some imaginary 'special trip.' Treat yourself *now*. Use them and revel in the extravagance.

I did not heed the advise from the corny e-mail. Instead of using all my accumulated miles to travel non-stop to Beirut kicking it in business class I chose to save my prized miles for some nonexistent 'special trip' and go with the deal. The deal included the most convoluted way to travel to Lebanon with twelve extra hours of torturous waiting and flying time. Yes, I compromised my comfort for value, yet again.

From California to Chicago to New York to Amman, four planes, five airports and thirty-six hours later, plagued with debilitating fatigue, I finally landed in Beirut, Lebanon. Set your breakfast tables with your finest china, wear that expensive underwear and use your flight miles today!

Chapter Twenty-Two

Beirut in September is warm. After my nightmarish trip I step onto the curb outside Rafic Hariri International airport and hail a taxi to take me the twenty minutes into the city. It's ninety degrees at midnight.

I had prepared well. The entire month of August was spent searching the Internet for everything Lebanese. My hostel was pre-booked—a walking tour scheduled, my Lonely Planet high-lighted with relevant information and important papers folded into the pages. And of course, I knew the correct fare for a taxi to get me into the city. I could tell you the *real* price of how much it costs to get from the airport into the city for fifty different places around the world, It's what I do. The unsuspecting driver pulled up to me, anticipating another naïve tourist. You just stopped for the wrong passenger pal. Twenty dollars. No more no less. The driver began to argue with me but I held my ground.

Exhausted but exhilarated to finally be in Beirut, I watch the city speed by from the back seat—nothing especially different from any other city in the world, freeways, billboards, tall buildings. I handed the driver the address of the hostel and he seemed to know the place.

He didn't. We stopped at a street corner and he asked a couple of guys working in an auto body shop if they knew where the hostel was. They didn't. Two more stops and finally a man points up the street to where I see a poorly lit sign. I get out of the taxi squint in the darkness to confirm what it says, Hostel Sofar. Bingo!

The driver claps his hands and says in accented English, "Yes! Hotel Sofar, there!" He grabs my backpack from the trunk, dumps it on the road, jumps back into his cab and speeds off, happy to be rid of me. Left alone, I begin to walk the rest of the way up to the hostel.

I pull my backpack around to my front as a slightly soft and not great barrier between me and whatever is out there that could kill me, and continue to make my way towards the scary looking hostel.

"Hello?" I question the air past the open door under the hostel sign. Nothing. My dad would be thrilled at this scene. I walk inside and see HOSTEL SOFAR spray-painted on the wall, with an arrow pointing to the next floor up.

Classy joint.

Climbing the stairs I fight the urge to run back outside, find another cab and stay at a fancy hotel for a few nights, blowing my accommodation money for the month. The building was old, no lights showed the way up the stairs or down the hallway. The wood creaked with each step. I'm pretty sure that I'm in one of those scary movies where the audience keeps chanting, "Don't go into the hall! Don't go up the stairs!"

So, like all good heroines, I go up the stairs and through the glass door at the top. "Hello?" Still nothing.

What the hell kind of hotel is this? The taxi driver had never heard of it, they have no sign, no reception. I look around for the REDRUM I am sure must be etched in blood somewhere close.

"Ahhh, welcome to the Hostel Sofar." A demon announced.

I saw eyes looking at me over a desk in the corner. I clasped my hand to my heart and it, thoughtfully, started beating again.

Not a demon but an old man rose up from behind the desk. He wore a thin white tank top and what looked to me like boxer shorts. Believe me, a hundred and fifty-year-old man in boxer shorts is not pretty.

"Please, madame, let me take your bag." My backpack outweighed him by at least ten pounds.

"No, it's fine, I'll just leave it here until I have a room." I thumped my backpack down on the tiled floor. "I am

Mia Coffin, I e-mailed you about a week ago that I would be here. I received a confirmation that you had a room for me. Here, I printed it out." I pulled out one of the papers stuck between the pages of my guidebook and handed it to him.

"Yes, my son does computer. How many tonight?" He answered in broken English.

"Oh, one, please." I said holding out one finger.

"Just, one?" The old man questioned searching behind me for my nonexistent companion. Like my father, he is probably wondering what the hell a young, blonde woman is doing by herself in Beirut.

"Please come to your room, you fill out register tomorrow. Where you come from? My English not so good, you speak French?"

"Uh, Je ne parle Français bien. I come from California."

"Very long way, you must sleep now. I make tea for you?"

"No, merci, just a shower and a bed." The man starts down a narrow hallway. I grab my backpack and follow him. He points through an open door at a dorm room with four beds.

"This your bed." He points, proudly.

I look at it horrified and take a deep breath. "Thank you very much sir, and the bathroom?" I ask, scared to see it. I'm thinking of the lovely hotel I could have had if I had run when I had the chance. My guide walks back into the hall and pushes open the first door to his left, "Voila!" He said, then without looking back, he continued shuffling back to reception and disappeared behind the desk. Within seconds his snores are rumbling down the hallway.

My room has a ceiling fan and an open window. Cars honk their way along the street below and music pounds from a distant dance club. Three backpacks are opened on the other three beds with clothes, towels and papers spilling all over the floor, but the place is deserted. I wonder who my roommates are and hope they won't come home tonight. I rinse off in a cold shower and lie on the single bed listening to the unfamiliar sounds of the city and watching the fan swirl above my head.

I should have been scared. I was alone and a woman in a foreign city. On my torturous journey over I finished reading Ilan Pappe's book about the ethnic cleansing in Palestine which alarmed me. The innkeeper might die at any moment. Oh, and my roommates could possibly be serial killers. But as I lay there in this unfamiliar place, I was completely and totally thrilled to be, finally, in Lebanon. After years of romanticizing this place, I was really here!

It was early, 5:30 in the morning, when I opened my eyes. Curled up on my left side, I focus directly in front of me, not even two feet from my face, onto a man's hairy back. Beyond the sleeping gorilla, there is another, and another. Awesome, I get to share my room with three smelly men-apes. The one on the far side near the window has his mouth open, with drool pooling onto his pillow. Gross.

All of my roommates are olive-skinned with black hair, maybe Italian, or Spanish. I didn't hear them come in the night before, and I'm suddenly embarrassed. I grab at my sheet and pull it up to my chin. What if *I* were drooling when they came in last night or snoring or my sheet had uncovered my leg and they all saw my naked thigh? As they say, you get what you pay for. And this luxurious room cost me all of thirteen bucks. Which in Lebanon means you're sharing with three hirsute men who, still, could possibly be serial killers.

I decide to get ready quickly before the Ted Bundys wake up. I had read that Beirut was quite western and accepting of lone women. Just to be safe though, I dressed in long pants, a long sleeved shirt and draped a scarf over my hair. I stuffed my guidebook into my purse and hit the streets.

They used to call Beirut the Paris of the Middle East. I had read Edward Said's account of his childhood home, the quaint fishing villages, the grand hotels, mountain resorts, remote waterfalls, meticulously uniformed waiters, and what caught my interest most of all were the people. Said explained that in the Lebanon of old, Jews, Armenians, Greeks, Syrians, Egyptians, Palestinians, Iraqis, Christians of all denominations, Muslims both Sunni and Shia would sit at dinner together, shop, go for walks, frequent the same hotels and cafes—all without a second thought. I hoped that I would experience something like that instead of the segregated ideological narrowness that I had read dominates the Middle East today.

As down and out as my hostel seemed, it was actually located in an up and coming part of the city. Gemmayze boasts nightclubs, bars, cafes, and a ton of foreigners. It didn't take me long to find a chic French café. The smell of fresh baked bread and rich coffee pulled me in from the sidewalk.

"Bonjour, Madame, qu'est que vous voulez?" A waiter in a perfectly starched, white button down shirt, black vest, black bow tie and white apron asks me as I sit at a small iron table.

Okay, Mia, don't embarrass yourself and be the stupid American… "Je voudrais un café au lait et un pain au chocolat, sil vous plait." My French teacher Madame Bancel, would be so proud!

"Very good miss," the waiter replies. OK, so he knew English was my native language, my accent may need a little work. Frenchie returns with the most delicious chocolate croissant and coffee I have ever had in my life. I ordered another round and basked in the mood of Café Paul.

An impeccably dressed man in a designer suit sat reading Le Monde, two Armani looking models wearing Wimbledon tennis whites laughed and sipped cappuccinos, and a beautiful couple with their gorgeous cherub children sat around a table near the window munching on pastries and big bowls of hot chocolate. Everyone spoke French, and I realize that if I closed my eyes, I might as well be in Paris. I have already been to Paris. After an hour I had had enough of the café, maybe it's my Gemini bursting forth, but the pretentious, elitist thing had already run its course. I wanted to experience the real Beirut and maybe hear some Arabic.

During the next eight hours I walked Beirut like a Mormon missionary, I swear I covered every square inch of that city. I walked along the Corniche, and past the Hotel Saint Georges. I sipped an espresso with some local fishermen and bought postcards from a shop in the Hamra district. I finally got to experience the things I had been dreaming of, and they were even better than I had imagined because they were real. I couldn't make up the laughs, looks, tastes and smells of that day. Of course most of the women I saw were wearing trendy blouses and short skirts, the Lebanese women in Beirut are modern and uber fashionable, while the silly American was attired in winter wear. Better to be safe than sorry, but I couldn't wait to take off all my excessive clothes when I got back to the hostel.

I finished my city tour at another café in the downtown area. I felt shabby among all the expensive shops and eateries. Picture yourself in the Venetian hotel in Las Vegas and you will know what the newly developed downtown section of Beirut looks like. Even the sky seemed unreal, painted with perfect baby blue hues and wisps of milky white clouds. Modern architecture and a pedestrian roundabout are dominated by a giant clock tower. Workers dressed in blue jumpsuits sweep the streets at every hour of the day—not a gum wrapper in sight, the place is immaculate.

Above the expensive shops that line the streets, are apartments with For Sale signs in their windows. It feels like a fairyland, very weird, very quiet compared to the streets in the Hamra and other less developed districts I saw that day. Gucci, Prada, Louis Vuitton, banks, banks and more banks. Not what I expected as my anthropological mind races to figure this place out. Whose money is rebuilding this city?

And who can afford a one bedroom apartment for $10,000 a month?

On my way back to Gemmayze, past Martyrs Square I stop at Hariri's newly built mosque that matches the downtown architecture, I poke my head through an open door in the massive Mosque. The first thing I notice is the largest most ornate and dazzling chandelier I have ever seen. The lighting in Versailles looks like an IKEA special in comparison. Again, the disproportion of wealth is astounding. Why would anyone spend that kind of money on a light fixture when they could pay for a new clinic or build ten new neighborhoods?

I run across the street back into Gemmayze and see an Internet café. I made my mom a promise ten years ago to contact her within forty-eight hours of landing in a new city. Our contact treaty was established after she saw a news report that a plane had crashed in Bombay, exactly where I told her I would be. I, of course was not on that ill-fated plane, in fact I was in the Philippines partying on Cebu with some Germans. When I finally e-mailed her, she enacted the contact treaty that still exists today.

Dear Mom, your fifth daughter is safe and sound in the beautiful city of Beirut! The journey was hellish, but you know me, always looking to save a buck. I had a long day of walking around and I am headed back to my lovely hostel to shower and have a nap. It's very hot here and I am fighting some wicked jet lag. I will write more when I see another place and I'm not so tired. Just wanted to let you know I am safe and holding up my end of the contact treaty. Please tell dad that there is nothing to worry about. It feels like I'm in Paris! Much love to you and the fam. Love, Mia

I dragged my butt up the stairs to the hostel reception. "You must be the American that arrived last night, sorry about my father, his English is not so great. My name is Moukhtar, but everyone calls me Mo." I introduced myself and Mo had me fill out the register while asking me how many days I was planning to stay and where I had been all day. I went into detail about my exciting day exploring the city. He was surprised at how much ground I covered. I wanted to ask him questions about the Lebanese culture, the different religions and how such an opulent chandelier could be hanging in that huge mosque when the Palestinian refugee's survived in the city without *any* electricity. But I was too tired. I apologized for being short but was desperate for a shower and a nap before dinner. Mo was kind and he was busy running a hostel, so he understood and wished me a good day. I washed my filthy body down and retired to my dorm room. Reading my itinerary for the next day's walking tour and that lovely fan put me right to sleep.

My two-hour nap turned into a fourteen-hour sleep! I woke up at five the next morning with the three sleeping gorillas snoring off their long night of debauchery. Hunger rumbles my stomach. I wonder what time the pretentious café with its pompous waiters opens. I could definitely set aside my judgment for another chocolate croissant and coffee.

Still not wanting to make my roommates' acquaintance, I quietly ease out of the room. I shower off, make myself a cup of tea in the communal kitchen, grab my book and climb the stairs to watch the sun rise from the roof. I sit in a broken plastic chair and notice small pockmarks in the cement walls.

Bullet holes.

I had defended my choice of vacation to so many people, that I nearly forgot the truth—this city had been at war for decades. As the sky lightened around me I saw more evidence of bombs, bullets, shells and conflict. In fact most of the older buildings brandish testament of what happened here. Sad and pointless. The destruction of all these beautifully crafted buildings and ultimately a culture. For what?

There are far more Lebanese living outside Lebanon than in. Most Lebanese are proud of their country and heritage. However, no matter how proud you are, when your home, school, work and daily existence is unsafe, you leave. Looking out at the sea, sipping my tea I think of how volatile this place is. How lucky I am to live in a stable nation. However much I protested and railed against the Bush administration, I had the right to do just that. My parents are quite conservative as are four of my eight siblings. But we are a loving, educated and tolerant bunch protected by an umbrella that is the United States. And that's what crosses my mind this lovely Tuesday morning on the rooftop watching the sunrise over Beirut harbor.

Thomas Friedman's "From Beirut to Jerusalem" had been schooling me for the past few days on the Israeli-Arab conflict. I continued my education for another hour before I had to put the book down and get some food. Friedman's a bit heavy when your stomach is calling. I'm sure there wouldn't be any peace resolution for the next few hours anyway so I descend the concrete stairs to pay for another night's stay and head out for my walking tour. It is seven, but the old man is still sleeping on his cot behind the desk. I quietly enter my room where the boys are still snoozing. I am filling my daybag with my Friedman book, a map of the city and a bottle of water when the hairy gorilla closest to me opens his eyes and says hello.

"Hi," I whispered back with a smile.

"Why do you wake up very early?" His English was heavily accented.

Still whispering I answered, "I am on vacation here in Lebanon for only four weeks and want to see everything I can. And I have jet lag too. I just flew here from California. Where are you guys from?"

"We are from Colombia. My name is Rene, that is Jesus and that is Carlos." He offered his hand and I shook it. "Nice to meet you Rene, my name is Mia, I am American."

He smiles and moves so that his sheet slips down to his waist "Why do you have a flag from Canada on your pack if you are American?" Rene, still half asleep whispers.

"Uh," I am pretty sure that I've been struck dumb by Rene's magnificence. Add to that, I am positive that he is very naked under his wafer-thin sheet. I tear my gaze from Rene's groin area and stare at my pack. Canada patch, right. "It's easier not to be the spokesperson for my government's war in Iraq while I'm traveling and so I thought…" Rene was looking at me like I was speaking gibberish, so I stop my political rant and smile, "I like the maple leaf." That seemed to satisfy Rene, the sexy Colombian naked guy who has been sleeping two feet from me for two days. "I am going on a walking tour, I'll see you later, Rene."

"We are leaving tonight so we go to a party later, do you want to come?" Yeah, I'm positive that my very Republican, Marine father would be delighted with the idea of his daughter partying it up in Beirut with three hot Colombian boys. "Sure, what time?" Marine Dad is at least a couple time zones away, good times.

"We will leave here at around ten, our flight leaves at six." Well, that doesn't make too much sense, but I tell Rene I'll be there and it is sure nice meeting him. He flashes another killer smile and goes back to sleep.

Chapter Twenty-Three

I don't often spend the kind of money it takes for guided tours, but I discovered this too good to be true walking tour of Beirut and signed up online. It promised five hours of walking around, learning the history of Beirut from a local. All the guides were recent graduates of the American University of Beirut and the tour boasted over thirty major destinations including the famous green line that divided Christians and Muslims into East and West for fifteen years, the old Jewish quarter and its recently rebuilt synagogue, the infamous Holiday Inn, and the Solidere project. At the end, they promised you'd be well versed on the tragedies and transformations of Beirut. Exactly what I wanted, so it better be worth my thirty bucks.

The walking tour met outside the gates of the American University of Beirut. I had sussed out the area yesterday so I knew it would take me about an hour to walk there from the hostel. At ten o'clock I was waiting in front of the giant banyan tree on Bliss and Clemenceau Street as instructed by the web site. Tourists began to congregate under the tree until there were fourteen of us.

A young guy who looked like a terrorist suspect I had seen on the FBI's most wanted posters inside a U.S post office jumps up on a bench and announces that his name is Ronnie and he is going to be our guide. I am about to follow a terrorist around Beirut. Dad would not be happy.

Ronnie began by welcoming each of us in perfectly spoken English then explained that our meeting place, the American University of Beirut, was founded in 1866 by the American missionary, Daniel Bliss. He proceeded to walk the fourteen of us through his beloved city, stopping Beirut traffic like he was a god.

After five hours, and more information that I could possibly retain, Ronnie brings the group to stop in front of a statue, a triumphant looking woman holding a torch above her head, and a man dressed in Roman-looking robes with two other fallen men at their feet. The bronze statue looms over our heads, along with the fiery afternoon sun.

Ronnie begins his final tour stop by touching his chest and speaking in Arabic, "Sahet el Shouhada." Then he translates and begins the story of this important place. "This is Martyr's Square, it commemorates the Lebanese nationalists who were hanged by the Ottomans on the 6th day of May 1916. The statue has been repaired several times after being hit by mortars and bullets. After the last civil war ended in 1990, though, the government decided not to repair the statues' bullet wounds as a reminder that even through conflict, beauty survives—it has become a symbol for all that was destroyed during the civil war." He pauses and then thanks all of us for joining him on the tour and for coming to Lebanon as tourists to be an example to the world that Lebanon is once again a safe and well-deserved tourist destination.

Every preconceived idea I had of Ronnie when I first saw him are gone. He turned out to be the most informed, polite and well-versed storyteller I could have ever wished for in a tour guide. At that moment I saw him as a movie star. The guy relayed the information so well because he cared. He loves his country. We all thanked Ronnie for an amazing tour and went our separate ways.

Without Ronnie's inspiration, I realized my feet were actually one size larger from swelling. When I finally hobbled back to the hostel, my room had been cleaned and the Colombians were gone. I showered off the sweat and city muck that had accumulated during the long tour and lay down on my narrow bed. Sleeping through an evening in Beirut is only accomplished with serious jet lag, copious amounts of alcohol or after a five-hour walking tour in 100-degree heat. The traffic and construction are a never-ending cacophony of hell. I sleep. I dream about the apocalypse, but I sleep.

Starving, and tired of the noise, I wake up at ten that night and find a note from the Colombians at the front desk: *Mia, Carlos, Jesus and I will be partying our last night at Beiruf. Come join us! Love, Rene.* Wow, he loves me already!

A service taxi took me across to the harbor and I followed the loud music to the top floor of a building near downtown. The bar was called Bey-Roof, because it is on the roof, in Beirut. Clever. I immediately discover that I am way under-dressed. The women are in sequined tops and tight miniskirts. The men, expensive suits, tight shirts and shiny shoes. Enter, the very American backpacker wearing jeans and the Walk Beirut T-shirt I bought from Ronnie. At least I have some lipstick on. Talking to anyone was going to be totally impossible over the deafening techno crap, so I went straight for the dance floor. After three Almaza's and a shot of arak, I had enough liquid courage to show off some not-so-hip dance moves under the disco ball.

I ran into Rene, literally, on the dance floor and he bought me another beer. Have I mentioned how pretty Rene is? Under the influence, he's even prettier. We danced and laughed until about four in the morning then me and the guys shared a cab back to the hostel. Carlos ran upstairs to grab all their bags. Jesus was passed out in the taxi. While Rene and I said our goodbyes, he gave me his number in Bogota and invited me to stay with him if I was ever in his part of the world. Carlos returned, gave me a hug and the three beautiful, hairy, Columbians headed off to the airport. We certainly didn't do a lot of talking over the last four days but they seem like a fun bunch of guys. I got a contact out of it, and where most people will never show up on your doorstep, I'm one of those who do. That's my fair warning for you—Rene, Carlos and Jesus.

My head was on fire the following day. Not with actual flames, but with the fire of arak on my brain. I needed to get out of this city. Must have quiet, kept swirling around in my throbbing head. Beirut, as lovely a city as it is, is very loud and very crowded and very dirty. Like any city, I can only handle about a week of it at a time.

Referring to my guide book, I found a port town just forty-five minutes north, promising quiet streets, ancient ruins, fresh seafood and with a fraction of the population of Beirut. I quickly packed my backpack and headed to Darwa station to catch a mini bus to Byblos, or Jbeil as it was known in Arabic. Most towns in Lebanon have two sometimes three names, just to make it that more confusing to get around.

Lebanese love their coffee, and so do I. After three strong espressos and a pastry at the Darwa bus station, I was feeling semi-human again. The forty-five minute ride in a crowded mini bus from Beirut to Byblos cost me one dollar. I love Lebanon. Great food, cheap and easy transportation, nice people, beautiful coastline, warm water, and old ruins. What is an anthropologist not to love? Byblos, the small fishing village, was waiting for me to discover her.

I found a little hotel that overlooks the sea and asked about a room. Sixty bucks a night, ouch! But I needed a rest and so I splurged. My room was on the third level, equipped with a freezing cold air conditioner and two queen size beds. I quickly changed into my bather, walked down the wood stairs to the beach and dove into the sea. The warm water felt like heaven. Cleansing the grime of the city, I floated on my back and stuck my chin out. Closing my eyes, I felt the hot sun burn my cheeks. Now this is what I was talking about when I dreamed of a Mediterranean holiday. I rinsed the salty water off in an outside shower and wrapped my sarong around my chest, tucking the cloth between my breasts, creating a flowing toga, and headed back up the hotel stairs.

A mass of caramel color fur lay on a concrete slab in the shade. At first I thought the dog was dead, but as I watched, I noticed its fur rising and falling with each breath. I bent down and touched its head. "I bet you're hungry." The animal lifted its nose and gazed at me with dark pools of sadness.

When I was in Vietnam I met two travelers from Scotland who killed a street dog out of compassion for the poor mongrel who would have perished in pain. Street dogs have been the topic of many heated debates among travelers. After an intense discussion of what responsibility we have as 'civilized westerners' to aide these animals that are miserably abused, an Israeli veterinarian who I met in Thailand summed it up best for me. He began with stories of his childhood in the Golan Heights surrounded by family pets. He went to University and studied veterinary medicine to make a difference in the lives of animals. He in fact devoted his life to animal care, so he certainly would be the expert on the love of animals. "It is not our place to kill these animals even if it's with good intentions. Allow nature to take its natural course," he said.

I still feel sorry for the street dogs and cats, and I feed them, love them, and shoo away kids who are abusing them. I sat with this poor animal for a few minutes, petting her head and promising to bring a scrap of meat. I named her Butterscotch after the color she had once been before the mange ate away most of her fur. I continued back up the stairs to the hotel lobby, found a comfy chair on the veranda and ordered a beer. My sister Tess claims that a beer will always cure a hangover. It does.

Looking out over the sea, sipping an ice-cold beer I reveled in the peace and quiet that is a small village, and I was feeling content that I had made the decision to leave the city. A young woman sat at a table near mine, she has short black hair cut in a hip style and huge dark eyes lined with black kohl. She looked like that French actress in *Amelie*. I smiled at her and said hello. She smiled back and said, "Bonjour," then opened her laptop and began to type away. It reminds me that I needed to e-mail home, so I asked her if I could borrow her computer to write a quick message.

"Bien sur," she replied and pushed her laptop towards me. I quickly got up from my table and joined her, thanking her for the use of her computer.

"My mom is so worried that I am traveling in Lebanon alone." I said, searching the screen for Yahoo mail.

"My mahzah has me call her every day," the girl replied in a thick French accent with a roll of her dark eyes.

I laugh, "Los Angeles is more dangerous than Beirut!"

"Is that where you are from, Los Angeles?"

"South of L.A., about an hour. Where are you from?"

"I am from Paris, but I am working in Asmara for the last eighteen months."

"Where's that?" I pride myself on geography but have no idea where Asmara was. The girl explained to me that it was the capital of Eritrea and because the country does not allow any non-government organizations including any humanitarian aide, she had been there under the guise of working for a gold-mining company from Sweden that works with the Eritrean government to find gold deposits.

"It sounds like a movie," I said.

"Yes, but not so exciting. I love the people of Eritrea and I want them to develop and flourish."

I was mesmerized by this girl. I quickly typed a letter to my mom letting her know that I was safe in Byblos and that I would be here for at least a couple of days to enjoy the sea. I thanked the girl and then asked what her name was.

"Nadine Nahas, my pleasure to meet you," she replied and raised her hand to shake mine.

I took her hand and introduced myself, "Mia Coffin, very nice to meet you Nadine. Thank you very much for the use of your computer, my mom will be able to sleep another night."

Nadine and I sat at the table together looking over the Mediterranean for the next two hours drinking beer, talking about our families, and how we made it to Lebanon. Nadine's father was Lebanese. He was born and raised in a village not far from Byblos, in Zahle. He moved to Paris when the civil war began in the early seventies, and met Nadine's mother while attending the Sorbonne. He worked for the United Nations and was assigned to the Sudan in the 1990's. He took Nadine to Sudan when she was nineteen—it had such an impact on her that she vowed to go back to Africa and make life better for the women suffering there. She began by working with Action Contre La Faim in Khartoum at a health center for mothers until she couldn't stand the bureaucracy any longer.

She moved back home to Paris and finished her undergraduate work in public planning, then applied for her masters in policy and planning at the Sorbonne. She became interested in Eritrea and tried to find an organization working there. When she learned that the country was basically a dictatorship, she was more determined than ever to find a way to get in and help. She discovered that their government was issuing visas to a company based in Sweden to research the possibilities of gold mining, so she had her father pull some strings and bingo—she is now there under the auspices of a Swedish gold-mining company.

During the last eighteen months Nadine had been making contacts with locals who were beaten by government officials for everything from their religious beliefs to protesting the practice of female mutilation. She had been in dangerous predicaments and felt she was losing the battle. "I am tired, Mia. It is so frustrating to make progress with informants then to lose them to fear and have to go back to zero. There are only ten of us in the group that I am working with and we all need time for ourselves. I managed to get off for seven days. Most of the volunteers have been in Asmara for over a year without leaving. The cover of working for the mining company will only last for another few months and I needed a break from that life, so I came here to Lebanon. My father always spoke of his country with such love, pride and nostalgia that I had to see it for myself. This is where my ancestors are from. I want to find the memories that my father holds."

Nadine is so passionate and lovely. I was embarrassed to admit that I am a simple American: my father is from New Hampshire, my mother from Utah, I graduated from a safe little University in Fullerton, California and I came to Lebanon because it sounded cool. Not exactly the fascinating pedigree Nadine came from or the devotion to save the world that she had.

Nadine has been at the hotel for two days and as we lamented the price of our rooms, we naturally concluded that I would check out of my room and move into hers the next morning: money problem solved, it would save us thirty dollars a night and why not, there were two huge beds in each room.

The sun had set and we were starving so we walked into the village for dinner. We found a quaint restaurant overlooking the little harbor. The Lebanese flag with its cedar tree emblem greeted the tired fisherman returning to their protected harbor built by the Romans two thousand years back. Nadine and I feasted on a stew with big chunks of white fish, ripe tomatoes, basil, carrots, onion and spices we couldn't place: Nadine guessed cumin, I thought curry. We dipped the fresh bread into the warm, spicy broth and slurped it down chasing it with a bottle of Sauvignon Blanc. I recounted some of my funniest travel stories, she told me of her life in Asmara. We talked about our families, our favorite authors, the war in Iraq and our hopes for peace in the future.

I moved my stuff into Nadine's room the next morning. She had packed a bag even smaller than my backpack. I am always impressed by how small some travelers' bags are, at how few things one needs to leave home with. We spent the morning at the beach, reading, swimming, napping and playing badminton with an ancient set I found at the hotel.

On our way up for lunch I saw Butterscotch sitting in her usual spot. "Hello, Butterscotch." I said, leaning down to pet her head.

"You know this dog?" Nadine asked.

"Yeah, we met yesterday, her name is Butterscotch."

Nadine looked at me like I was crazy, then added, "Poor thing, she just has babies after babies, we should get her fixed so she doesn't have to bear any more puppies."

I thought of the Israeli vet, and said, "It's not our place to take care of these animals."

"Of course it is! This dog has never been loved or cared for in her life." Nadine said angrily.

"OK, before we adopt all the street dogs in the world, lets go eat. We can bring Butterscotch a treat on our way back down." Nadine walked ahead of me speaking French and throwing up her hands in disgust.

I came to Byblos because it was near the sea and I needed a break from the city. I had no idea that it was such a historic area until Nadine asked me at lunch if I had been down to see the crusader castle.

"No, I haven't explored Byblos at all except for the hotel, the beach and the restaurant near the port last night." I answered, a bit embarrassed that I had no knowledge of the unique history of the area.

"Then it's the perfect place to begin our tour of this country. Allons y!" Nadine said and began towards the village. She gave me a quick history lesson while we walked down to the ruins near the coast. "The Phoenicians founded this port town five thousand years ago. They were an enterprising maritime trading culture who began to trade their cedar wood for papyrus from Egypt. They traded all over the Mediterranean up the coast to Turkey, Italy, Spain and back to North Africa. They sold their cedar wood to Egyptians who used its essential oils for the mummification process, cosmetics and insect repellent. Then the Romans took over a few thousand years later and built their temples atop the old

Phoenician site—then the crusaders came and built their castle to defend it from the Muslims."

I looked at Nadine with astonishment. "How the hell do you know all this?"

"I took a class at the Sorbonne, History of the Middle East."

"Wow, I guess you did, and you must have gotten an A!"

We paid the entrance fee and opted for a guide, always an important addition when there are ancient ruins and handsome college students for hire. Our guide was called Adonis. "Is that your real name or your tour guide alias?" I had to give him a hard time with that Chip n'Dales stripper title. He promised that he was born with it, and then explained that he was a Phoenician. Silly me, I thought Phoenicians had gone the way of the dinosaurs, apparently untrue, since I had met several people in Lebanon so far that had described themselves as Phoenicians.

Adonis helped me out by starting at the beginning. The very beginning— like thirty thousand years ago when Neanderthals were cruising around Europe. Evidence of early habitation was found on this site during the Neolithic period. Then the Phoenicians, a sub group of Canaanites built their city here and since then it's been taken over by the Assyrians, Persians, Baibars, Romans, Christians, Ottomans and finally the French.

"Wow!" I said to Adonis and Nadine, "Everyone wanted to live here, it's like how California used to be, great weather, fertile soil, nice beaches, where the *in* people want to be!" They looked at me like I was a complete idiot. "Sorry," I apologized. "Please proceed with your tour, Adonis."

Adonis continued only slightly confused at my interruption about hip Californians.
" Most people think that Adonis was a Greek god, but he was around long before the Greeks adopted him as their own.

Phoenicians built temples to their god Adonis 1550 years before Christianity took over. Temples erected to Adonis, Aphrodite, and Baal are found all over this area. The Phoenicians invented the first alphabet, which was later adopted by the Greeks and Romans. The Phoenicians never deserted this area, they simply adapted to the ruling people and today are mistaken for Arabs. But I am not an Arab. I am Phoenician and my name is that of a great god who was resurrected and is worshiped to this day. "Adonis, that's a huge name to live up to," I joked.

After two hours of walking around the ruined crusader castle with Adonis in the sweltering heat I was ready for a beer. We invited Adonis to join us at a tea garden just outside the entrance to the castle. He agreed, and the three of us talked for the next few hours over several beers, (Adonis did not drink alcohol, he opted for sodas) plates of hummus, and fresh bread. He entertained us with stories and histories of his beloved country. Of how Phoenician myths, religious practices and gods have evolved into today's modern religions.

Chapter Twenty-Four

Lebanon is only 240 kilometers from tip to tip so you can make day trips anywhere in the country. Nadine and I used Byblos as our base and took mini busses to different places every day for the next three days. We woke up early each morning and spent a few hours at the beach, reading, swimming and playing with Butterscotch then went on a daily adventure. Our first day we took a minibus an hour up the coast to Tripoli and got lost in the massive souk buying scarves, spices, and lots of crappy tourist junk we didn't need.

We visited an Ottoman house turned museum that was built in 1540 exquisitely furnished with antique kilims. Next we hit the famous Al Muallaq Mosque—we weren't allowed inside because it was Ramadan, but we hung out in the courtyard with its ancient olive and orange orchards. We sat on a curb eating taffy the locals call hallab and watched a young street performer who rapped in Arabic. He was actually very good—I wish I had a connection with Jay-Z to sign this kid for a record deal.

We invited the rapper to lunch with us and he ordered us a local feast of shawarmas doused in fresh yogurt, bread with artichoke hummus and cokes. Then we polished off five slices of fresh baklava and wrapped up the rest of the pan for the boy to take home. His name was Ahmad, he was eleven but looked younger. With some French, Arabic, English and lots of sign language, he told us he lived in the Beddawi Palestinian refugee camp with his mother and five brothers. His father had been killed, but how he died was unclear—Ahmad charaded like he had a machine gun and mowed a few times back and forth spitting out the sound of gunfire, pretty sure he was enacting his father's death.

Ahmad was the sole provider for his family, making money by singing on the streets of Tripoli. So sad, but this kid was surprisingly happy and hopeful. His favorite rapper was Snoop Dogg and he sang 'Drop it Like it's Hot' with all the clicks and pops for us. He sang every word and sounded just like Snoop. He had us laughing on the outside and crying on the inside. When I meet special kids like Ahmad, I want to help, but how? A few cakes for his family and twenty bucks made his week. Nadine and I returned to our safe little hotel in Byblos that night singing Snoop songs.

On our second excursion we visited the cave complex in Jeita, about thirty minutes southeast of Byblos. The cave was massive, we walked for forty minutes into the depths of the grotto yelling, "Echo!" and trying to remember the difference between stalactites and stalagmites. On the boat that takes tourists through the cavern cruise I overheard a guy speaking American English, I asked where he was from and it turned out he was a professor at Stanford University. He had a driver so Nadine and I hitched a ride with him to our next stop, Harissa, just twenty minutes from the caves.

Harissa is a pilgrimage site set high above the city of Jounieh with a massive statue of the Virgin Mary at the front gates of a Maronite cathedral. There were hundreds of tourists walking up to pay respects to the Virgin. And, as I saw from the top, several young kids scratching their initials into the marble. I guess that's a universal phenomenon just so everybody knows that J.S. hearts M.R. forever. Our new professor friend ditched us on the highway back to Beirut—he said he had a meeting with several bankers and had to get back, so he didn't have time to drop us off in Byblos. We just flagged down a mini bus, paid our dollar each and were back in our favorite tea garden within the hour.

Nadine and I went for an evening swim, fed Butterscotch some salami we stole from the breakfast buffet then headed back into town to plan our next outing over dinner. She was excited to visit the small village where her father was born and see if she could find the house he grew up in and hopefully a family member to meet—so we decided to head to Zahle the next morning.

The 170-kilometer trip took us three hours in four different minibuses. Finally, after descending into the valley, we reached Zahle and quickly realized it wasn't a village, but the third largest city in Lebanon. They call Zahle, the bride of the Bekaa valley, because it is and has been the breadbasket of Lebanon for the past 300 years. Located at the base of the great Lebanese mountains with its rich soil and consistent water source it's naturally the agricultural powerhouse for the region. Also strategically stationed between Damascus and Beirut, it became a melting pot for immigrants traveling between the two cities. With less conflict in either capital, a lot of those travelers decided to stay put in the fertile valley. From 1920 until now, its population quadrupled. That explains why Nadine's dad remembered his birthplace as a small village.

The church of St. Elias was our first stop and we hit pay dirt…sorta. The nun in the administration office spoke no English but a little French. She explained to Nadine that Nahas was quite a common name in the area and she would need more information on her ancestors to find out if they were recorded in the church's archives. Nadine had an address where her father was born and the name of the midwife who delivered him. Nadine unfolded the note her father had written and showed it to Sister Ghoukassian. The nun's eyes lit up and she drew us a little map of where to find the house. She wished us, "Bon Chance" as we walked out of the church office and followed her sketch to the family home about eight blocks away.

Nadine was muttering away in French, probably what she was going to say when she met her long lost family members. I warned her against romanticizing the situation, suggesting that perhaps they had moved as her father had warned. We arrived at a huge brick house complete with freshly painted green shutters on three stories and a wraparound veranda on the first level. The gardens were well kept with perfectly manicured topiary spirals growing on either side of the front walkway.

"Maybe Captain Von Trapp is home?" I joked. "Knock already!" Nadine straightened her back and patted her hair then rapped on the huge green door with a brass lions-head knocker. We waited. Nothing. She banged again. We waited for a minute then she went around to look in the giant window behind the hedge. I followed her and cupped my hands against the window. The furniture was covered in white sheets and cobwebs covered the ceilings.

Nadine looked at me with disappointment, and we turned away. "Sorry my sweet girl, looks like they have been gone for a while." I touched Nadine's shoulder with sympathy. "It always sucks when you have envisioned how something will go and it doesn't go that way at all. Trust me, I'm the queen of expecting how perfectly a date, a job or a trip will turn out and it sometimes is the *opposite* of what I imagined." Nadine just stared at the big house with sad eyes. "You know Mia, I wanted to come here with my father to meet our ancestors—so if I didn't succeed this time, it's OK. My dad and I will make a trip back here together and, with him at my side, I bet we'll find what we're looking for. This is still the village of my family, so lets go enjoy it while we're here. Merci, Mia, for coming with me all the way out here."

"Don't thank me! I wouldn't have seen Zahle if not for you, and your quest for your heritage." We hugged and started to walk back the way we came.

"My father worked in the vineyards every summer," Nadine began, "and he spoke fondly of harvesting grapes and being proud of the wine he helped produce. Lets go visit a winery in honor of my father and the Nahas name." We had a renewed mission—it was a beautiful summer afternoon and we were starving.

We found a winery slash restaurant near the center of town called Bahy Family Wines, and because we were celebrating the Nahas family that afternoon, we chose it. Jean

Bahy was there to welcome us. The tour began with a quick video of the history of wine making in the Bekaa valley. It said that the Phoenicians began making wine five thousand years ago in this valley and were credited with introducing wine and viticulture to Europe. Nadine whispered that the French should send Adonis a thank you card. We giggled. Jean marched us down into the underground caves built by the Romans. There were tunnels cut into the rock where huge oak barrels and ceramic pots lined the cold stone walls. Jean talked about the varietals grown and how his ancestors were wine makers for the Romans, how they would transport their wine in huge ceramic pots to the great Temple of Dionysus in Baalbek.

We finished the tour back upstairs where Jean invited us to sit and taste samples along with a homemade lunch. It seemed we had been transported to a piazza in Tuscany, the air was crisp and not so hot as Beirut, we sat on a shady patio overlooking the Bardouni River, which was rambling through the distant vineyards. Clusters of ripe grapes drooped on trellises above our heads. Jean's wife made kebbe zahleweieh, ground meat stuffed in bread, and yogurt. Fresh baked bread, cheeses and fruit were brought to us along with glass after glass of sweet white wine. All in all I'd say we made up for not fulfilling our initial mission of finding the Nahas family. I'd rather hang out with the Bahy family anyway.

Jean insisted that we go to Baalbek and see the mighty Temples he spoke of. Baalbek was only forty minutes away and to miss experiencing the greatness of the temples was a tragedy when we were so close. But it was already past three and we had a long ride back to Byblos. Nadine only had one day left and didn't have time to go to Baalbek. I still had almost a week to come back, so I promised Jean that I'd make it to Baalbek and see the Temples where his ancestors supplied the wine for many a pagan party. We thanked Jean and his family for the spectacular lunch and tour then walked back through the city to find a minibus back to Beirut.

Zahle felt more European than Middle Eastern, horse-drawn carriages clip-clopped down the wide cobblestone streets lined with red geraniums and variegated ivy spilling out of hanging baskets. Children's shouts of playing filled the air and couples walked in the afternoon sun. Was it the wine or was this the quaintest place on Earth? We walked through the souk and Nadine bought her father a delicate engraved wood box. I picked up a brass tray and some trinkets, along with the bottle of Grenache I bought from Jean, my bag was overflowing with more crap I didn't need.

We stopped at one more café before getting on the bus and met another guy calling himself a Phoenician. Nadine and I needed to get to the bottom of this, so ordered a bottle of wine and invited our new friend, Abdul to educate us. After two bottles of wine and lots of flirting Nadine had a hypothesis. "Listen Mia, the reason why these Lebanese call themselves Phoenicians is the same reason Iranians call themselves Persian, they were once the greatest civilization on the planet, they invented mathematics, chemistry, and engineering, their ancestors were enjoying running water and wearing silk pajamas while Europeans were living in the dark ages. They want to be associated with their great past that lasted for thousands of years, not with their recent governments that have been in place for the last fifty years. They are embarrassed how the country they call home has regressed into Islamic law. These people went from inventing the wheel to stoning fourteen-year old girls."

Nadine *did* have a point, but she was drunk, and so was I and it was ten o'clock at night in the middle of Lebanon. So we said our goodbyes to Abdul and got on the bus where we both immediately fell asleep on the ride back. Neither of us woke when the driver reached the end of his route. The driver yelled back to us, "Hallo! Beirut here! Cola station!" I paid him ten dollars for our journey and hailed a service taxi to drop us at Darwa station. Another thirty-minute minibus and two bucks later, we arrived safe and slightly more sober at our hotel in Byblos.

Waitress dreams filled my sleep: a very thirsty guest was asking for soda refills, but the soda machine was four blocks from the restaurant so I was running all night making sure he had fresh Sprites. Anxiety-filled waitress dreams follow me around the world.

I woke at ten, exhausted from my dream and very thirsty for water. Nadine hadn't stirred yet. She was scheduled to return to Asmara the next evening. I wanted to make our last day in Byblos memorable. By memorable I didn't mean hung over, but that's how it worked out.

"I'm going into town, I'll be back in a bit," I whispered to the still sleeping Nadine. She mumbled something about staying in bed then taking a swim with Butterscotch. I left her sleeping and quietly closed the door behind me. My head was throbbing. I think I drank four entire bottles of wine yesterday. The hotel restaurant offered breakfast until eleven every morning. I went down and ordered a cup of coffee and an aspirin. Sitting on the veranda sipping my coffee and watching the waves roll onto the rocky beach made me feel better—another perfect day in this ancient Mediterranean wonderland. I felt so lucky to be here, and to have met up with Nadine, my new, smart, funny and kind friend who I knew would stay in touch with me, unlike most travelers I meet who swap e-mails and invitations that are never realized.

The morning sun warmed my shoulders as I walked down the now familiar road into the small town. I thought about Nadine. She was leaving and I'd be on my own once again. Part of me would miss her, but part of me knew it was time to rely on myself again. Nadine had seen a purse she liked a few days before but said she couldn't afford it. I went back to the shop and had the saleswoman wrap it up as a going-away gift. The cozy tourist shops, filled with hookah pipes, Lebanon fridge magnets, and every trinkety souvenir you could think of sucked me in and by the time I felt my stomach growl it was already one in the afternoon. I made my way back to the hotel hoping Nadine hadn't eaten yet so we could share lunch.

When I opened the door to our room I was surprised to see that the curtains were drawn and Nadine was still in bed. She must have been drunker than I thought last night. I bent down to talk to her when I saw a massive bruise on her left arm, just above her elbow. I couldn't see very well in the dark room and hoped it was a mere shadow. I walked over to the window and pushed open the drapes allowing the bright sun to fill the room. Instantly my fears were realized—it was a bruise that bloomed into a horrible blackish, green color all the way up from her elbow to her shoulder. I sat on the bed, her back towards me, her left arm jutting out of the covers to reveal the horrific blossom of color.

"Aaaahhhh, Mia where were you?" she murmured.

"What the hell happened to your arm, girl?"

"I, heard you leave this morning so I got up to see if you were at the restaurant. They told me you just left, so I decided to go for a swim. I saw Butterscotch on the stairs outside scratching his fleas, so I decided I wanted to give him a bath. No one cares for him and he needed a bath to get rid of his fleas."

Nadine was not making sense.

"Nadine, what are you talking about, I need to know what happened to your arm, it looks very bad." I tried to keep her from babbling about Butterscotch to find out who hurt her. But, her jabbering continued, "She has no one to look after her and she is filled with painful fleas, I wanted to help her and make her clean for once in her life." I watched Nadine muttering about that stupid dog for another two minutes, all the while seeing her arm swell and change color right before my eyes. Her wound was getting worse and I was getting worried. I touched her arm and she shrieked in pain.

"Sorry… OK…I won't touch it again, but I need to look at it closer." I tried to calm her down but she was probably in shock and wouldn't stop talking about Butterscotch. Then I saw the puncture wounds, near the inside of her arm on her bicep muscle, dark blood and yellow fluid seeping from two small holes in her skin. Bite marks.

Chapter Twenty-Five

"Did Butterscotch bite you?" I asked in disbelief. That dog was so passive and loving for the entire time we had been there.

"Ce nest pas sa faute," Nadine slipped into French.

"Nadine!" I roared, "Did Butterscotch bite you?" When Nadine answered it sounded like she was drugged, like she had a mouth full of honey, "Oui, I mean yes, Butterscotch bit me, but it was not her fault, I took her down to the sea to bathe her. I had her lathered up with soap... and was trying to force her into the sea... to wash her off. She got scared... she didn't understand what...I was doing to her, she was only defending herself, she had no choice. Oh Mia, there is much pain in my arm, I am so sleepy, please close the curtain so I can sleep."

I had no idea what the symptoms of rabies were, but I knew I had to get Nadine up and to a hospital as soon as possible. "What time did this happen?" I asked as guilt ripped through me that while I was shopping Nadine was being mauled by a rabid dog. Nadine didn't acknowledge me, she was whimpering and mumbling in French.

I ran down stairs, past reception out to the street where several taxis were usually parked waiting for passengers. I bent down and through the passenger's side window asked how far to the closest hospital. The driver did not respond right away, he was drinking an espresso in a plastic cup and reading a newspaper propped onto the steering wheel. He just looked at me with a blank stare. Come on man, I thought, please speak English and please rush Nadine to a hospital with western standards, and please make her OK.

"There is small clinic in town, but they close now. Big hospital in Jounieh and Beirut." He answered slowly, trying to find the words in English. I remembered when I was on my walking tour with Ronnie we passed the American University of Beirut Hospital.

"OK, I need you to take me and my friend to The AUB hospital."

"Better is Fouad Khoury Hospital."

"Fine, whatever damn hospital! I just need to go very fast, wait here, I'll be right back with my friend." I turned and ran back to the room. "OK, my girl, we are going for a ride." I said as I rushed in and went directly to Nadine. I lifted the sheet off and saw she was still wearing her bathing suit. Shit, I have to dress her. Stay calm Mia, just get a T-shirt and put it over her head, find her shorts…there's no time, you don't have time to dress her, she is not well, she is going to die. Relax Mia! She is not going to die. "Can you stand up, Nadine?" I asked as soothingly as I could with blood rushing to my head.

"Je suis fatigue, Mia."

"Yes, I know you're tired, but you have to get up and come with me, now. Listen Nadine, this is important, we need to get you to a doctor right away." I spoke to her while I lifted her body into a sitting position, her feet grazed the floor. "Good, now let's stand up, can you walk?" I scooped my arm around Nadine's back and helped lift her to her bare feet. "Perfect, now slowly, lets walk to the elevator, you can do this," I said, trying to convince both Nadine and myself as we shuffled along the floor. Nadine was wearing her bathing suit, I had my purse slung over my shoulder and the bed sheet scrunched up under my arm—all one needs for a trip to the hospital.

The woman at reception stared at the half-naked girl with the giant purple bruise and her crazy companion drenched in sweat with a hotel bed sheet under her arm. Clearly, she did not know what to say, so she wished us a good day as we walked to the waiting taxi. I draped the sheet over Nadine and sat holding her in the backseat. "Please hurry," I begged the driver. I heard the crack in my voice but

I didn't want to start crying in front of Nadine or the taxi driver. I just held Nadine and prayed that she was going to be all right.

To ask a taxi driver in Lebanon to go fast is redundant, but this guy was on a mission and got us to the emergency entrance of Fouad Khoury Hospital in forty minutes. Nadine was on a gurney and wheeled away faster than any hospital in the States would have taken. I stayed behind in admittance to fill out paperwork and answer questions while Nadine was being, "made comfortable." Doctor Hourani introduced himself to me, and began explaining Nadine's condition, but all I could concentrate on were his long thick eyelashes. Focus Mia, ...

"Your friend is lucky to have you, she is resting and will be on medication that will keep her very drowsy through today until early tomorrow. We have begun the series of rabies treatments and fixed her IV with morphine for the pain and a sedative to induce a healing sleep. You may visit her tomorrow and she will be able to leave in two days time." I thanked the doe-eyed doctor then went outside to the hospital garden and sat on a bench warmed by the afternoon sun and wept tears of relief, hunger and exhaustion.

At a nearby cafe I ordered maroush kalaj and a Sprite. The sun was setting and I was drained. I took a taxi back to Darwa station then a mini bus to Byblos and walked the route back to the hotel in the warm evening. When I arrived alone the woman at reception asked about my friend. I told her Nadine went to hospital in Beirut—that I needed to check out, and I wouldn't be returning. I went to our room and packed my things. I did my best to pack Nadine's bag and stuck the purse and card at the top so when she opened it she would receive my gift.

I spent the night on a pull-out chair next to Nadine's hospital bed hoping she would be OK. At six the next morning I heard Nadine asking for water in a sleepy voice.

"Good morning, sunshine, it's good to hear that you're thirsty! I was worried about you." I smiled at Nadine over her bed, handing her a plastic cup filled with water.

"What happened?" Nadine's voice was a whisper.

"Butterscotch bit you when you tried to wash her, you silly girl, you spent the night in the hospital and you are on a rabies treatment for the next two days," I explained.

"I am leaving tonight," Nadine protested.

"I don't think the handsome doctor would agree, he said you have to stay and finish the series of five shots." I delivered the news with a sigh.

"No, I have to be back tomorrow, they need me in Asmara." Nadine challenged me. A nurse came in right then to shoot Nadine up with another dose of the sedative she was taking intravenously.

"No, please, I need to go, I need to be discharged and go home, please, I need to talk to the doctor," Nadine pleaded with the morning nurse. The nurse looked at me and I nodded, agreeing that we needed to speak with the doctor before Nadine was pumped up with more drugs. The doctor didn't arrive until noon. By then, Nadine had physically taken the IV out of her arm and was dressed in her clothes when he walked into her room.

"Evidently, you are determined to leave, and I cannot force you to stay, I can only give you a prescription for the rest of the rabies treatments and wish you the best," the super cute doctor advised.

Nadine was inflexible on staying one more night at the hospital. She promised that she would finish her rabies treatment in Eritrea even though she was convinced that Butterscotch didn't have rabies and she would be fine. The other volunteers were counting on her to be back. I agreed very hesitantly with promises and vows from my friend that she would take it easy and see a doctor in Asmara. The hospital discharged her and we took a taxi to Rafic Hariri airport. I waited with her as she checked in for her flight on

Yemen Airways to Sana'a Airport. She had her new purse stuffed full with all her travel documents and books. Nadine reassured me that the five-hour flight would be easy with her pain pills. I laughed nervously when we heard the final announcement to board.

"I love you my sweet girl, please take care and e-mail me the minute you are home," I told my dear friend. She agreed and hugged me with her left arm. "Merci pour tout. Mia, I'll see you in California soon." Nadine was crying. I stayed at the airport terminal until I watched her plane take off into the night sky. I caught a twenty-dollar taxi back to the hostel and slept like a baby in the same room I had shared with the Colombians. This time I was alone, the three other beds lay empty.

Chapter Twenty-Six

I was disoriented for several minutes when I awoke with the hot sun on my face—the curtains wide open. The Columbians had always kept the curtains closed. But this morning my room was bright. I felt happy. I worried about Nadine, but it was seven o'clock in the morning so she had landed and had been back in Eritrea for six hours now.

After Jean's description of the temples of Baalbek, I knew that was my next adventure. I interrogated Mo at the front desk about Baalbek, where to stay, what to see and how long I needed. Mo answered all my questions, gave me a hotel name—Mt. Olympus and reassured me that travel around Lebanon was safe, easy and cheap. I guess I was just anxious being alone again. I knew I would be fine. I had five days left on my trip and was excited to see the places that Nadine and I had missed—Baalbek, and the ancient twin cities of the south, Saida and Tyre.

The New Zealand symphony played Adagio for Strings, and then Gorecki's Third Symphony filled my ears. My Ipod ran out of battery power as the minibus began its trek down, back into the Bekaa valley. For two hours I watched as the scenery changed from the city sprawl to brick houses perched on hillsides. Nadine and I saw all this on our way to Zahle— but then came the desert. I started to notice the Hezbollah flag slowly replacing the Lebanese flag about twenty minutes before reaching Baalbek. And when I finally arrived in the city center it was a world of yellow and green fluttering in the wind with its AK47 and promises of liberation emblazoned in Arabic. The party of God—who can compete with that? As I exited the minibus with my backpack I thought, we're not in Kansas anymore!

Hot, dusty, dry and windy. Women were all wearing the long black dress with their faces completely covered in black. I stood where the minibus had dropped me and felt instantly blonder and whiter than ever. I felt the stares and judgment. Don't be silly, Mia, these people don't hate you, no one is staring at you. I saw the green sign for the Mt. Olympus Hotel and walked across the street to check for rooms and prices. A giant man with a full beard wearing a long white dress and pants underneath met me at reception. He reminded me of a Mujahideen fighter shown on CNN. I tried to act like there were tourists swarming around, like I wasn't the sole tourist this guy had ever seen. He was very welcoming, offered me coffee and showed me all the rooms available, which was every room. I decided on a bed in the dorm room for ten dollars a night. "Is this your slow season?" I asked over a cup of very thick dark coffee.

"No, just this morning, a French couple left. And we have been fully booked for the last few weeks," he lied. I asked him about the ruins and the best time to see them. He sat down across from me in his office and pointed out old photos of him sitting with Yasir Arafat. Him in full army fatigues as a young man. His office was filled with books and dusty cabinets. He took out a tin box and dumped out several old coins. Telling me they were found at various archaeological sights around the city and were from the Roman period. I bought one for thirty dollars. A delicate Filipino woman interrupted our chat and he excused himself to scream at her in Arabic. I went back to my room and found my scarf stuffed down at the bottom of my backpack. Draped it around my head and shoulders and walked through the village to the entrance of the best-preserved Roman temples on earth.

The black blobs that were women passed me. I couldn't see their eyes through the mesh covering their faces. The men stared at me. I thought they would be used to seeing tourists, but maybe it was because I was a woman alone that I got such looks. I tried to ignore the feeling that I was not welcome. Several kiosks were set up before the entrance to the ruins, there was a sad camel dressed with carpets slung on his back that you could sit on and take a photo, snow globes with the temple of Jupiter reconstructed as it looked in its heyday and old Roman coins sold for five bucks—I got ripped off.

Men called out half-heartedly to me, "Buy souvenir!" It was very hot, it was Ramadan, the holy month of fasting, so everyone was tired and hungry. The wind picked up and blew dust in my face. Finally, I made it to the entrance and approached the ticket booth. "One, please."

The man in the booth looked out at me through his cage. "English."

Not sure if that was a question or accusation, I answered, "Yes, I speak English." He handed me a pamphlet written in English then added, "twelve thousand." I paid the man then walked through a narrow tunnel where several men sat playing chess and drinking tea.

"English," one of them said. I smiled and said yes. He stood up and presented his documented authorization that was encased in a plastic envelope attached to a rope around his neck. Like he was an FBI agent flashing me his creds. "Madame, my name is Raffi Fadi. I am commissioned by the UNESCO world heritage site to be a guide. You will be very interested to know that I have been a guide here for thirty years and it will be my pleasure to take you through the greatest Roman temples on earth today for the very cheap price of twenty dollars.

Wow, how could I resist that?

Raffi turned out to be the best twenty bucks I had ever spent in my life. This guy was a walking wikipedia. We spent two full hours exploring the great temple of Jupiter. Raffi pointed out the altar and described the strange ceremonies that the ancient pagans preformed in honor of their gods. This was once the largest place of worship and religious ritual in the entire Roman Empire. When Raffi left me, I sat on a large rock outcrop and imagined what this place felt like two thousand years before. Heliopolis, the city of the sun, was a huge Roman city where thousands of people lived, loved and died. They worshiped Bacchus, drank wine and had orgies under the night sky. This place was bountiful with resources, rich in culture, knowledge and learning. And now, a forgotten ruin in the dessert of Lebanon. Sad.

I was reminded by Raffi to keep my ticket so I could return later that evening without paying again. He told me not to miss the temples at night, when they were lit up. I was thirsty and starving, but didn't want to eat in public because most of the people were observing Ramadan. I stopped at a little shawarma restaurant, ordered a sandwich and bottle of water to take back to my room at the hotel. There were no windows it was cool and cave like. I lay on my bed and slept the hot afternoon away, my belly full, and my dreams filled with Roman goddesses wrapped in fine linen dresses with summer flowers woven into their long hair.

Two hours later I woke shivering in the dark room. I checked my travel clock and saw it was 4:52. I walked outside to the bathroom and washed my face in cold water. Hot water was not offered in the hotel during the summer months. You didn't need it, but I love my hot showers no matter how hot it is outside. I wanted to see the temple in the evening, Raffi told me how beautiful the columns looked with the lights shining on them. So I walked the ten minutes through town to the temples again. I showed the ticket agent my stub and he passed me through. The guides were gone for the day and the site was completely deserted. I walked back through the old temple, listening to the birds and honks from outside the walls. It was lovely, but sad that there were no tourists here to appreciate this amazing artifact. I felt safe, and I made a point that when I got home, I would tell everyone how this ancient Roman complex was more complete than any other found in Italy, Greece or Turkey. I thought maybe I could sell tours here, I was just so perplexed why such a magnificent place was empty of tourists. I thought of how my father reacted to me coming here, fear. Fear had been pumped into our heads by the media. Fear sells.

The site closed at six, so I found an exit and walked the perimeter of the walled complex. The sun was low and I took photos of the ancient columns against the pink sky. I found a stream and saw that there was a homemade dam put in place to flood a grassy area. I knelt down and felt the cold water, still dreaming of the ancient people who lived here so long ago. A crack snapped me out of my daydreaming and a flock of birds in a tree above my head rushed out with their wings clapping. Another crack, and it occurred to me that I was hearing gun fire. I had walked for twenty minutes around the back of the ancient site and there was no one around me. I was completely alone and suddenly very scared.

I turned back immediately and heard another shot. I hurried back in the direction I had come from. A bird fell from the sky only yards from where I stood. Blood pumped out of the grey-feathered breast. My breath caught and I felt like I was going to cry. Just keep walking, Mia, they are just hunting birds. I heard several more shots while I walked through the grass, back to where I had exited the ruins. I followed a narrow road. A Jeep Cherokee slowly drove behind me. I stepped off the path and into the bushes so they could drive by me, but the car stopped and a very handsome guy about 26 smiled at me and said, "You like see Baalbek? I drive you we get soda." I normally would not get into a car with a total stranger. But all my experiences in Lebanon with Nadine so far had been great. We met the nicest people and had some great conversations that we wouldn't have had if we had just stayed in our room at night. With his nice smile, my judgment went out the window and I thought, I'm not doing anything else tonight, might as well hang out with a local and talk to him and his friends about modern Baalbek and find out the culture. I jumped into the passenger seat and immediately saw a rifle on the floor.

Chapter Twenty-Seven

He saw me look at the gun, he smiled and said, "I shoot bird." I smiled back and said, "Yes, I hear many shots tonight." I wanted out of the car instantly, but I tried to act cool, and convince myself that I was fine. We would go to a local restaurant, have a few cokes, meet his friends, talk about what they do and what they want for their future, exchange e-mails and call it a night. He made a right-hand turn, away from my hotel and gunned the engine. We were driving on the main road within seconds, heading out of Baalbek. My stomach turned and I knew this was not good, but again, I pretended not to be concerned and looked out my window at the setting sun over a giant mosque where the last prayer of the evening blared from loudspeakers affixed to the minarets. I took a photo of the mosque, then turned the camera to him and quickly took a shot of him. I looked at the speedometer, 100 miles an hour. "Too fast, please slow down," I urged, trying to hide the shaking in my voice.

"You like sex? You like hash?" he said, looking much older than I first thought.

Panic. "No, I want to go back to Baalbek. I don't want sex. I don't want hash. Please take me back now." I was pleading and felt tears rising. Panic. I automatically opened my car door thinking that I could jump, but I knew immediately we were going way to fast and I slammed it shut.

He reached over to his door and pushed the master lock button, my door locked with a click. My stomach dropped like I was on a roller coaster being hurtled down forty stories. I looked around desperately, trying to figure out where we were. The road was dark, there were no street lights and no moon. We were not on the road that I had taken that morning into Baalbek. We were driving east, into the desert hills beyond Baalbek, toward Syria. This was not Byblos with its mixed culture, educated people and wealth. This was completely different. It was the desert of Lebanon where unemployment is sky high, fundamental Islam rules and the people are desperate.

An e-mail that my mom had sent me years before popped into my mind. It urged women who had been kidnapped, to do everything possible not to be taken to the second location. I knew I had to get out, even if I got hurt or died during the escape, at least I wouldn't be taken to wherever he had in mind. I had to jump from the car. I waited for him to slow down on a turn. When he finally did, I was ready. The first left turn he took was still too fast. We past cement buildings under construction and dusty trails up the hills. The next right was slightly up a hill and I knew this was my chance to escape. I clicked the lock open, threw the gear into park with my left hand and opened the door with my right. In one move, my legs were out of the car, running alongside. The man grabbed my left arm so hard it surprised me. I had never been grabbed so fiercely in my life. His aggression only fueled my determination to get the hell away. I wrenched my left arm away and was free of the car.

I turned and ran as fast I could down the slope and back to where we had just driven. I saw a gas station with a light inside and pulled at the double glass doors. They were locked. I looked back and saw that my kidnapper had continued driving up the hill away from me. He had apparently abandoned his attempt. He was letting me go. I saw a building with a light on across the street from the gas station, I tried the door, and it opened. I was hysterical, crying, and breathless when I ran into the small restaurant. There was one man sitting down on the very back table with three women and a little boy. It looked like they had just sat down to break their fast for the evening. The man stood and looked at me, annoyed.

"Please," I whimpered, "I need a taxi to Baalbek! Please excuse my interruption, can you please call a taxi for me?" The man made no move for the phone and seemed very calm for having a western woman run into his restaurant in the middle of Nowhere, Lebanon crying for a taxi.

"Please, join my family and eat, I shall have a driver take you to Baalbek, but, now you sit and drink and share our dinner." I really had no choice. I sat next to one of the women and smiled at the little boy. I was shaking uncontrollably, but tried to slow my breathing and calm down. I dried my eyes and blew my nose with a tissue the man handed me as he sat back down at the table. All three women wore the long black dress and scarf-head cover getup, but pulled back the veil while they ate. They continued to eat and sip on Sprites. The man handed me a bottle of Sprite. I nervously sipped at the sweet liquid while the women stared at me, with no compassion, with no emotion.

"Tell me what happened to you," the man asked casually over a bite of his dinner. He had no interest in me at all. I should have checked myself, but I felt safe. I started to cry again as I explained what had occurred. I reached for my camera and shakily displayed the photo I took of the driver. The man took my camera and passed it around to the women who spoke in Arabic. As one of the women was quietly speaking about the picture on my camera, an old Mercedes Taxi pulled up and the driver walked into the restaurant.

I immediately jumped up and said, "Oh, a taxi, I'll take it into Baalbek." The restaurant man said something to the taxi driver in Arabic and the taxi left.

"You cannot trust any taxi here. I will call a driver to take you back," the restaurant man said to me. Then he added, "You were looking for hashish?"

My heart dropped, "No, of course not, I only thought we would drive to my hotel and have a soda and talk about your country." That didn't sound right the minute I said it. Could I really have been that naïve only an hour ago?

"Why did you go with the man if you are alone," the man asked me. He was right, I looked guilty, but I just wanted out now. I didn't want to explain my careless decision to jump into a car with a man in a foreign country who barely spoke a word of English and had a rifle riding shotgun.

"It was my mistake," I confessed, "I just want to go back to Baalbek now."

Restaurant man pulled out his cell phone, and after three phone calls and about thirty minutes, a car pulled up outside and a girl walked in. She was wearing western clothes, jeans and a T-shirt, no head scarf, her hair was light with dyed blonde streaks.

"Ah, here is your ride," the restaurant man stood up and greeted the girl. They spoke in English, "Here is the girl who needs a ride to Baalbek," he explained looking at me. "I think you will feel much safer with a woman." I thanked the women sitting at the table for sharing their meal with me, but they didn't respond. I walked out and thanked the man for calling a ride for me and apologized for the inconvenience and for interrupting his dinner. He was already walking back into the restaurant without a goodbye. The girl got into the passenger side and I climbed into the back seat. A young boy about fifteen sat in the driver's seat. When I got into the back I looked at the driver, he looked crippled, like he had polio or something, his left leg was withered and his left arm was twisted. I heard the lock click into place. The boy had locked all the doors. The girl looked back at me and asked with a smile and easy-going mood, "Where do you come from?"

"Canada," I answered, wishing my American passport wasn't in my purse. The boy pulled out and headed the wrong way, back up the hill to where I had jumped from the car. I quickly asked, "Are you taking me to Baalbek—this is the wrong way."

"We will go to my house first," the girl looked back at me, suspiciously. Then she added, "You can be my friend on Facebook?" Instantly I recognized the car, I was in the back seat of the Jeep Cherokee that I had jumped from and we were headed back up the hill!

"Please, please take me to Baalbek, I do not want to go to your house. Please forgive my rudeness but I must get back, I told the hotel owner I would be back and he will be very worried," I said with panic setting in again. Hoping that they thought someone knew where I was and would alert the police if I did not return that evening. This was not the case though. No one knew where I was, no one cared if I returned to Baalbek.

I had rolled my eyes at my mom when she pleaded with me to e-mail her more than once a month while I was traveling. And now I was back where I thought I had escaped, back in this car, going back up the hill to the man with the gun. And the group who 'saved' me at the restaurant called these people when they saw I had the photo of the man. I had visions of the American who got beheaded in Iraq. Why? Why do these people want me? Is the whole village in on this? Am I going to get where they are taking me and see the man in the restaurant with his wives and little boy cheering on my death? Are they going to torture me? I have nothing to give, my parents will be so worried when they hear I've been kidnapped and my captors want millions of dollars for my safe return. They will have to sell their house and go bankrupt for that amount of money. Stop, Mia! You need to stay calm, keep your wits about you, and think. You can think your way through this. You're an anthropologist, don't think from your own perspective, think from *their* culture.

An anthropologist? You just graduated from college and you think you're a full-blown anthropologist? Mia, you're dead, they are going to take you to a basement and chop off your head. You are not doing fieldwork here, you are being kidnapped and you are going to die. Screw your ethnocentricity and get out of this car, Mia! All that went through my head in one second, the next second I tried to open my door while the boy ripped up the hill.

"My brother said you would try and jump out again," the girl smiled back at me like we were friends on a casual outing. The man who kidnapped me was her brother...great. "My brother will sell you the hash and we will take you back to Baalbek. You meet my family and have food with them, we can be friends on Facebook."

What the hell was this weird hospitality thing about sharing a meal? No thanks people, I'll pass on being kidnapped, fed chicken and Sprite, browse our common friends on Facebook, then get beheaded. "No, please, I do not want hash, I just want to go back to Baalbek, please. I will pay you to take me back now," I implored, but the girl just looked ahead and smiled to the driver.

We drove another twenty minutes up into the hills east of Baalbek. There were no streetlights, and the buildings we passed were dark. I followed the dusty road as the headlights flashed the way. I tried to memorize where we had come from but the boy turned so many times up the hill, I forgot how many. I began to cry. The jeep came to a stop in front of a brick house and the boy clicked off the door locks. The three of us got out of the car and walked to the front door that was wide open. The girl took off her shoes and went into the small room, then the boy with the lame left side took his shoes off, so I followed suit, like I was willingly there, having dinner with this family.

I looked down to see an older woman and man seated on a large carpet with an infant and a little girl about five years old. They were eating and when we arrived they smiled and pointed to the food. "These are my grandparents," the girl explained, "please join us for food." Then the girl scooped the baby up and said, "This is my little boy, his name is Mohammed, the praised one." The boy driver limped over to the old woman, said something in Arabic, then sat and began dipping a piece of bread into a bowl of yogurt sauce. Perfect, just a little friendly get together with their kidnapped friend.

The man who kidnapped me then walked into the front room with a sinister smile on his lips. I backed up through the front door and was outside near the jeep. The girl,

Mohammed on her hip and her older brother followed me outside. "You are crazy!" I accused him. He laughed at me. I looked behind me, complete blackness, there was no-where to run. I was lost. I had to talk my way out of this or die here. "No, do not say my brother is crazy, he was only selling you what you asked for. We only want to sell you your hash." His sister was trying to calm me down. She was right, name-calling was probably not the best angle for my release. The siblings argued in Arabic for a minute in front of me, and then the girl took my hand and said, "Please, come in and share our dinner."

I went with her and her crazy brother followed us back into the front room. Grandma smiled up at me and held up a scrap of bread for me to take. I took it, smiled, said "Shukran," and kneeled down on the carpet. I felt like throwing up. Tears brimmed my eyes, I tried to smile at the little girl sitting there with her family. "Mickey mouse!" The little girl said to me then hid behind her great grandma. There was a Mickey Mouse button pinned onto my purse strap that my niece had given me before my trip. "Yes, this is Mickey Mouse, do you like Mickey Mouse?" I asked, taking the pin off my purse and offering it up in my palm to her. Everyone was watching me—the old couple, the boy driver, the sister, the crazy brother, the little girl and baby Mohammed. How could this nice family murder me? The little girl slowly reached for my outstretched hand with the encouragement of her great grandma. "Thank you," the little girl said in a soft voice. "You're welcome," I said smiling through my fear.

"Please, you need to talk to my brother now," the sister told me and I looked up at the crazy man who was waiting for me to follow him. I thought it hard to believe that the sister would allow me to be led away to my death while the family dined in the same house, so I followed him. Down a short hallway, past an open window, then down a few stairs to a room on the right side, directly under the front room where the family was sitting, having dinner. Crazy led me through the doorway into a small brick room with a concrete floor. He walked to the center of the room and pulled on a string that lighted a single bulb in the ceiling. Cardboard apple and peach boxes lined the walls from floor to ceiling, but I didn't think he was here to sell me produce. He hefted a box down from the top of one of the peach box towers and put it on the ground in front of me, lifted the lid and took out a rectangle wrapped in clear plastic and tin foil.

Crazy unwrapped the layers of plastic and presented what looked like a large chocolate bar to me. "One hundred dollars!" His white teeth peeked through his lips as he smiled at me.

"I do not have one hundred dollars and I do not want any hash. You make a mistake. I need to go back to hotel," I said as calmly as I could, hoping I wouldn't make him angry. Crazy grabbed the back of my hair with one hand and shoved the hash into my nose with the other, his face was almost touching mine. "You want hash, I bring you here to buy hash. Now you buy or I take sex from you." His breath smelled like garlic and his spit landed on my lip when he said 'from'. He let me go and I quickly wiped my lip with the back of my hand. He carefully wrapped the hash back into the layers of plastic and finally covered it back up with the tin foil, placed it back into the box where about twenty similar packages were stored, replaced the lid and put the peach box back on top of the others. He looked at me with his scary smile and walked out of the room closing the door behind him. Without a second of hesitation I turned the doorknob but it was locked.

Chapter Twenty-Eight

I listened to Crazy walking back up the concrete stairs then his voice, speaking Arabic. He was fighting with his sister. I stood in that windowless room filled with boxes of hash, wishing Nadine had been with me, or that I hadn't gotten into a car with a stranger, or that I had anyone on earth that knew where I was. There was no way that Crazy would allow me to live after he had showed me his stockpile of hash. Why did he show me? I have watched Good Fellas way too many times to know that they *have* to whack you after they show you where the goods are hidden.

The door to my prison room creaked open and the little girl from upstairs stood at the entrance. "Mickey Mouse," she said to me holding the pin I had given her. I held my finger up to my lips and said, "Shhhhhhhhhhh." She had come alone, not to save me but to show me how she loved her Mickey Mouse pin, I would have thanked her but I couldn't waste a second of my freedom so I stepped past her and without a moment of hesitation, ran up the stairs then jumped out the open window. I had no idea if it was a one-foot or a thirty-foot drop, but I didn't stop to think, I just vaulted out of that house.

As I dropped through the warm air I felt giddy, I had escaped again. But I knew I had to move quickly. I landed with a thud on something soft, a bag of sand in a burlap sack sat next to a pile of bricks. I thought how lucky that I hadn't landed on the bricks but didn't pause. Through pitch darkness, I ran down a hill. I didn't allow myself to breath or cry, I just ran as quietly away from the house as I could. My feet levitated over the gravel path. I ran without getting tired. I ran with no direction. I slipped down a hill but felt no pain. I just ran.

My feet were wet with blood, the gravel had cut into the flesh of my bare skin. I ran. Down and left, down and right, I was lost in the dark. I kept running. I looked behind me, wondering if Crazy and the nice family had discovered my escape. Sweat ran down by back, my face, I wasn't conscious of it but tears were streaming down my cheeks, my nose was plugged up with snot. I allowed myself to stop. Mia, you need to get it together. But I couldn't permit myself to relax or believe that I was safe. I had already thought I was safe, once tonight—when I wasn't!

I leaned up against a brick building near the path I was running down. There were no lights, but I could hear someone speaking several floors above me in the building. I wanted to run up the stairs and find someone to help me but I was paranoid. I couldn't trust anyone in this village now. I began to walk, following the gravel path to my right. I saw a light, then another, I was back at the highway. Under the streetlight I felt naked, if Crazy came looking for me I was a sitting duck, totally exposed.

I saw bright white headlights coming my way, and I started breathing so hard I was sure that I would faint. A large truck passed and relief flowed through me. I was positive it was going to be Crazy in his Jeep. I would never get into a Jeep Cherokee for the rest of my life. Another pair of headlights gunned toward me, and I realized that a minibus should also be coming along this highway headed for Baalbek. I would just have to wait here, alone, under the streetlight. No problem. I finally had to put my purse in front of my mouth to stop myself from hyperventilating as each car whizzed by.

I saw the minibus long before it saw me. I flapped my hand downward the way locals make transportation stop. It worked. The minibus moved over three lanes and halted on the dusty shoulder where I stood. I ran ahead and pulled open the sliding van door to see seven men in full military fatigues with their AK47's. I gulped and prayed that they weren't in on the kidnapping. "Baalbek" I beseeched the driver and after he nodded at me and answered, "Na'am." I slammed the door behind me and nearly sat on one of the soldiers' laps, it was so crammed. I held my breath and pretended that it was totally normal for a lone, western, blonde woman to stop a minivan twenty miles outside of Baalbek at night, with bleeding bare feet.

It was business as usual for the minivan, a clank on the metal ceiling with a coin directed the driver to stop, and a person flapping their arm in a downward motion on the side of the road meant, pick me up. No one knew I had just been kidnapped or almost killed. No one cared. We stopped and picked a man up, dropped two soldiers off, picked up another, dropped three more with no one even looking my way.

Mt. Olympus Hotel was lit up ahead in green neon, I pounded my coin on the ceiling and said, stop please. The driver stopped and I paid him five dollars without waiting for my change. I ran straight for the Hotel, passing through the open doorway with an absurd feeling like I was finally home. The giant Mujahideen-looking man stood from behind the reception desk when I ran in. "Ahhhh, there you are. I began to worry when you took so long to come back. Baalbek is no place for a woman alone."

No shit, Sherlock. But instead of saying anything, I ran straight into his arms and started to cry hysterically. The poor giant Mujahideen stood there in shock trying not to touch me. But I just needed to pretend that he was my dad for a minute. I had kept it together through the mini bus ride and even through two kidnappings I had never really fallen apart. Now I was going to lose it, I didn't care who I upset.

Finally, after a few seconds, I was able to calm myself enough that I could speak again. I pushed off from his giant chest.

"Something not so good happened?" he asked the obvious, taking a few steps away from me. He looked worried, like I might grab him again.

"Something terrible happened to me tonight, a man took me— here I have his picture on my camera." I tried not to shake as I showed him my camera, but I couldn't help the convulsions that racked my body with giant shudders. Crazy's face lit up the display screen and I actually shuttered as I looked into his face again. "I need to call the police," I said. "I need to call the police!" I said again because I wasn't sure that I was making sense to anyone.

Mujahideen looked at Crazy and then back at me. "You," he glared at me, "you asked this man for hashish!" he accused.

All night everyone had been accusing me of this and now I wanted to scream and maybe lose it again. "No!" I yelled. "No! I do not smoke hash, I don't want hash, I never said anything about hash!"

The man took a drag on his cigarette and blew out his smoke casually. In the sudden silence, I realized that I had been screaming rather loudly. I glanced around at the deserted hotel. And then, as I realized that I was totally alone with another man who thought I wanted hash, fear started to crowd the edges of my consciousness.

"I would advise against calling the police." He took another deep drag on his cigarette. I moved away from him and glanced out the still-open front door. I could run, but to where?

"This city and my hotel do not need any more bad press," he continued, stubbing out his cigarette. "And I need a good score from the Lonely Planet guide book. You will like me on Facebook, right?"

More bad press? Clearly I should have done my homework on this city. I pride myself on being prepared before I go anywhere. In this case my research was directed at the Roman times, from 2500 years ago—however, I neglected to read up on what has been going on for, oh, say the past twenty years here.

"Yes, I will like you on Facebook." What was it with these people and Facebook? "I will not go to the police, I will just take a shower and go to sleep now, thank you very much."

"Good, good, this is good. And you don't tell anyone about this, right? If you tell, say it happened in another city, yes? And if you need to cry again, I will get a woman for you."

"Sure, right, whatever," I answered the owner and went to my room. Who *are* these people? I planned to go directly to the police, to tell my story so that Crazy would be punished, but after the way restaurant guy and the Mujahideen guy reacted to my story with disregard and accusations, I decided not to tell one more person about what happened. I just wanted to leave. I felt very alone, very scared and very naive.

I locked my room door behind me, went into the bathroom and stared at my face in the mirror. I let out a breath and with it a waterfall of tears. My chest heaved like I was not in control of my body. I crumpled on the floor and cried like I had never cried in my life. And then I remember what the hotel owner had said about me needing a woman if I was going to cry again. That made me smile a little through my tears. Yes, I needed a woman. I needed my mom. I took a cold shower and scrubbed the blood off my feet and ankles. I washed my hair three times to get the dust and memory out. I made sure the door was securely locked and went to sleep alone in the windowless room at the Mt. Olympus Hotel.

I was awake long before my alarm went off at five. All night I had dreams of Crazy, he was torturing me by pouring hot water onto my feet. The cuts on my skin weren't as bad as I first thought, after I cleaned the blood off, I saw there was only a shallow scratch under each foot. The pain had subsided. But rage had taken over. After three in the morning, there was no sleep for me. Just waiting, watching the clock so I could get up and leave. I wanted out of this place, this city, this country. Fear had turned to anger.

No goodbyes or thank you's to anyone. Resentment fueled me, across the street, into a minivan and back to Beirut. I stared out the window the entire three hours damning Lebanon and its people in my head. No smile passed my lips for the children or women. In fact, I found myself glaring at the women. Traitors.

I looked out at the dirty city and rolled my eyes thinking, they can take this place, their shit country and go to hell. All the good times were forgotten. The love I had for this place was gone, the beauty of the people and their culture was ruined for me. I just wanted out forever.

The minivan stopped at the end of its route, Cola station. I got out and immediately hailed a service taxi straight to Czech airlines office. I regretted now more than ever not using my flight miles. The cheap flight I bought flew me home via Prague, Frankfurt and London before getting back to LA. The cost of being cheap.

"How may I help you?" The woman at the desk asked in her clipped eastern European accent.

"I need to go home." I felt tears well up and physically shook my head to make them stop. "Now. I need to go home now."

"Okay?" she said confused.

"I am booked on a flight that leaves in three days, but I can't stay here anymore. Please, please don't make me stay here anymore."

I noticed that her nametag said Ava. My sister Paige had a dog named Ava. I almost said that, but then realized that, really, no one wants to know they share a name with a dog. She clicked on her computer, squinting and then clicking the keys some more. She had impossibly long fingernails and they made a really obnoxious sound on the keys of her computer. "Well, as you Americans like to say, I have good news and bad news." She huffed a small laugh.

I was not in the mood. I didn't laugh or smile at her, oh so funny, American joke.

"Anyway, there is a flight this evening."

"Perfect! I'll take it." suddenly I loved Ava and her awful fingernails.

"Yes, well, the bad news, I'm afraid is that you have a tier three ticket. There are no changes permitted with a tier three. You will have to purchase entirely new passage which is another five hundred dollars." I actually contemplated, for about two seconds, putting five hundred dollars on my Visa. But let's be frank here people, I'm cheap. Tail between my legs, I left the Czech airline office and caught a service taxi to the hostel.

Papa was at the reception with a huge smile for me. "Beinvenue Mademoiselle! Moukhtar no here, you need bed tonight?" I was partly glad that Mo wasn't there, I was in no mood to detail the events from my previous night. I promised myself that I hated everything Lebanese—that I would hibernate for two days in the Hostel Sofar and happily leave on my scheduled flight never to return to this hellhole again.

The heat was oppressive in my dorm room. I took a cold shower and sat on my bed with the fan whirling at full speed. I found a giant paperback in the reception and escaped into a George Martin fantasy novel. Kings, duels, dragons, and maidens filled my afternoon and into the evening. The book was over a thousand pages, perfect, I had three days.

Papa came into my room after an hour with a cup of freshly made tea, he offered up the mug with a grin, "Tea pour vous mon ami." I took the steaming cup of sweet tea and said merci as Papa padded out back to his desk. I tried to keep Crazy out of my thoughts. I tried not going over and over what had happened last night.

I had to leave the hostel at some point to eat and write an e-mail home, but there was a fear inside of me, an innocence lost. Not that I was some innocent child before the incident, but I was bitter, angry and searching for someone to blame beside myself. I went to sleep early, without dinner. I heard a couple come into the dorm room late that night, but I turned to the wall pretending to be asleep. For me, Lebanon had become a prison. I wanted to do my time and go.

Chapter Twenty-Nine

I slept poorly again. I woke up tired and hungry. I longed to go home. The ordeal kept running over in my head, I needed to release it. To purge Crazy from my mind. I wanted to tell someone what had happened to me, to confide in someone, anyone. But I promised myself I wouldn't, not even my family would know. Especially not my family, I didn't want them to worry, I definitely wouldn't tell my parents. My dad would freak. He would contact the State Department to demand Lebanon be upgraded from the mere travel alert to—if you go there you'll die status. My mom would never think I was safe traveling ever again.

Nothing like this calamity had ever happened in my years of traveling alone and I blamed myself. It was my fault that I got into a car with a strange man. I would have never in a million years done that in Los Angeles or anywhere in the States. What were you thinking Mia? I made a mistake, I got away and it was over, so stop running it through you brain. But my hate for Lebanon was still in my belly, or was that hunger? I *was* starving, but I was too scared to leave the safety of the hostel.

My roommates were waking up and talking about how excited they were to be going down south today. Yeah, that was *me* four weeks ago! If they only knew how ruthless the Lebanese are...

"Good morning." The guy chirped to me.

"Hello." I said back with a please don't talk to me face, that apparently he didn't read so well.

"Been here long?"

I wish I could afford a room by myself. "No, just arrived yesterday from Baalbek."

"My wife and I are so excited to see Baalbek, you know they have the most complete Roman ruin in the world?"

Yeah, and great hash too! "Yeah, I know, I saw it, it was amazing." I said dismissively.

"Who are you traveling with?"

Clearly this guy needed a friend. "I am alone, I've been traveling around Lebanon, but I'm headed home in a couple days."

"Really, all alone, I could never do that! Where's home?"

Sometimes I feel like wearing a sign around my neck that reads: I'M AMERICAN- I'M ALONE. "I'm American, how about you two?"

"We are Canadian, from Vancouver."

Liars. "Really? Are you really Canadian or do you just say you are?"

"What? Why would someone lie about being Canadian?"

Evidently this guy hasn't watched CNN in like ten years. His wife returned to the room with wet hair and introduced herself. Her name was Jen and his was Kosta, his parents were from Greece so he got the name. We sat and talked for another few minutes and they asked if I knew a good place for breakfast. I told them about Cafe Paul and started to draw them a map when Jen invited me with them. I was starving and there is safety in numbers, so I agreed.

My oath of silence to the world didn't last long. I told Kosta and Jen the entire episode, tears and all (never tell me a secret you want kept). When I reached the part that I got to the hostel and hadn't left to eat, they officially adopted me for the next two days. I refused their charity at first, but they persisted, convincing me that *they* needed me as their tour guide Ha! After breakfast of ham and cheese croissants and perfectly foamed cappuccinos we walked to Darwa station and headed for the southern city of Saida in a minibus.

Forty kilometers down the coast from Beirut is the flourishing city of Saida. I had planned to come here, but after Baalbek I'd committed myself to rot in my room rather than continue my trip. I was already glad to have escaped my self-inflicted confinement. The sun was shining, people were out and about and the Earth had continued to turn.

Our first stop was the Crusader castle built in 1228. We paid our two-dollar entrance fee and accepted the offer for a guide who repeated a schpeel very similar to what I heard in Byblos—Welcome to the oldest and most important Phoenician city in the world...

After an hour with our tour guide I was well versed in the long history of Saida and felt relived that I left the safety of the hostel to explore the south with Kosta and Jen. Walking along the corniche after our tour we stopped at a restaurant overlooking the Mediterranean sea. The day was hot, but the breeze was delightful. The possibility of recovering from the incident crossed my mind—sitting there comfortably, laughing, enjoying my new friends' company and feasting on fish and chips.

I loved that afternoon, maybe because it came on the heels of a disaster, but my wounds, both physical and emotional, were healing thanks to the friendship of Jen and Kosta. The three of us wandered through the old souk with vaulted wood ceilings. Above a brick archway a sign announced that St. Paul and St. Peter had their last meeting on that sight. Vendors sold homemade soap, fresh sweet-cakes, antique carpets, and hundreds of different spices displayed in huge baskets. Cumin, nutmeg, anise, cloves, and mixes of rose tea. My senses were aroused. I felt inspired again.

We left the ancient city and headed back to Beirut as the sun began to set. I sat quietly in the minivan watching the giant orb color the sea. What beauty! What history! My imagination had returned, I thought of the people who built this place, fought for it, loved it through the centuries. The people of Lebanon, that's what made the place so special. My healing was inspired by these people. The Lebanese who had been kind, generous and gracious to me. Papa, Mo, Steve,

Adonis, Doctor Hourani, Jean, Raffi and all the others who taught through example to forgive and love.

We ate dinner in a cafe near the hostel. Jen fished out her ten different handmade bars she bought at the soap factory that afternoon. She made me close my eyes, then held them to my nose and asked me to guess the flavors. Cinnamon, lavender, rose, sandalwood. Back at the hostel I thanked my new Canadian friends for allowing me to tag along with them, they had no idea how much it meant to me. My determination to stay miserable and sit in the hostel for the rest of my trip, melted away. I wouldn't let Crazy ruin all my experiences from the last month. I slept well in my dorm room that night with the fan spinning above our heads drowning out the sounds of the city.

My last full day in Lebanon started at Cafe Paul's with Kosta and Jen and plans to head south again, past Saida, to her twin city of Tyre. Again, we crammed into a minibus and were off. I smiled at a little boy sitting on his mother's lap. Angelic, innocent he smiled back, then stuck his tongue out at me. I laughed and thought to myself how children are the same all over the world. There is a universality about us humans—as much as we want to be distinctive from one another and claim originality, our delicate species thrives on love. In actuality we are all the same, insecure, triumphant humans. A love filled me, a kind of familiarity among these people. I loved the Lebanese people again.

The first thing I noticed were the UN troops with their baby blue berets marching through town. The feeling in the southern cities is much different from the wealthier, Christian parts of Lebanon. Scars from the war were evident—bullet riddled buildings and bombed out structures. The PLO had used this town as their headquarters throughout the late1970's and into the 80's and 90's making it a target for American made— Israeli dropped, artillery. The people of Tyre rebuilt after their homes and businesses were destroyed. Then another attack, then more construction, I wonder if the people have any hope for peace left.

The Roman theatre is what Kosta was interested in, so we took a taxi to the entrance near the harbor and walked around the old Roman columns and ruined hippodrome. The day was oppressively hot, so Jen and I skipped the grandiose tour and sat under the shade of an oak tree watching fishing boats sail into the harbor. Kosta took off to inspect the archeological excavations—that seemed stalled to put it mildly. War trumps the preservation of historic relics.

I couldn't leave Lebanon without one more swim in the warm sea, so we rented a cabana on the sand and spent a few hours during the hottest part of the day sipping on cold beers and swimming in the warm Mediterranean. Kosta tried smoking apple tobacco out of a hooka pipe—then coughed uncontrollably until people started to stare—then laugh. Kids played at the water's edge, old men strolled on the sand in speedos, girls flirted with boys playing soccer. The scene was familiar, it could have been anywhere in the world, except fifteen miles south was the border with Israel.

This land has experienced death, hate and misery like no other place on earth. For thousands of years Tyre has seen war. Alexander the Great conquered it in 332 BC, and anywhere the Bible says Jesus went, forget about it, everyone fights over it then! I felt sad for these children growing up with uncertainty and hate for your neighbor. As an American I felt thankful for my freedoms yet guilty for my government's decision to aide Israel's never-ending bombardment. Twenty thousand Palestinians live in destitute conditions— not permitted to hold jobs or be incorporated into the Lebanese community, in the Bourj el Shemali refugee camp in Tyre. The camp was built as a tent city in 1948 to accommodate a few hundred people, while they waited to return to their land after the Israelis forced them from their homes. The Palestinians thought they would be here a month, maybe two, its been sixty years. The first generation born into these camps grew up listening to their parents lament their natural right to return to their homeland. The resentment towards the Israelis turned to hate. Add thirty years, poverty, hopelessness and presto, you get bitter angry young men. Then militant Islamists adopted their cause and by 1978 rockets began being launched into Israel killing innocent civilians. And so it goes.

We again made our way back up the coast to Beirut. Kosta and Jen sponsored my going away dinner in a fancy restaurant in the Ashrafieh discrict. I thanked them for letting me join them for another great day that I wouldn't have experienced if I had stuck to my hell bound plan of misery—wasting away in my room feeling sorry for myself. Kosta and I began to debate that one can be anti Israel without being anti-Semitic. "I have nothing against Jewish people or the Israelis, it's their government's apartheid policies that I disagree with. I wouldn't want to be judged based on my American government's war mongering ideals." I began my rant, when Jen stopped us and proposed a toast, "No politics over an expensive meal." Thanks Jen, I'll drink to that! One thing was agreed upon and that was Lebanon is a fantastic country with friendly people, amazing history and delicious food. I added, great looking guys as Kosta rolled his eyes and Jen winked at me in agreement.

Waiting to begin my thirty-hour journey home, at Rafic Hariri airport the next morning I reflected on my month. This mysterious ancient place had put a spell on me. Lebanon my beloved.

I never did tell my parents about Crazy.

Ruins of Roman temple in Baalbek

Call Me Ishmael
New Zealand

New Zealand

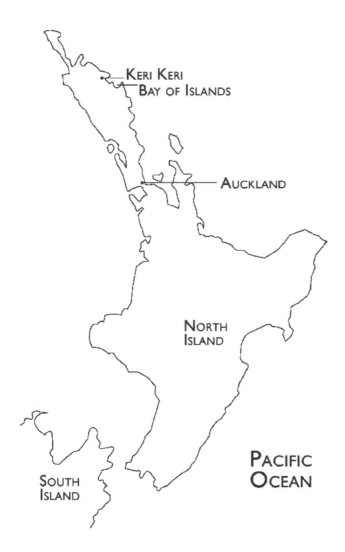

Chapter Thirty

People talk about my passion for travel like an illness that needs to be exercised from me like a demon. Once my mom gathered up five of my sisters to start an intervention in hopes of making me 'normal'. One reason people discourage my traveling is that I don't do anything productive while I'm away. I plan a trip, save money, take off and return home, broke. This time things would be different, I was combining travel with business! I had a purpose to go to a faraway place, not just an appetite to relinquish my obligations and split.

The first time I went to New Zealand, I learned two secrets. First, it's total paradise—the people are genuinely nice, the weather is beautiful, and there's not an ongoing civil war...bonus! Secondly, I found that Kiwis (what the locals call themselves) recycle everything and it's totally acceptable to buy second hand clothes, books, cars, whatever. In fact they encourage keeping things in good condition so they can be reused. Wow, what a concept. Coming from Southern California where we trade in our cars every two years and wouldn't be caught dead in a pair of used jeans, this was quite refreshing.

The notion of reusing things coupled with the high literacy rate in New Zealand got me thinking. I could take used paperback books, which are virtually thrown away in Southern California and sell them to those environmentally friendly New Zealanders. I would be able to combine my wanderlust with a moneymaking business and finally legitimize my travel bug.

I carpeted my neighborhood with flyers asking for used paperback books and in a week I had sixty grocery bags of them on my doorstep. Minus the three bucks for the ream of paper, my business was pure profit after the first seven days. I collected books from garage sales, donations and library book sales for the next ten months, carefully storing my precious cargo into apple boxes. I didn't want to waste money buying packing boxes, so I made a deal with my local grocer to save his produce boxes for me to pick up every night. I stored the full boxes of books in my room until they started to take over. I gave my desk away and replaced it with a homemade apple box desk, my mattress became a platform bed, and with lamps perched on them, I created apple box nightstands. I could fit about thirty-five books in each box and I had one hundred and twenty seven boxes filling my room in my apartment.

My goal was to collect five thousand books, that meant another eighteen boxes and since my room couldn't fit one more, I finally rented a storage unit and broke the news to my two roommates that I would be moving out of the apartment. They feigned sadness, then quickly rented my room to one of their friends. The plan was in full swing, I gathered books by day, waited tables by night and managed to take two classes to keep my student health care current.

Admittedly, I got a little ckoo ckoo as I neared my goal. I would covet stranger's paperbacks, asking if I could have their book when they finished. My mom ended the insanity by appealing to her favorite resource, the church. In eight days, the church sisters delivered the last six hundred and thirty books to my parent's home, putting an end to the collection frenzy and meeting my goal of five thousand paperback books. Never underestimate the power of church ladies.

Try telling people that you are going to be a bookseller in New Zealand. I was met with the most hilarious expressions and comments like, "Bring a jacket, it gets cold during winter in Europe," and "What language do they speak in Zee-land?" And my favorite, "When are you going to find a man and settle down?" I didn't listen to the nay-sayers. I was determined to show people that I could travel and make money at the same time. I had returned home broke too many times to fail. And besides, I was an American and a Coffin, taught by my country and parents that I could succeed at anything I put my mind to. Well, I had my one hundred and forty-five apple boxes securely locked in a storage unit, super high expectations and a backpack, now I just needed my ticket.

I combed the LA Times travel section to find the cheapest ticket to Auckland. In tiny letters at the bottom of the page I read, 'Circle the Pacific.' New Zealand was in the Pacific, right? I looked closer and I saw, Auckland, Sydney, Jakarta, K.L., Bangkok, Hong Kong and a little 999.99 incl tax right below the heading. I think it's a shame to get a round trip ticket without stopping somewhere. I mean, if you're going to fly over ten hours anywhere, there's always a place in between to stop and see. One time I flew to Istanbul and discovered a stop in London and Frankfurt that only cost an extra sixty dollars. The key to remember is to allow yourself a few days, not hours, to check a city out. In my case, I am not satisfied that I really get the essence of a place without a two-week stay.

I dialed the number on the Circle the Pacific ad. An Indian guy answered.

"Air Brokers Travel, Bob speaking, how may I help you?" Why foreigners change their beautiful names to assimilate into American culture I'll never understand. The Vietnamese girl, Tracy. The Persian guy, Tom. The Chinese man, Mike. Really? I truly believe that Americans can learn how to say Mai-ling, Reza and Pei. Maybe it's my anthropological voice crying out for diversity.

"Yes, hello, I am calling about the ad in the Los Angeles Times Travel section that shows a flight to circle the pacific for a thousand dollars," waiting for the guy to announce that it was a typo.

"Yes, you choose three stops and you must complete your travel in one year."

"For nine hundred and ninety-nine dollars including tax?"

"Yes, ma'am."

"I would like to go to Auckland in about two weeks."

"I need your exact date of departure and the two other destinations, please."

"Oh, OK," referring to the ad I said, "Um, how about K.L. and Hong Kong and I'll leave in two weeks from today." I had no idea what K.L. stood for, but I'd find out.

"So, departing LAX on thirty October and stopping in K.L. and Hong Kong for how many passengers?"

"One, please."

My ticket arrived in the mail three days later and the next fourteen days were crazy, getting ready to leave for my year's adventure. That was my plan, to sell my books in New Zealand for nine months, then take the last three months to travel through South East Asia, and be back the next November to start fall semester at the University. After choosing a shipping consolidator out of Long Beach harbor, I rented a U-haul truck and enlisted my twin brothers, Martin and Michael to help load up the apple boxes.

The storage company was unhappy that I only used their space for one month. Americans and their storage units––I could write a thesis on the absolute absurdity of working your butt off to buy things, then putting them in a concrete box and paying to keep them there year after year. Weird.

My books were shipped off and they would arrive in Auckland three weeks later. I opted to pass on the extra insurance—unaware of how often shipping containers get lost at sea. That information I learned the hard way, as well as how very strict New Zealand's immigration policy is. Some things in life have to be experienced firsthand to really grasp—like a broken heart, a flat tire on the side of a California freeway or, having an immigration officer at the Auckland airport relay the information that Americans are only eligible for a three-month travel visa.

Chapter Thirty-One

Upon arrival at the Auckland International Airport in New Zealand, I tried to explain that I needed the extra six months to really explore the country and get a feel for the culture, I left out the part where I wanted to sell five thousands books without a permit.

Mr. Very-serious-don't-mess-with-me-immigration-officer responded curtly, "You have three months." His accent was adorable and I knew I could find a loophole. Maybe I could marry a Kiwi and stay forever. Reality is not my strong suit.

On my first trip to New Zealand, I discovered a little town up the coast from Auckland that I fell in love with. Keri Keri is located on the East coast of the North Island, about 240 kilometers north of Auckland. An agricultural Mecca, Keri Keri is nestled in a sheltered bay with green rolling hills, thousands of small islands dot the coast. I was driving along a country road and stopped at a table set out at the end of someone's driveway. On the table sat several plastic bags filled with berries, avocados and apples, and a hand-written sign announcing— FRESH PRODUCE—3 DOLLARS EACH—a mason jar with money in it let you make your own change.

It was an honesty system, unknown to a Californian for at least a hundred years. A bit confused, waiting for the owner of the property to approach me with a shotgun, I carefully picked up a bag of fresh blackberries and added my three New Zealand dollars to the jar. I waited to be questioned, arrested, or shot at, but I was alone with the bags of fruit along the side of a deserted road in the shining sun. So—people in Keri Keri, New Zealand just trusted each other? At that moment, I decided I would get back to that place.

It took me nearly two years, but I was back. Getting off the three-hour bus ride from Auckland to Keri Keri the next morning, I instantly recognized the place and felt confident that this is where I should make my home and sell my books. As I was walking from the bus stop to the Youth Hostel, it started to sprinkle, so I ran the rest of the way trying to keep my backpack dry. The guy at the front desk had an English accent, so I asked him how long he had been in New Zealand.

"Five years, now."

I told him that all *I* wanted was nine months, and asked if he knew how I could extend my three-month tourist visa.

"Canadian or American?" he asked.

"American," I said with a wince like it was a bad word. He told me that it was possible to extend your visa but it wasn't guaranteed, "Especially for Yanks." he added chuckling.

"Just because we Yanks beat you Poms in the war of Independence doesn't mean you have to be bitter," I said sarcastically. Then he reminded me that New Zealand was part of the Commonwealth of Britain and that he could stay as long as he liked and work legally.

"And if you had been one of our colonies, *you* could stay in New Zealand too." A child's laugh interrupted the colonial debate—a cute little guy on the floor behind the desk wearing a Spiderman T-shirt and diaper.

"Hello," I said in a high-pitched mommy voice.
The front desk guy said, "Say hello, Skylar," then added that it was helpful to be married to a Kiwi to get a visa to stay in New Zealand. So that was it! I had to keep my eye out for a Kiwi husband.

Jet lag was killing me. Usually I fight it and try to stay up, but I needed a solid two-hour nap before I could even think of exploring. I walked through the common area past a pool table, a TV, stacks of games and books, bean bags, and chairs all set around tables connecting to an open kitchen. I found DORM ROOM #1 which had four bunk beds and a huge window. I plopped my backpack on the floor next to a lower bunk, lay down and quickly fell asleep to the sound of rain on the tin roof.

I had no idea where I was when my eyes opened four hours later. I remembered a plane journey and a toddler called Skylar. I focused on the slats of the bunk above me. I'm in a bunk bed.

"Good morning, lazybones," a girl's blonde head swung from the upper bunk. I was staring at her face upside down.

"Hi," I said, groggily.

"You have been sleeping the afternoon away."

"Yeah, I just arrived from California and the time difference is just brutal."

"My name is Gwenda, from Dusseldorf."

"Hello Gwenda from Dusseldorf, I'm Mia from California and I'm starving." Gwenda shared her spaghetti with me in the common area, then beat me at five games of pool. She had been living in the hostel for three weeks on a break from her University where she was studying agriculture—and had become a great pool player in New Zealand.

Gwenda explained that because of the constant rain she had been stuck at the hostel for days. We hung out the rest of the night playing Scrabble while she taught me German swear words until jet lag defeated me again at nine o'clock.

The sun never came through the window the next morning, the sky just became lighter and lighter shades of gray. I was waiting restlessly so that I could get up and eat. I rose from my lower bunk, took a shower and went to explore the village. I treated myself to a restaurant breakfast, something I rarely do when I have access to a kitchen, but I allowed myself to sip a cappuccino and devour a croissant and egg sandwich at a darling outdoor café run by an Austrian guy. I was wasting time! I had three weeks to buy a car, find a place to live, rent a store to sell my books before they arrived from the States—and go to a bank.

I deposited my 8,000 American dollars in a new account and walked out with a receipt reading 12,400 New Zealand dollars, validating my residency. The conversion rate made me feel rich. But being frugal (my sisters call it being cheap) I knew I had to be very careful not spend too much.

Kathy Broadbent had a Farah Fawcett hair-do and a huge smile filled with crooked teeth. "Welcome to Broadbent Realty, how may I help you?"

I told her that I was looking for a house to rent in town. I wanted to establish myself before I mentioned my illegal book business and the shop I would need to rent for that. Kathy was so nice, we sat over two cups of tea while she talked about how she and her husband Simon, had opened the realty office when their boys left home for University eight years ago. She promised to pick me up and show me around once she had made the appointments with the owners.

I stopped at the New World Supermarket on the way back to the hostel and bought some spaghetti, tomato sauce, broccoli, and a pack of mint biscuits (cookies to us Americans). They have a generic brand called *No Frills* which has plain white packaging with the contents starkly written in black—BEANS, SUN LOTION, BEER. No Frills products are half-price, so I was instantly a no-frills customer.

The communal kitchen at the hostel had quirky hand-written notes saying, PLEASE HELP TO KEEP THE KITCHEN TIDY and PLEASE LABEL YOUR FOOD OR IT WILL BE THROWN IN THE BIN.

I made myself a cup of tea and ate my mint cookies while I watched Gwenda annihilate a Dutch guy at pool. The English guy who ran the front desk was sitting on the floor reading an ABC book to Skylar. I joined them and offered them a cookie. Of course—it was raining. So I spent the afternoon hanging out with my new hostel friends playing pool, Scrabble, Pictionary and eating mint cookies until I was sick.

After four more rainy days I had a new posse. Tim and Rachael, Skylar's parents, ran the hostel. Paul, the Dutch guy, had skippered a yacht from Tahiti. Alon, the Israeli guy, was dodging his army duty by traveling everywhere except Israel. Ben and Valerie, the English couple, were on holiday from teaching English in Korea. Steve, the Scottish guy, had been on the road for twelve years, working as a carpenter. Natalie, the Swiss girl, was traveling on her father's money, and having an affair with Steve. And, of course, there was Gwenda who schooled us on the detrimental effects of genetically-modified seeds that were taking over the farming industry. I wonder what they thought of me, Mia, the American girl with a Canadian flag patch stitched to her backpack who shipped five thousand books from California to New Zealand.

Chapter Thirty-Two

I bought a car for eight hundred dollars three days later from a German couple who had been exploring New Zealand for the past six weeks. I named her Sunny because she was an orange 1973 Datsun Sunny. When I pulled into the hostel parking lot I beeped the horn. Ben, Valerie, Gwenda and Paul ran out to check out my new wheels. We all packed into Sunny and drove down to the Dairy for ice cream. When we returned, I saw Kathy Broadbent talking to Tim at the front desk.

"Hi, Kathy."

"Hello Mia, looks like you've got driving on the wrong side of the road sorted."

"Yeah, I'll need some practice before I drive down to Auckland with all those roundabouts and some new windshield wipers if the rain keeps up like this."

"Welcome to New Zealand in November!" she laughed as it began to sprinkle. I invited her into the kitchen for tea.

She sat across from me and started, "Listen, Mia—Simon and I have agreed to offer you a place in our home while you are here in Keri Keri." I looked at her puzzled, but she went on, "Our boys are all grown and we are left with a huge house that we don't use half of. We have a large downstairs with a separate entrance, kitchen, living area and three bedrooms. All the boys' things are there, but we can clear them out for you, if you'd like to stay." She had shown me three different rentals the week before—all too expensive.

"How much would you charge per month?"

"Absolutely nothing! We would be happy to have you. Our youngest, William, is staying in Simon's cousins home in Surrey and we understand how it is to be young and poor."

"I'm not poor..."

"I know. We just want to offer it to you. And if you find another place, or are uncomfortable with us old folks, then you don't have to stay."

"Thanks so much, Kathy, I would love to come and stay with you. But, there's something I need to tell you." (How should I reveal to her that 5000 books are about to land on her doorstep?)

The property was more like a farm, with a long driveway lined with apple, peach and avocado trees. A clothesline stood in the garden with white sheets blowing in the wind. An old boat covered with a tarp sat on a trailer near a freestanding garage.

Kathy and Simon met me in the back as I pulled Sunny around. They gave me a tour of my new place. Kathy took the sheets off the line and told me they were for my bed. Simon opened the garage door and showed me where I could store my books when they arrived. After Simon made an exquisite roast lamb dinner with fresh tomatoes and eggplant from their garden, I lay in my freshly made bed, listened to the rain and thanked my lucky stars for my good fortune.

About ten days later, Gwenda ran over from the hostel to tell me the Auckland dock yard called the hostel and left a message for me that my one hundred and forty boxes had arrived. I called the dock guy, "One hundred and forty-five boxes, right?"

"No, ma'am, I have one hundred and forty boxes here, and you will be charged sixty-five dollars per day that your cargo sits in my warehouse." He must be mistaken, but I knew I had to hustle down there so I would avoid another sixty-five dollar charge.

"OK, I'll be there before three." Gwenda and Paul drove down to Auckland with me to pick up the books. A single cassette tape came with Sunny when I bought her from the German couple, so on the way down to Auckland the three of us listened to Bob Marley's Legend album eighty times.

In Auckland driving was a different story than in the country. I asked my co-pilots Paul and Gwenda, if I could turn left on a red light. No one knew, but then someone honked behind me. I guessed that was a yes. I rented a one-way trailer from U-haul and hitched it to Sunny—just in case driving a stick shift on the wrong side of the road in a foreign country wasn't difficult enough. We arrived at the docks just in time to see a locked gate.

"Please, please, please," I pleaded with the huge Maori guy manning the gate. I had a vision of me, Gwenda and Paul sleeping in the trailer eating Cup o'Noodles, and listening to Bob Marley until the next morning.

"Take it easy girl," he said, "It's just lunch time, the gate will be opened again in an hour."

I parked Sunny near the locked gate, and we killed time by walking for an hour around the huge industrial part of Auckland docks. I treated lunch at a Korean BBQ, the tastiest thing I had eaten in three weeks.

This is the part where I learned the hard way that buying extra insurance is a good idea. The dock guy was correct, one hundred and forty boxes had arrived from California. That meant—one hundred and seventy five of my books were floating in the Pacific somewhere. I was bummed out. But when I travel, I try to keep two things in mind: (1) it could be worse, and (2) always hope for the best. My dad's favorite Bible scripture popped into my head, Romans 8:28, "All things work together for good."

I wasn't completely sure how losing five boxes of my precious books could be a *good* thing, but at least I had the majority of my books and perhaps the five boxes were safe and sound on some Polynesian island where the locals could now read Tom Clancy and John Grisham to their hearts' content. Amen.

It rained thirty out of thirty days that November. I ate ice cream, played pool, and read every day. I hefted an apple box into my room one day when I ran out of books to read. I must have picked the box that the church ladies donated because it was filled with Testimonies from the gospel and romance novels. So I caught up on saving my soul and sex. I had been in New Zealand for a month, and was getting depressed and fat. My books were safe and sound and dry in Simon's garage but I had no prospect of a shop, and the rain was unrelenting.

The first sunny day was December 6th. I waddled into town to sign up for the gym. Unfortunately, I discovered there was no gym in Keri Keri, but I did find Angie's, a second-hand clothing shop.

A bell attached to the door announced my presence. A Maori woman, about sixty years old sitting behind a desk, sewing a patch on a pair of jeans looked up at me and said, "Hello, how may I help you?"

We started chatting about business and she admitted that she had been thinking of hiring some summer help. I had an offer for her. If I could set up some of my books in her shop, and work three days a week with no wage, she could work the other three days and put my book money aside for me. Angie would save money on paying for staff, and I would have a place to sell my books. A deal was struck and I spent the next three months selling Angie's used clothes and my books. It was a perfect match. To attract tourists passing by, I hung an extra sign under Angie's, reading 'And Books.'

Keri Keri is an international port town. People from all over the world sail to the Bay of Islands to stop and recover from their long journeys across the Pacific. They pick up supplies—like books—lots and lots of books. I sold one couple from Wisconsin thirty paperbacks at once. They were headed to the Mediterranean via India and Africa then onto the Caribbean. They were not unique— "boaties" came in every day and bought my books. I got to hear stories from Americans, Australians, Europeans and South Africans about life on the Ocean. I met local Kiwis too, who bargained for used clothes and laughed at my accent. I felt like I belonged and started to make friends with the locals.

The rain had finally stopped and I started running the trails up to the waterfall and down to the Stone Store. I lost the ice cream pounds and felt great. I was achieving my goal of traveling and making money. In fact, I had broken even after selling eight hundred books. Now it was pure profit—and I had a free place to stay. My only problem was my tourist visa. It was about to expire—I was faced with deportation.

I borrowed one of Kathy's dresses and high heels for my big day at the immigration office in Auckland. My visa was expiring in three days, it was the second of February and the sun was blazing. By the time I got Sunny parked and found my way to the immigration office I was drenched with sweat from the heat and anxiety. I had no plan if I was denied. There was no way I could sell my books and be on a plane in three days. I was prepared to plead, beg, and cry if it would help. I thought of the Mexicans living and working in Southern California. They were as desperate as I was, just to live and pay their own way by working. I'd been working side by side with Mexicans at restaurants over the years. Often, they work three jobs for years—contributing to our tax dollars—and still are denied a green card from American immigration. I hoped New Zealand would be more lenient with me.

I took a number and sat in the waiting room. I kept going over in my head the story I would tell. I brought my bank statements proving I had sufficient funds to support myself. I had my onward plane ticket—evidence that I was planning to leave. I turned and asked my neighbor how long she had been waiting, and where she was from. Two hours and from the Philippines, she answered. The room was filled with South East Asians, I smiled at her and wished her luck. Ten minutes later my number was called—I thought they had made a mistake because the Filipino lady had been waiting far longer. I walked to the window and gave a woman my ticket. She directed me through the door to her right.

A man met me behind the door and asked me to follow him. I followed him to a windowless office. A metal desk, a computer, a stack of files. It was cold. A poster on the wall read, *Over stay and pay*! Another showed a picture of a man in handcuffs with, *You do the time because it's a crime!*

I was very nervous.

"Passport, please."

I handed him my passport.

"Are you nervous, Ms. Coffin?" he asked looking up from my passport.

"No, sir." I was sweating.

"I see your tourist visa is expiring in three days and you have filled out an extension request to stay in New Zealand for another three months?"

"Yes, sir," I wanted to throw up.

"You are staying up in Keri Keri, eh?"

"Yes, sir."

"Heaps of rain up that way, eh?"

"Heaps."

"All right, Ms. Coffin, you are sorted. I've granted you an extension of three months. You are to leave New Zealand by the first of May," he said while writing something on the stamp in my passport with his pen.

"Cheers man, thanks very much."

"Cheers, you take care now, Ms. Coffin and enjoy the fruit up north, eh." He handed me my passport and out I went past the lady still waiting in the reception. Not sure what that was about, but glad to be white that day. Something is definitely wrong with the immigration system in the States and in New Zealand, but I wasn't going to be a crusader on that day. I legally had another three months in paradise. Hurray! I ran out of there!

When I drove Sunny into the yard where Kathy was taking her laundry off the line. She asked worriedly how it went. I told her I have another three months! She hugged me and sighed with relief. I treated Kathy and Simon to a celebratory dinner that night. They were truly becoming my family and I loved them very much.

Chapter Thirty-Three

My life became a comfortable routine. I watched the shop Mondays, Wednesdays and Fridays, then hung out at the hostel at night or had dinner with the Broadbent's. My days off were spent exploring the North Island in Sunny. Ben, Valerie, Gwenda and I went up to the North Cape and camped on the beach. Simon let us take his boat. So a few days a week we hitched the twelve-foot tin boat with its fifteen horse power engine to Sunny and went fishing. Natalie and I couldn't bear to touch the worms, so we baited our hooks with fresh cooked shrimp, bait that was mostly eaten by Ben and Paul.

My books were selling faster than I expected and money was rolling in. I had finally found a business that permitted me to travel and make money. One hitch was immigration. I couldn't keep extending my tourist visa. Immigration would get suspicious when I returned to New Zealand for nine months out of every year.

My husband idea wasn't panning out either. Hostel romance didn't foster long-term relationships. I would meet a cute guy, hang out with him for a day or two, then he would leave—not too encouraging. But, I had been allowed three more months, which seemed like an eternity, so I didn't worry about how I would need to extend my visa again before my trip to South East Asia. I was having so much fun *and* making money.

Natalie, Steve, Ben, Valerie and I went fishing one Friday after I closed the shop. While we were motoring to our favorite fishing spot we saw a moored yacht flying the recognizable red flag on a buoy. Scuba divers. We slowed and came along side the yacht.

"Hello!" the guy yelled out from the deck.
We all waved back and yelled, "Ahoy!"
"Howsit?" the guy asked us as we approached.

"Great, just going fishing, you going for a dive?" Valerie yelled over our engine.

"Yeah mate, the viz is brilliant," His accent was English. Then Ben recognized him from the sporting goods store in the village.

"Hey, Kevin, is that you?"

"Cheerio, Benny, howsit?" Kevin smiled and zipped up his wetsuit.

"Cheers, Kevin, have a great dive!" Ben called back while we were speeding away. We didn't catch any fish—we just talked about learning how to dive, all afternoon. None of us were scuba certified and we all agreed to branch out from our fishing trips to try scuba.

The five of us met at the sports store in the village the next morning to talk with Kevin about how we could get scuba certified. He told us that he would give us a discounted price if we had six people interested in the course—I signed up Gwenda without asking her—and the deal was set.

The six of us were to meet at the community pool at seven sharp the following Monday morning. The rest of Saturday and the entire Sunday was spent at the hostel interrogating Paul with every question about diving. He had gotten certified years earlier in Holland and reassured us that it was easy, fun and valuable knowledge that everyone should have. I called Angie to cover my Monday and Wednesday shifts, promising to work her shifts the following week.

March is a beautiful month in Keri Keri. However at seven in the morning, the community pool is freezing. Kevin Lyons, our scuba teacher, was trained in the British Royal Navy. His wife was a PE teacher who ran ten miles every morning, and his two children held national records in kayak racing and swimming. The Lyons family would hike Mount Cook for fun, and complaining was unheard of. So when I began to whine about how cold I was that Monday morning, Kevin scolded me—"Scuba diving is a serious business!"

He began the first lesson poolside, recounting stories of divers who drowned due to panic and misjudgment. We had begun the CMAS course, the most difficult scuba course known on Earth, guided by a man with zero compassion or sense of humor. Awesome.

Friday morning, my alarm went off at nine. I had to open the shop at ten— and I couldn't feel my legs. The last four days had been the most grueling, horrific and intense of my entire life. Timed laps in that freezing pool with a weight belt strapped to my belly, workout drills around the track, mock emergencies created on the bottom of the pool, and written tests from the CMAS workbook.

After each nightmarish day we were sent home with reading assignments, and tested on the material the following morning. Dive tables, buoyancy compensator devices, equalizing, depth gage, safety stops, mask clearing, buddy breathing, underwater signals, various water entries, nitrogen air tanks, emergency rescues, diving after flying—ask me anything, I knew it and was prepared to dive anywhere in the world under any conditions, except, I couldn't move my legs. I hated Kevin—the tyrant drill sergeant from hell with no empathy whatsoever for normal humans.

The final written test was administered bright and early Saturday morning. All six of us passed in the ninety percentile and received our CMAS scuba cards that afternoon. Kevin invited us all to his home to celebrate that evening. I certainly didn't ever want to see the man again, the guy tortured me for a week and made me barf up my tuna sandwich after inflicting the bottom-of-the-pool test on me after lunch. No thanks guys, I'd rather stick hot pokers in my eyes than party with Kevin and his over-achieving family.

Ben and Valerie forced me to go. And, in the end I actually had fun and finally got to meet the thoughtful, amusing and pleasant Kevin. His wife, Ellen, was human too, and by the end of the night we had planned our first diving excursion as card-carrying CMAS scuba divers.

The weeks passed quickly, my bank account was growing fat with book sales and I still had two thousand books left. Apparently, it was the busiest summer for boaties ever in Keri Keri and I was reaping all the benefits. I was reading like a mad woman, hiking, diving, fishing, and playing tons of pool with Gwenda and the gang. I was having the best summer of my life. I felt so independent and proud of myself. Then the gang started to disperse—that's what happens when things are going great. The same is true for bad times, you just have to wait a while and everything will inevitably change, whether good or bad.

Ben and Valerie left for Korea the last week of March. We had a big going- away party for them at the hostel. I was sad to say goodbye to my limey friends who I bonded with through certification-hell week. Paul took a skipper position on a yacht going to Seattle a few days later, then Alon took off to Thailand— which left the hostel very quiet. Boredom set in, and a plan began brewing.

Natalie and Steve tried talking me into taking a sailing course from Kevin Lyons.

"Not just no, hell no!" I answered. They converted Gwenda and worked on me for three days trying to convince me of how sailing would benefit me throughout my life. Of how I could crew a boat anywhere in the world and make money. I countered by reminding them that I was a bookseller and already had my business. They were relentless and came up with every reason known on earth to sail. Finally Gwenda persuaded me with her cunning trickery of tears! "Please, Mia, I can't do this alone," She blubbered.

"Fine, I'll do it, just stop with the crying!"

It was a huge decision, but I agreed to take the sailing lesson with Natalie, Steve and Gwenda. Kevin Lyons would take us out on his thirty-six foot sloop, the Honey Bee, for one week and teach us how to be competent ocean-going sailors. The instruction included learning all the sails, knot tying, line functions, dingy training, navigation, emergency and safety techniques, and capsize recovery. One full week of sailing instruction, eight scuba dives, with all food and beverages included, cost one thousand New Zealand dollars. A week on the ocean being taught by Kevin Lyons—God help me!

Departing Keri Keri bay on April Fool's day was probably not the best idea. The Honey Bee was packed and ready for the week's adventure at sea. She was weighed down with pre-made casseroles, fresh water, fruit, ice, four novices and one beaming captain.

While we were cruising out of the sheltered bay, Steve popped a beer, "To Aoteroa!" he cheersed to the sky.

"Oye!" Kevin yelled out from the stern. "No alcohol at sea! Absolutely none, until we are moored safely each night. This is not a cruise ship! Sailing is serious business! If you want to learn, you may as well learn right from the get go that a ship is not a democracy, it's a monarchy, pure and simple. One ruler, one captain and his rule is absolute. Right now, I am your captain! There has to be total and complete compliance with the system. It's been that way for generations at sea and we're not going to change it now. I will not tolerate any ill behavior or questioning of my authority on this vessel. Is this understood?"

Uh-oh, Kevin was in full tyrant mode. Steve poured his beer overboard and apologized for the misunderstanding.

We motored for about thirty minutes before we made it out of the inlet and into the bay. Kevin cut the engine and called us all to the stern. "Alright, let's hoist the main and the jib. Set a course of 110 for the Poor Knights islands. Natalie, hoist the main!"

Natalie took ahold of the main halyard, started pulling and we watched as the halyard led through its various fairleads and blocks up and over the mast slowly hoisting the yellow and white sail to the top.

"Two block it and tie off the halyard to that cleat," Kevin pointed to Gwenda, who stood at the base of the mast.

Gwenda took the line and put a couple of half hitches on the big metal cleat, securing it tightly. Kevin yelled instructions to Steve, and they hoisted the jib, next. Natalie wrapped the jib line counter clockwise onto the metal spur. We were sailing.

Kevin, wearing a huge grin, began to unwrap a bright yellow sail.

"What's that?" I asked him.

"This, my dear lady, is what your thousand dollars bought me, a new spinnaker." He proudly announced. "Now that we're clear, I'm dying to get her up, and see how she goes." He began hefting his prize to the bow and ordered me to follow him. "Attach the shackle on the halyard to the head of the spinnaker," he commanded, whatever the hell that meant.

Obviously, my total cluelessness showed on my face. Kevin let out a frustrated sigh and reassigned me a different task. "Just hold on to this line and hoist when I tell you." I watched as he expertly tied off, lifted and unfolded the beautiful sail. "The red stripe identifies the port side, the starboard is determined by the green," he advised, but I was totally lost and felt out of my element completely. I didn't know the difference between port, stern, or the head—that's why I was taking a sailing class!

"Strike the jib! Let go the jib halyard," he yelled to Natalie. "Bring her in!" he yelled to Steve. "OK, Mia, hoist the spinnaker!" I began to pull the rope hand over hand until I felt the wind grab the sail and it blossomed into a great yellow flower with a huge explosion, Woooop!

Right then the rope started running through my hands at thirty miles an hour. I clung to the line thinking that if I let it go, Kevin's precious sail would be lost to the sea. I closed my hands tighter trying with all my might to slow the rope, but it kept flying through my clenched palms.

Immediately, Herman Melville came into my mind. I tried reading Moby Dick several times, but just couldn't get through those tedious pages and pages of detailing and cataloging every last line, sheet, block and tackle on the entire Pequod. His intricate descriptions, expounding and elaborating on every single working piece of that ship was lost on me. Oh, how I wished at this particular moment that I had persevered through those monotonous details to the end, perhaps I would have learned exactly what the hell a spinnaker was and how it was hoisted. My lament about deserting the white-whale tale was interrupted by something flying into my eye—it was my skin.

Chapter Thirty-Four

"Let go of the rope!" a distant voice called.

"Let go!" another voice. My mind raced! I would be the hero! I was going to save Kevin's new sail from the depths of the ocean! I held on to the rope as tight as I could while it ripped my palms off.

The rope came to an end and it flew out of my grasp and high up into the air. Oh no, I thought, I lost the sail. I watched Kevin and Steve grab armfuls of the yellow, red and green cloth and muscle them back onto the deck. It hadn't flown away. I looked down at my hands in slow motion… nothing… they were fine, no blood, no pain, they were perfectly white. Almost blue-white, like a corpse.

The next instant the blood burst from the open wounds. I raised my hands above my head and warm blood ran down both my forearms and into my arm pits. Still no pain. I was in shock.

Kevin yelled at Steve to secure the sail and stuff it into its bag. The boat was rocking and I had to grab ahold of the rail line, my bloody hand slipped immediately and I went down. I caught my chin on the foreword cabin as I fell, my hands instinctively raised to break my fall. Blood was everywhere. My palms were virtually gone, a layer of skin had been ripped off by the flying line. I lay on the deck, wedged between the cabin and the alley, face up with my palms crossed over my chest like a mummy.

Kevin's face appeared above me. He was kneeling over me and speaking but I couldn't understand him. Bloody limeys. "We need to get your hands cleaned up, Mia." My hands were heating up, like someone put hot coals in my palms, then the pain hit me full force and my world went dark.

My mom always tells me that you forget the pain of childbirth or else you wouldn't have another baby. The human body is truly amazing. I woke up forty minutes later, wrapped in a blanket below deck, Gwenda patting my forehead with a damp towel. The blood was cleaned up under my arms, and my hands were wrapped in wet ace bandages with ice packs. They felt like they were on fire. "Ouch." I said, with a grimace.

"She's conscious!" Gwenda yelled to the upper deck. Kevin, Natalie and Steve all came running down below.

"You gave us a scare, my dear," Kevin confessed.

"How'ya feelin?" Steve added in his Scottish brogue.

"*Now* can she have a beer before we moor?" Natalie asked Kevin with a hint of sarcasm. She popped open a Steinlager and handed me a Vicodine. After eight beers, and one more painkiller I didn't feel much till the next morning.

The five of us had a serious meeting the next day to determine if we were going to head home and call it quits because of my injuries. I assured everyone that I was fine, my hands would heal and I didn't want to ruin everyone's trip. One of nine children, I was versed in being a martyr. "It doesn't martyr to Mia," my sisters would tease. Seriously, I didn't want to be a burden, and I hadn't seen my damaged palms up to that point—they had been wrapped in bandages since it happened.

I masked my pain and self-pity with beer and Vicodines for the next two days as I watched my shipmates learn how to sail a dingy, go on dives and race each other in knot-tying competitions. I was unable to join in any of the tests. I took the cool, wet bandages off at night to dry my palms—they looked like raw hamburger—but kept my hands covered with the bandages through the long days.

The first two nights we moored off Poor Knights Islands, about twenty-five kilometers off the coast of Keri Keri. The Honey Bee was tethered so close, I could see the grasses, birds and red dirt on the rocky island. The islands are a marine preserve and no one is allowed to set foot on them. I was seasick and dying to go ashore and explore. All I wanted was stable ground for an hour or two, but all I got was a rocking boat. I sat behind the tiller and read my paperback, listening to my shipmates laugh and play in the water.

"Brilliant viz! I can see for thirty meters!" Steve yelled from the surface to the others as they ascended from their dive. Sure glad I paid a thousand bucks for this.

During the third afternoon the wind picked up so much that Kevin decided it was too dangerous to stay another night at the Poor Knights. We set sail back to the coast at about three in the afternoon. Three hours later the sun was setting, the wind was howling and the Honey Bee was slamming into ten-foot waves. Natalie, Steve and Gwenda were learning to tack into the wind, back and forth.

Their progress was slow. I was freezing, my hands were sore and I knew I couldn't go below or I would be sick, so I sat on my bench, behind the tiller and watched my ship mates sail. I got sick anyway, I wretched over the port side into the wild Pacific Ocean then wiped my mouth with the back of my bandaged hand. The sea was rough, the sun was setting and Kevin was scrambling to get us into a sheltered bay before dark.

His hopes were thwarted by the wind and at nine o'clock that evening we were still battling to get the boat into a safe haven. Kevin took advantage of the situation and taught the four of us some of the details of nighttime navigation, star recognition and handling the helm in rough seas.

I felt discouraged and depressed. I sat sick, tired and cold on deck and gazed out at the black ocean, watching the dingy hit the water behind us. Whack! Whack! Whack! With every hit, a burst of luminescence would light up the ocean like magic dust from Tinkerbell's wand. The silver lights against the black ocean was so appealing I wanted to drift off my bench and slip under the water. No one would notice I was gone. My pain and misery would be no more. The hull slammed down onto a wave and I grabbed onto the line to keep myself from actually going overboard. Pain shot through my hands where I had grabbed the wire. They were bleeding again.

"Land ho!" Kevin shouted. I was so done being on that Godforsaken boat, tears welled up in my eyes at the prospect of land.

We moored in Whangamumu bay at about midnight. There was no dinner and no stories or laughing that night. We were all exhausted, cold and hungry and went to sleep with few words.

Dawn broke over the most spectacular sight I had seen in my life. A white sandy beach led up to a green slope, blessed with a flowing waterfall surrounded by wild yellow ginger and giant ferns. The bay was sheltered on both sides so the Honey Bee rested in calm seas, dead calm. Not a whisper of wind on the water, the sun was blazing. The only sound was the waterfall ashore, cascading down into a deep pool.

"Anyone for a hike?" Kevin better not be messing with us!

"Really?" We all waited with bated breath and desperate faces.

"Come on, you whimps!" Kevin called while bringing the dingy alongside the Honey Bee.

Land, glorious land. No wonder Captain Cook liked this place. Although my body was on land, my legs didn't get the memo, and I was rocking and rolling for the first few hours. We had a picnic of fresh bananas, tea, and lemoncake, then hiked into the tropical forest and bathed in the fresh pool at the base of the waterfall. Gwenda washed my hair for me, which felt like heaven. Since the accident, I hadn't taken my hair down, I couldn't, my hands were useless. We returned to the beach and napped under a huge Kauri tree on the site of an old whaling station. My palms dried out for the first time in four days, there was yellow puss forming under the blisters and the pain was inching down my wrists. I hiked back up the slopes of the bay while the other four went for a dive off the beach. I snapped a photo of them emerging from the crystal clear water. A pang of jealousy ripped through me as I heard them laughing and recounting their fantastic dive, while I was stuck on land with my throbbing hands. Kevin, Steve and Natalie took the dingy back to the Honey Bee to gather dinner fixings and the sleeping bags. We made a fire and barbecued lobsters in their shells, drowned them in butter and washed them down with a Marlborough Sauvignon Blanc. From the beach we could see an old concrete ramp rising from the sea with a winch at its top. A rusted iron wheel and spokes sat bolted to the winch with the date 1836 driven into the metal.

Hundreds of thousands of Humpback, Right, Minke and Sperm whales were slaughtered right here in this peaceful bay. Whalers scheduled their carnage every May when the giant mammals migrated southward towards the Antarctic to mate. We sat around the fire, our bellies full, our faces bright, staring into the flames and felt the loss of those gentle giants.

Chapter Thirty-Five

I went for a scuba dive the next day. Everyone convinced me that my hands would be fine—the salt water would help heal them and it would be a shame if I didn't experience the incredible visibility at least once during our trip. Gwenda strapped my tank to my BCD, secured my weight belt over my wet suit and put my fins on so I could save my hands for only what I had to do. I started to bake in my wet suit while I waited for everyone else to gear up on deck.

"Just jump in the water and wait for us, Mia," Kevin commanded. I jumped overboard. Immediately the cold ocean water filled my neoprene suit and cooled me down. I pulled my mask over my eyes and nose and instantaneously gaped at the largest fish I had ever seen in my life, swimming straight for me.

"Aaaahhhhhhgggg!" I screamed.
Kevin rolling his eyes called down to me from the deck, "What now, Mia?"

"There's a fish bigger than a line-backer down here with a giant mouth coming straight for me!"

"That would be a grouper, Mia. Relax, he's harmless, he won't eat you. Take your mask off, and don't look if you're scared."
I hated that man! I pulled my mask off my face, inflated my vest and treaded water, watching Gwenda strap her tank onto her vest, praying she'd hurry. I was imagining Jaws swimming beneath me waiting for the perfect angle to seize my thigh and take me down.

"Hurry up, Gwenda!"

The five of us bobbed on the surface listening to Kevin. "Right, Steve and Natalie are buddies, Mia and Gwenda are buddies, stay with your buddy the entire dive, I will lead the way. We'll descend together and at twelve meters we will begin to travel clockwise around the rock island. Keep the land on your right at all times. Watch your bubbles to identify the 'up' direction. When we have traveled around the entire rock, we shall ascend together and meet for a safety stop at four meters." He gave us the OK signal with his hand formed like an O, and we all held up our O's to him.

I descended on the mooring line, down, down, down all the way equalizing my ears and breathing normally. I checked my depth gage until it hit twelve meters. I stopped and waited for my buddy. We proceeded around the giant rock outcrop, giving each other O signals. Huge grouper swam past and I looked at Gwenda with wide eyes and pointed, she looked back at me with wider eyes through her mask and held her hands three-feet apart, concurring with my amazement.

We gestured to different oddities—a giant lobster, a bright blue clam, an orange starfish. Gwenda pulled my arm and pointed to a rock, I looked at her, confused, and she took her hand and made a snake signal with her hand. I looked at the rock again, and focused on the spotted head of a Moray eel with his fangs bared. I quickly swam backward and saw Gwenda laughing under water.

Thirty minutes into the dive I noticed it was a bit harder to breath than it had been. I checked my depth gage and read twenty-five meters. Holy shit! I had never been that deep before and I panicked. I wanted to shoot up, but I knew I needed to relax and go up slowly. I found Gwenda's eyes and shoved my depth gage into her view. Her eyes got big and I signaled my O, then the thumb up, then my flat hand gradually going up. She gave me an O. We ascended to twenty meters. I gave her an O. She returned the O. Seventeen, fifteen, eleven. O? O. We finished circling the rock at twelve meters, then after fifty minutes, we started our ascent. We had lost the others at the start of the dive, but it didn't matter, we had each other.

The Honey Bee was twenty-five yards away when we surfaced. The ocean was choppy and I was cold. I put my regulator back in my mouth, inflated my BCD a few pumps so I would float and began the swim to the boat. Gwenda climbed the ladder first so she could help me up. She made five trips up and down the ladder, hauling my tank, weight belt, mask, snorkel, and fins to the deck. Then I climbed up myself, somehow, without using my damaged hands. No one had arrived on the boat yet, so we dried off in the sun and laughed about our exciting dive.

"You were so scared when you saw the depth gage was at twenty-five meters!" Gwenda joked.

"Not even close! I was totally calm, you were the one that freaked out!"

"What if they die down there, and we have to sail back to shore alone?"

"Why would you even joke like that Gwenda?"

"Because I haven't the first clue how to sail after this lesson and I know you don't either!" We laughed and hoped they would surface soon.

Kevin came up with five huge lobsters, so we enjoyed another superb lobster dinner paired with a jammy New Zealand pinot noir on the deck under a blanket of stars like I had never seen before in my life. The sky looked like we were inside a black hefty bag that someone poked a billion holes through and let the light shine through. We moored in Woolley's Bay, just south of our dive site and fell asleep at nine o'clock, sunburnt, full, and happy.

I woke up at four in the morning, very unhappy. My teeth chattered with cold and my head and hands were on fire. I lay there quiet for an hour, waiting for another person to stir. Another hour went by, then Kevin got up and took a pee off the deck. He walked below and put the kettle on for tea.

"Kevin," I pathetically whispered. He walked over and looked down at me.

"You look like shit, Mia." He put his palm on my forehead.

"I feel like shit, Kevin."

"You are burning up, girl—let's see those hands." I turned my palms up and offered them to him. They were yellow with puss and blood. "Right, I think the sailing lesson has ended for you. We must get you to a doctor."

"I'm not being a whimp?" I asked, searching his eyes sarcastically.

We sailed all day up the coast. I kept apologizing to the crew, but they assured me that they were completely content with the trip and ready to go home, even if it was one day early. Kevin joked that everyone had earned their sailing certificate except for "the gimp".

I slept most of the way back, feeling like death. Gwenda and Natalie made sure I had enough water to drink, and plied me with Vicodines. But I couldn't keep any food down. My fever broke at around five that evening. I sipped hot soup and allowed Natalie to clean my hands with hydrogen peroxide. My hands bubbled with infection. We sailed into Keri Keri inlet at midnight. Kevin docked the Honey Bee to allow us to go ashore, then motored to his mooring and spent the night on the boat.

Steve drove the rest of us back to the hostel where I spent the night so Rachael could take me to her doctor the next morning. Natalie gave me some medicine from Switzerland, I sipped it like a tea and the stuff knocked me out like Mike Tyson. When Tim and Rachael saw my hands the next morning, they asked why I hadn't come home sooner." "I guess, I was being Mia the Martyr," I joked.

"Let's get you to the doctor," Rachael said. I was worried about the cost but I knew at that point my hands desperately needed medical intervention. I couldn't dodge it any longer.

Chapter Thirty-Six

Keri Keri community clinic was a blast from the seventy's—retro architecture meets the Brady bunch house, painted ugly shades of army green. Rachael helped me fill out the forms because my hands were still useless and the pain was constant now.

Natalie had been feeding me Vicodine since the accident, so in actuality I hadn't ever felt the real brunt of the pain. I explained this illegal drug detail to the doctor with a tone of apologetic apathy. I was sorry that I was popping highly addictive pain killers that were never prescribed to me personally, but not at all sorry that the pain had been dulled for the past six days.

When the doctor unwrapped my hands, she actually cringed. When a doctor recoils from a wound, it's never a good sign, right? She confirmed I had stable and aggressive staphylococcus aureus. I had two questions: What in the hell does stable and aggressive mean? And can I keep the Vicodine?

Stable meant that it was better than serious. Aggressive meant that it was a very good idea that I had come to the doctor that day and not the next, and staphylococcus aureus meant I had a Staph infection. And no, I could not keep taking the Vicodine. Doctor Karlson drained the puss blisters and while I was crying out in pain, she assured me that a surgical cleanse would be far more painful. I asked her if there was a resident anesthesiologist on call to put me out. She actually rolled her eyes, and muttered something about Americans being big babies.

Dr. Evil explained that I was lucky the infection had not reached my blood stream, and prescribed me a two-week supply of antibiotics. She bandaged up my hands and gave me specific instructions on how to clean them, how often and to call her if the pain exceeded, "Quite bad". I wondered if Kiwis took a shot of whiskey and bit on a length of leather during major surgery.

Rachael was waiting for me in the reception with a concerned look. "Howsit, Mia?"

"I've got a stable case of staph infection," I reported.

"At least it's not serious or critical," Rachael said, relieved. Was every Kiwi versed in medical states? I walked to the receptionist and asked how much I owed for my visit with Doctor Karlson.

She looked at me, perplexed. "Sorry?"

"How much is today's visit going to put me back. I don't have insurance so may I have your cash discount?"

"Sorry?" she said again, staring at me like I was not speaking English.

Rachael interrupted me, and apologized to her. Then asked when my follow-up appointment was scheduled, and if my antibiotics were ready. The crazy receptionist, still staring at me, handed Rachael the two-week supply of antibiotics, explained when and how many to take per day, then gave her a little card with 'April 21, 10 a.m.' written on it. "If you or Ms. Coffin have any questions or if the wounds worsen, please call at any time, thanks for your visit."

We walked out. "What just happened?" I asked Rachael, my hands lifted like a surgeon going into the operating room.

"What just happened is called a public health plan. We pay taxes, and the government makes sure that its citizens are healthy and taken care of."

"I pay taxes, and my government uses it to spread democracy, not so much care for their citizens health."

"You mean you have to pay for basic annual exams, like a pap smear or a physical?"

"Of course, that's why I haven't been to the doctor for years."

"What about when women have their babies?"

"It costs thousands."

"I thought America was so advanced."

"Yeah, if you're rich, we have the best treatment money can buy." My hands were throbbing and I was done discussing my country's nonexistent health care policy. Rachael drove me to the Broadbent's and left me in the care of Kathy who doted on me for a week, making sure my dressings were changed and that I took my medication, four times a day. I slept, took Advil (a sorry substitute for Vicodine) and read The Clan of the Cave Bear series, taking strength from Ayla, the strong, blonde heroine.

Angie only opened the shop four days during the "off season"—April through October. She pledged to me that she was completely happy watching the shop and didn't expect me to work my shifts when I was suffering. I thanked her again, and told her I would call in a week's time to report how I was feeling.

Summer was coming to an end. I felt the frost in the night air. Kathy brought me a wool blanket to put over my duvet, she cut the last of her dahlias and made a gorgeous arrangement for my room. My hands healed slowly, but surely.

Gwenda went back to Germany. Her thesis project had run out of extensions and she needed to save the world's agricultural dilemmas. I would miss her funny, spontaneous personality. What would I do sitting in the shop alone for the next three months without Gwenda to sign me up for trouble? Angie called and told me my books had completely sold out during the last ten days, and to bring a couple boxes down. I told her I would be there bright and early on Monday morning with books galore. I was bored and needed to work anyway.

Two weeks since my diagnosis, and I was back to report all good news to Doctor Karlson. She examined my hands and gave me a clean bill of health. She pointed out where I would probably show permanent scaring on my palms. Then asked if I wanted a cup of tea. This was nothing like the States where doctors didn't have the time of day for you.

"Sure, I switched my work days with my boss, so I don't have to go in today," Doctor Karlson was surprised that I had a job. I expounded on my special circumstances, importing my books, living with the Broadbent's—and told her my plan to go through Asia on the way back to California. She asked about immigration and I recounted that story as well, relaying how easy it turned out to be for me to extend my tourist visa.

"I wouldn't count on getting lucky twice, Mia." She was right, I only had ten days before my extension expired. I assured her that I would get down to Auckland that week. I invited her into Angie's for a free paperback book of her choice.

"Do you have any Vonnegut?"

"Heaps. Come by any time. Thanks, Doctor."

Six days later, on the 27th of April I finally made it down to Auckland to get my visa extended...again. This time, I knew what to expect, so I wasn't nervous and didn't get dressed up to impress. I gave Steve and Natalie a ride down. They were taking off to Australia for a few months of backpacking, then onto India.

Part of me was jealous that they had found love. Now they had each other to share traveling with and I had no one. I romanticized the idea of having a man to share all my crazy experiences with. But the thought of a relationship exited as fast as it entered—who needs that headache? I dropped Steve and Natalie at a Hostel in Parnell and wished them luck. "Keep sailing and diving," I urged them.

"Learn how to let go of the rope when you're told to," Steve laughed. Natalie gave me a baggie filled with ten Vicodines. "Just in case you find yourself in pain again." I hugged her, wished them well and was off to the immigration office.

Same parking, same cute Maori guy at the gate, same reception filled with South East Asian families. I took a number and waited with a paperback. I was reading why ancient civilizations collapsed, according to Jared Diamond, when my number was called, again, ahead of almost everyone waiting there. A woman greeted me without a stitch of makeup on, her hair pulled back in a fierce blonde bun. She directed me to her office and asked that I please have a seat across from her. *Diana Brown* was etched into a plastic plaque on her desk.

"Passport, your onward travel ticket and evidence of sufficient funds please." I pushed my documents over the desk to her. She opened my passport and began typing my information into her computer. "Right, Ms. Coffin?"

"Yes."

"You entered New Zealand on the first day of November, extended your stay here last February second for a period of three months, your application indicates that you are requesting another three months. For what purpose, Ms. Coffin?"

"Um, I am staying up in Keri Keri and I just love it. I would appreciate the opportunity to be able to travel around a bit, perhaps to the South Island. I just ran out of time to see and experience the culture as I would have liked." Wow that sounded like complete crap.

"Right." Without looking up at me she opened the two envelopes I brought—one was my airline ticket to K.L., the other was my last bank statement showing thirty-three thousand New Zealand dollars.

"How has twenty-one thousand dollars been added to your initial deposit on November third, Ms. Coffin?"

"Um, oh, that. My mom gets super worried about me traveling alone, and wired me money, just in case. She doesn't travel and doesn't really know how easy and affordable traveling alone is, and she thinks I could …" shut up Mia, just shut your mouth and stop spewing nonsense.

"Do you have evidence of the alleged wiring of the funds?"

Alleged? Was she accusing me of lying? "Uh, no."

"Right. Please wait here, Ms. Coffin." I watched Diana Brown stand and leave the airless room. I was definitely going to jail. My mom wired the money? What possessed me to say that? My mom has nine kids. I can just imagine me calling my mom—Hey mom, can you send me twenty-one thousand dollars? She would break into hysterics and say—Oh, sure Mia, let me just get out my checkbook and hey, let's make it an even fifty grand! That's a good one, Mia—then promptly hang up on me.

Diana Brown walked back in the room and sat down behind her desk. She smiled at me and passed my two envelopes and passport back. "I am sorry to report, Ms. Coffin, but your request for another extension has been denied. You must leave the country of New Zealand on or before the first day of May. If you fail to adhere to the laws, an immigration officer will be obliged to detain you, deport you and revoke your status, thereby labeling you as an unlawful non-citizen. You shall never be permitted to set foot in this country again. Good day, Ms. Coffin."

Chapter Thirty-Seven

I have no recollection of walking out of her office, through the reception, down to the parking lot and into my car. I just remember suddenly being in Sunny, crying my eyes out. There must be an appeal process, right? I can't just leave my books, my car, my life. Still, there's no way I was going to ruin my chances of returning to New Zealand. I drove back to Keri Keri, and for the next three hours, I went through denial, anger, sadness and finally acceptance.

I had three days to leave New Zealand. First, I called Cathay Pacific Airlines and booked a ticket to K.L. They flew twice a week, leaving on Tuesdays and Saturdays. Well, I couldn't leave the next day, so I booked the Saturday flight on May 2nd, hoping I could extend my visa twenty-four hours.

Next, I called Diana Brown, expecting to plead for leniency—and another 24 hours. Her office was closed. I highly doubted she was in the business of doing me any favors, anyway. So I called Doctor Karlson and lamented my predicament, hoping she wouldn't say, I told you so. She didn't. She turned out to be my angel. She had endless connections in Auckland who pulled some strings and I had my twenty-four hour extension faxed to her office by the next morning.

I parked Sunny in the hostel driveway with a sign reading, FOR SALE, $800, O.N.O., then in smaller writing, I wrote, SEE TIM FOR DETAILS. Tim and Rachael agreed to sell Sunny for me if I couldn't sell her in the next four days. The hostel was full, but the season was coming to a close fast.

All I had left was the book situation. I had thirty-eight boxes left, that was about thirteen hundred and thirty books. I had paid $800US for that stack of thirty-eight apple boxes sitting in Simon's garage. I could make $3,200US, if I sold them at Angie's. Problem was, I had to be out of the country in four days. What to do?

I walked into the village and stopped to talk to Kevin at his sporting goods store.

"Cheers, Mia, howsit? Sorry I couldn't give you a sailing certificate after the trip," Kevin scrunched his nose up as he looked down at my hands.

"No worries, mate, it was a blast!" I joked back.

"How're the hands healin?" Kevin's accent was a cross between English and Kiwi.

"They're tip-top, mate." I said in my best Kiwi accent, raising my hands, bandage free. "Hey, Kevin, I was wondering if I could rent the space next door for a one-day Blowout Book Sale. I got the boot from immigration and need to take off pretty quick, here." Kevin owned the space next door to his sports store and he was planning on putting treadmills and exercise equipment in during the winter months (my suggestion). But for now the space sat vacant.

"Of course, Mia, what ever I can do to help, it's yours." I'm pretty sure he still felt badly about my accident, so I thought I'd milk it.

I thanked Kevin and walked over to the print shop. I took a piece of paper and wrote, HUGE ONE-DAY BLOWOUT BOOK SALE THURSDAY APRIL 30 — 8 a.m to 5 p.m. MAIN STREET KERI KERI NEXT DOOR TO SPORTS MART! I made sixty copies then cut them in half. I had one hundred and twenty flyers to distribute in a day-and-a-half. I bought a roll of packing tape and went to paper the village with my flyers. Next stop, Angie's.

The bell rang when I opened the door—I'd miss that little bell. "Hey, Angie, howsit?"

"Hello, my dear girl, howsit?"

"Not great, Angie, I have to leave New Zealand this Saturday for a bit."

"How long's a bit?"

"A long bit, I'm afraid." I didn't want to cry, but suddenly my eyes felt suspiciously teary. I hadn't really thought of saying my goodbyes to people I loved. I had been in task mode ever since the drive up from Auckland.

"Never mind, love, you'll be back." Angie was a good friend.

"So, I am having a book sale at Kevin's on Thursday, and whatever I can't sell, I thought I'd leave here with you, if that's all right?"

"Of course, dear, just tell me where I can send you your money."

"Angie, please! You have given me so much, and I am just so grateful that you allowed me to sell my books here for as long as I have. I know our deal was that I'd be here until July. So, I thought if I gave you a few books, you'd forgive me for taking off early. Actually Angie, you'd be doing me a favor if you took the leftover books. I don't want any money for them, I just want to thank you and I don't want to start blubbering."

"Come here, my dear!" Angie hugged me tight. "Of course I'll take whatever you have left over, how can I help at the sale?"

"I don't need anything else, Angie. I just gotta go put these flyers up, set up the sale, sell my car, pack and get out of here before your government throws me out for good!"

"Well, get going my girl, and stay in touch."

"I love you, Angie."

"I love you too, my darling girl."

I walked back to the hostel, stopping at every light post and shop window to tape up a flyer. "Any nibbles on Sunny?" I asked Rachael who was manning the reception.

"Not yet, sorry Mia." Skylar had a crayon in his grasp and started to color the wall. Rachael scolded him, "Not the wall, sweetheart, keep your crayon on the paper." Looks like Tim had a painting job in his near future. I taped-up a flyer in the window and told Rachael I was going to drive Sunny down to Paihia Harbor to hand out flyers to the boaties.

"Good luck, Mia!," she called back, her hands full with her little terror.

Paihia is a quaint port town, south west of Keri Keri, with a huge harbor where all the boaties sail into from their international journeys. I walked down each dock, saying hello, and handing my flyers to people working on their boats. I was tired, and sun burnt after three hours of walking around taping my advertisement to every surface I could find.

I stopped into the dock shop to tape a flyer up and have an ice cream. I sat at a small table enjoying the best ice cream in the world, and watched a couple talking to the guy at the desk about how to get up to Keri Keri. They had American accents, so I eaves-dropped—I heard them say they were looking to get down to the South Island. When they walked out, I handed them a flyer and told them that I was on my way back to Keri Keri, if they wanted a lift.

"We'd be much obliged, miss," the man sounded like Rhett Butler.

"No worries mate," I assured him.

"Well, it sure sounds like she's got the local dialect down, wouldn't you say, honey?" He said to his wife.

On the twenty-five minute drive back to Keri Keri, I learned that Dean and Barbara Bowen were from Savannah, Georgia. Dean had been a Public Defender for the last thirty years for Chatham County, and his wife Barbara taught Marine Biology at Skidway Institute of Oceanography. They had retired a year before, sold their house, bought a yacht, and sailed away. Their four children thought they were crazy for not wanting to settle down and be their on-call babysitters for the thirteen grandchildren.

Their yacht was in dry dock, having its keel reconstructed after a close encounter with a reef off Cook Islands. They were headed to Keri Keri to rent a car.

"Why don't you guys just rent a car in Paihia?"

Dean answered, "Well, we checked out a couple of rental places in town, but all the cars were too big. Barb and I just need a small thing that doesn't use too much gas. We didn't budget on staying for so long but our boat will be in dry dock for three weeks, so we thought we'd take advantage of our crummy luck, and do a little sightsee'n. Barbara wants to go down to Queenstown and visit a workin' sheep station."

"Are you guys gonna try bungee jumping?" I asked. "They invented the bungee jump, the first one is down there off the Kawarau Bridge."

They both laughed, "No, we think we'll pass on that."

"What about buying Sunny from me?"

"Who's Sunny?" Dean asked.

"Sorry, Sunny's my car. She is a 1973 Datsun Sunny. I am selling her for eight hundred New Zealand dollars. She runs great. I took her to a mechanic before I bought her, and have only put about 600 miles on her since November. Do you want to test drive her?" I started to pull over to the left, before Dean could protest. "We only have about ten minutes left till we get to Keri Keri—test her out, see how she feels," I insisted.

Dean got into the driver's seat and moved the seat back, adjusted the rear view mirror and pulled the seat belt across his blue Members Only jacket. I popped the Bob Marley tape out, so Dean could concentrate, and we were off.

"Who owned the car before you?" Dean asked not taking his eyes off the road.

"I bought her from a German couple staying at the hostel in Keri Keri— they drove all over both islands for three months. So Sunny already knows the way to Queenstown!" I told Dean to make a left, then a right into the hostel parking lot.

"If you guys want to talk about it, you can walk into town from here and let me know later. I am just going to finish passing these flyers out around town." They thanked me for the ride and told me they'd think about buying Sunny. I went in to say hi to Rachael.

"Howsit?" Rachael asked. I told her about my afternoon in Paihia, passing out flyers to the boaties, and how I hoped I could sell the last of my books. Dean and Barbara walked through to the reception only a few minutes later. I was surprised to see them, thinking they must have left something in Sunny.

"We want to buy Sunny," Dean announced. "We would like to take her to a mechanic, if that's OK with you."

"Yeah, of course," I answered. It was already four in the afternoon, so I asked them if they wanted to drive Sunny back to Paihia, find a mechanic there in the morning, have him check it out and decide then. We agreed on three hundred dollars collateral, and they took off in Sunny. I felt sad. Rachael looked at me and asked what was wrong.

"You are a bit touched in the head Mia you should be happy that you sold your car that quickly." I knew I was lucky to find a buyer but it just made the reality that I was leaving New Zealand…real.

I walked to the Broadbent's that evening, feeling lower than a snake's belly. My book business and trip to New Zealand had been successful, I had accomplished everything and more, I was just feeling sorry for myself, and wished for another few weeks to wrap things up. Simon made my favorite dinner and turned my mood around. By the end of the night the three of us were laughing at my good luck in Paihia that day. Simon offered me his car to haul the rest of the apple boxes into the village in the morning. He had a big SUV but it would still take me five trips to get all the boxes out of the garage.

In the morning I came up with a plan to put all the boxes in Simon's little runabout, then haul the boat into town in one trip. I wonder what people thought as they watched me unload thirty-eight apple boxes from Simon's twelve-foot tinny into the vacant space next to Kevin's Sporting goods store. The rest of the day was spent unpacking books and displaying them in the front window and on tables inside.

At around three, Dean and Barbara popped their heads in the door. "Howdy, Mia, the folks at the hostel said we'd find you here." Exhausted and hungry, I asked if they would like to join me at the café three doors down for lunch. We shared a veggie pizza and drank cream sodas. Dean gave me another five hundred New Zealand dollars, and thanked me again for Sunny.

He figured it would be tremendously less expensive than renting a car for three weeks. The boat builder at the dockyard offered to buy it from them when their keel was fixed, so it ended up a win-win for everyone.

They invited me to Savannah whenever I got back to the States. Barbara went into a short history lesson, enthusiastically explaining that Savannah boasts the oldest standing house of worship, the First Baptist Church built in 1833. Plus, it was the only city spared from being torched by the Yankees during the Civil War. And, I knew Dean would defend me if I got into any trouble and needed a lawyer. I was sold.

We walked back to Kevin's and they picked out twenty paperbacks. I gave them a family-and-friends discount and wished them luck on their journey. I joked that they may want to pick up another few cassette tapes to listen to for the next three weeks on the road. We hugged and they took off, leaving me car-less, but with eight hundred bucks, the same amount that I bought Sunny for six months earlier. I walked home as the sun was setting over my lovely Keri Keri.

Chapter Thirty-Eight

I had waitress dreams all night. I looked out at a packed restaurant and I didn't have a pen that worked, I forgot all the table numbers and the chef told me we were out of everything on the menu. I'm sure it sounds like a silly dream to those who have never worked in a restaurant, but it was so real I woke up drenched in nervous sweat. I never wanted to wait another table again. And I didn't have to, at least today. I had to get my butt out of bed and sell thirteen hundred books!

I opened the doors for business at seven-fifty, with a bunch of one's for change, and a pot of coffee. Nine long hours later, I had sold eight hundred and thirty four books and made two thousand seven hundred New Zealand dollars. Thanks to all the Kiwis who bought horror novels, and Boaties who bought everything else!

Tim helped me pack the rest of the books back into their apple boxes. There were only twelve boxes left, four hundred and sixty books. We hefted the boxes into the back of Tim's truck and dropped ten of them off at Angie's. The two other boxes I gave to Tim for the hostel's Book Exchange. I took two books out to read on my trip, a huge Ken Follett that has over a thousand pages and Herman Melville's, Moby Dick.

Friday, May 1st was spent saying my good byes, closing my bank account and offering huge thank you's to Kevin, Angie, Dr. Karlson, Tim, Rachael and the Broadbent's. I packed up my small backpack and basked in my accomplishments—knowing I would return home—not broke!—for the first time from a trip. The summer was over and a part of me was happy to be leaving, three months ahead of schedule. I'd have six months to travel around South East Asia before my Circle the Pacific ticket expired. I certainly had enough money this time to explore a while, and I could afford to take some college classes when I got home. That evening Rachael and Tim threw a little going away party for me at the hostel. None of the old gang were left, but the three of us sat around the kitchen table and reminisced about the past six months of fun.

My last morning in New Zealand, Kathy made a breakfast spread for me. Simon was babbling that he wanted to drive me down to Auckland, but I had already bought my bus ticket the day before. "Simon, I will be fine! I'm not having you drive six hours there and back!" My farewell to Kathy and Simon was bittersweet. How could I thank them for being my surrogate parents? They were the best.

I boarded my bus in Keri Keri at noon to catch the Cathay Pacific flight that departed at 5:45 that evening. I arrived at Auckland Airport and got in line at the Cathay Pacific desk.

A petite Samoan woman took my ticket and passport when I finally got to the end of a very long queue. Her gold nameplate announced that her name was Maria Hunt. "All set, Mia Coffin," Maria announced with a big smile, after clicking away at the computer. "Straight through to Kuala Lumpur." And she pushed my ticket back towards me.

"Where?"

She blinked at me and then pulled the ticket back. "Kuala Lumpur, girl, says right here that's where you're headed." She pointed at the K.L. on my itinerary."

So that's what K.L. stood for, Kuala Lumpur! "Where the hell is Kuala Lumpur?"

Maria just laughed, obviously it wasn't all that strange for people in her line not to know where they were going. "Well, it's where you'll be at in about nine hours, girl. And you're leaving New Zealand right now, if that helps any. You might want to get a good travel book about Malaysia." She winked at me, "That'll be where Kuala Lumpur is." And she laughed again. A really loud and deep laugh. A few of the people behind me had obviously heard Maria as her voice did not at all match her small body type. They were having their own chuckles at the stupid American who bought tickets to countries, willy nilly.

"Malaysia," I said, nodding to everyone around me. "Good to know."

Fortunately, the rest of my check-in went by without a problem. I breezed through immigration with permission to enter New Zealand in the future. When I reached my gate, I sat and pulled Moby Dick out of my pack. I turned to the first page, determined to get through the entire story this time, and started reading.

Call me Ishmael…

Kevin, Steve, Natalie and Gwenda after their dive in Whangamumu bay

Special Thanks

David & Nadine Bartholomew, Malia, Steve, Kela, Makena & Mitchell Nahas, Melani, Jon, Emmalani, Owen & Pearl Stapp, Mele, David, Tess & Jack Brobeck, Martin, Allyson, Koa, Roman, Wesley & Violet Bartholomew, Michael, Karla, Kai, Kahili, Makala, & Kapono Bartholomew, Moana, Miguel, Ocean, Isla & Viva Amador, Momi Bartholomew, the Brown family, the Chalmers family, Jennifer Ford, Ben Lyons, Rene Karlson, the Whittall family, Bud Short, Jon & Peggy Feder, Victoria Bernal, Kevin Bias, Frank Castro, Sean Prince, the Deda family, Dina Solomon, Suparno Djamoen family, Bronte Bernal, Joshua Holoai'a &'Umiamaka Dang and Tabu Grill (for providing endless waitress dreams).

About the Author

The author was born and raised on the island of O'ahu in Hawai'i where she currently lives with her husband. She is working on her second novel and loves to hear from readers at Miafranciscoffin@gmail.com
Or find Mia Francis Coffin on Facebook.

Made in the USA
Charleston, SC
08 November 2016